£5-00

THE VITAL SPARK

Almost the first thing Haydn Scott had ever said to Lee was that it was dangerous to cross his path, and as he began to encroach more and more into her life she could see what he meant. It was obvious that he intended to take over her family business—was he going to take her over as well?

THE VITAL SPARK

BY

ANGELA CARSON

MILLS & BOON LIMITED
17–19 FOLEY STREET
LONDON W1A 1DR

First published 1979
Australian copyright 1979
Philippine copyright 1979
This edition 1979

ISBN 0 263 73075 1

Set in Linotype Plantin 10 pt. solid

Made and printed in Great Britain by
Richard Clay (The Chaucer Press) Ltd., Bungay, Suffolk

CHAPTER ONE

'WE could do with a delivery like this every day if your crop will stand it, Miss Ramsay.'

'Why the sudden demand?' Lee opened the back doors of the Mini van and stood aside while the plump little greengrocer bent down to lift the first stack of tomato trays into his arms. She eyed him with some trepidation. He was short, as well as stout, and three trays one on top of the other came up to his chin. Lee hoped he would not try to add a fourth, and so risk blocking his vision. In an endeavour to save himself an extra journey across the pavement into his well stocked shop, he would court disaster if he tripped over the pavement edge, and she was not too sure who would then be liable to pay for the fruit. Polrewin could ill afford to pay for wasted produce.

'It's that caravan site further down the coast.' He deposited the first load, and came back for more. 'These toms are just the right size.' He peered through the clean paper cover that fitted like a hat over each tray, with its oblong transparent window in the middle to show up the contents as well as protect them, and the name of the flower farm emblazoned on the side.

'They're not very big,' Lee said doubtfully, 'but they are a nice flavour.' She felt proud of their first crop of tomatoes. They represented a good deal of hard work, as well as the first real return on the capital she and Jon had poured into Polrewin.

'The flavour's fine,' the greengrocer agreed, 'but it's the number to a pound that sells them. Most of the folk who come caravanning have got children with them and they don't want a big tomato. Kids would rather have a medium sized one each than share a big one between them. It saves arguing about who's got the biggest half, see?' he smiled, with the resigned wisdom of a father of three.

'Dad takes the van down there every day now, and the

stuff sells like hot cakes.' Betty, the eldest, sauntered out to the front of the shop, prepared for a friendly chat, and Lee smiled. It would be beneficial to Betty's figure if she ate more of her father's fruit and salad than whatever was responsible for the superfluous pounds that pressed against the seams of her flimsy dress, and threatened the stitching's desperate endeavours to hold the two sides together.

'A caravan holiday would be fun.' Lee watched patiently as trays of lettuce followed the tomatoes until the interior of the van became a bare space, and the greengrocer slammed the back doors shut.

'That's the lot, Miss Ramsay.' He scribbled busily for a minute or two, then ripped off the top sheet from his pad and carefully adjusted the carbon paper for the next copy. 'Here's your tally for this lot. I'll settle with your brother at the end of the month, as usual.' He nodded in a friendly fashion and bustled off, and Lee carefully tucked the tally into her jeans pocket as she sorted out her ignition key and turned towards the van. It was invaluable to herself and Jon that Mr Dunn did, in fact, settle promptly at the end of each month, without argument or delay, and she blessed the fact that Polrewin had been fortunate enough to capture the greengrocer's regular order. It had been a major factor in keeping their new venture afloat until now.

'Caravanning's all right, I suppose.' Betty Dunn strolled across the pavement with her, not to be denied her chat. 'Me, I'd sooner go to one of those places on the French coast. Where you can sunbathe, and get a tan, like.' She pressed plump hands to her fluffy blonde head and sighed. 'Not that I'd cut much of a dash in a bikini,' she admitted ruefully. 'Not like you.' She eyed Lee's diminutive figure and slender waistline with unmalicious envy. 'Some folks have all the luck,' she grinned. 'There's you, with a tan most folks have to pay a fortune in air fares to get, and here's me lives in the same place, and all I do when the sun shines is go red, and peel.'

'It's having black hair, it makes you tan more easily,' Lee offered what comfort she could. 'And if all you do is peel in a heatwave, there's no point in spending money going abroad,' she consoled with a laugh.

'Ah, but there's always a chance you'd meet someone special if you went to that place where they hold the film festival,' Betty said hopefully.

'You mean Cannes?' Lee's attention was on her ignition key. 'I don't suppose the stars have much time for sunning themselves on the beach when they go there, they'd be too busy working,' she hazarded, not really interested in Betty's romantic daydreams.

'P'raps, but at least they'd be there,' the plump blonde was determined to hold on to her dreams at all costs. 'Now here, you never get anyone like that,' she grumbled discontentedly.

'We get yachts, and private boats coming into the harbour,' Lee felt obliged to cheer her up. 'And plenty of holidaymakers all the season, to say nothing of artists and photographers, and so on.' Surely the influx of summer visitors to the attractive little fishing town should be diverse enough to satisfy even Betty, despite her romantic notions, Lee thought, hiding her amusement with difficulty.

'Ah, but not anybody special,' her companion persisted. 'Not any film stars like they get in France, or—or– I don't know, though,' her tone changed, and she perked up visibly. 'Now, he's more like it!' she breathed ecstatically.

Lee turned and followed the direction of her gaze. Betty belonged to the wrong generation, she reflected, and resigned herself to being trapped for the next ten minutes or so, instead of making the early start back home that she intended. The fluffy-headed nineteen-year-old would have been better fitted to the era that packed the stalls of the local cinemas, and hero-worshipped the celluloid lives of the Hollywood screen lovers. Instead, she had to be content with the local bingo hall, and obtain her vicarious pleasures through the pages of the brightly coloured magazines that decorated the racks of the paper shop-cum-tobacconist next door.

'That's Vince Merrick, the son of the hotel proprietor.' Lee raised her hand to the tall, fair-haired man of about her own age who was walking across the far side of the pavement where it curved with the bend of the bay. He waved back, his face lighting as he caught sight of Lee, before he made a resigned gesture that meant he could not stop, and dived into the door of the local bank. 'Surely you've seen him before?' Vince's fair hair and blue eyes made him acceptable enough to look at, she thought, but she would not have thought him star quality, even by Betty's unexacting standards.

'Not him. I mean *him*.' Betty's pointing finger succeeded where her limited vocabulary failed. 'The one coming off that cabin cruiser—look!'

Lee obligingly squinted against the dazzle glinting from off the water in the harbour, and looked in the direction Betty indicated. She was just in time to see a tall athletic-looking figure leap lightly from the deck on to the top of the guard rail of a large white cabin cruiser with a broad scarlet band setting off the dazzling white of her paint, and walk nonchalantly, hands in pockets, with a catlike surety of tread along the length of the narrow rail. He scarcely paused as he came to the end of it, and measured the distance between his own boat and the one moored next to it, before he flexed long legs and stepped across the gap, and calmly used the second boat as if it was a public footpath placed there expressly to help him come ashore, though this time he walked on the deck and not on the rail.

For some reason his cool assumption that he had the right to use other people's boats for such a purpose nettled Lee. 'Show-off!' she muttered disparagingly, but nevertheless she watched with more interest, wondering what the self-assured stranger would do when he reached the end of the second deck. The water was still deep between the second boat and the exposed part of the beach, with only a small dinghy lazily moving up and down in the water at the end of a line between himself and dry land.

'I hope he gets his feet wet,' she muttered vindictively. She did not like holidaymakers who assumed, because they came to Tarmouth for a couple of weeks during the summer, that they were entitled to go where they pleased and do what they liked. The second boat was a fishing smack, and was owned by one of the local families Lee knew.

'He won't—look, he's pulling the dinghy towards him.'

Sun glinted on rich, tawny-coloured hair as the man leaned down and pulled at the painter holding the row-boat. A quick tug from hands tanned a dark shade of teak brought it to the desired position, and with another testing tug at the other end of the rope where it was fixed to the rail, the tall stranger swung lightly over the edge of the fishing smack. His feet sought and found the length of the dangling rope, and he slid down it and into the dinghy. His movements had the accustomed grace of someone who had done the same thing a thousand times before, and with easy familiarity he balanced lightly in the rocking boat, and used one oar as a scull. A quick pull sent the dinghy the full length of its tether towards the beach. Before it snagged against the taut rope and upset his balance, he foiled Lee's unexpressed hope and leapt across the intervening shallows, and gained the sanctuary of the dry pebbles on the other side.

'Ooh, I wouldn't mind him for my partner in the dancing,' Betty breathed on a gusty sigh, referring, Lee knew, to the forthcoming traditional procession that lent a yearly air of carnival to the little town, and was an added attraction to people in holiday mood who revelled in the colourful floats, and the chance to join in the gay gyrations along the crowded, narrow streets. The locals enjoyed it just as much, she suspected, despite their would-be indifferent attitude that it was a show put on purely for the sake of the holiday visitors. Certainly most of them managed to put in an appearance at the more formal dance held in the evening after the procession, at the Royal Anchor Hotel.

'He'd probably tread all over your feet,' she assured Betty, and although he was out of earshot, the stranger looked up as he reached the top of the harbour steps, almost as if he sensed they were discussing him. His eyes met Lee's dark gaze full on, and she felt a distinct sense of shock. They were as tawny as his hair.

He's like a lion, she thought. And for some reason, she shivered, although the sun was hot enough on her bare arms. Not a lion with a mane; he wasn't of the jungle variety. The thoughts passed unbidden across her mind. This man was more like a—a—mountain lion. Yes, that was it. A creature of the high, open places, cat-footed, and supremely sure of himself. And when he wanted to be, completely ruthless.... She tore her eyes away, aware of a strange feeling of breathlessness, as if she had been running. She focussed out into the harbour, trying to make it seem as if she had been looking out there all the time, and the stranger had merely got in the way of her gaze when he reached the top of the steps. The thing she focussed on drove the rest of the breath out of her lungs in a dismayed ejaculation. Her dark eyes took on a look of sheer consternation, and she opened her mouth to call out.

'Don't shout. You'll unbalance him if he looks up.'

How it happened she did not know. She did not see him move. But somehow the tawny stranger was by her side, his strong, long fingers gripping her arm, and his own eyes turned to watch the small boy busily trying to emulate his own performance along the top of the guard rail of the fishing smack.

'He'll fall.' It came out in a frightened whisper.

'He will if you've got no more sense than to shout at him.' The stranger's tone was taut, commanding her silence. 'The only thing that's keeping him on the top of that rail is concentration, and sheer good luck,' he added grimly.

'You're hurting.' She became conscious of his fingers, digging into the soft flesh of her arm above her elbow, bruising, with a clamp like a vice.

'I daren't risk you shouting at him.' He loosed her arm immediately, and she reached up and rubbed it with her opposite hand, her eyes angrily inspecting the red weals marking the place where his fingers had gripped her.

'If the child falls on to the dinghy,' he continued as if she had not spoken, 'he's likely to break his neck.'

'If he falls into the harbour, he's just as likely to drown,' she snapped.

'I hardly think so.' He measured the distance between himself and the fishing smack with a knowledgeable eye. 'I'd reach him before he went down for the third time.'

His tone conveyed the same arrogant assurance that brought him ashore by such an unorthodox route rather than bother to unlash the dinghy from his own vessel, and implied that he was quite capable of coping with any such eventuality with ease. Anger simmered inside Lee as she rubbed her ill-used arm in silence. The child—he looked about seven or eight years old, and she she did not recognise him as a local, he probably belonged to a holiday-maker—came to the end of the rail, and more by luck than good judgement fixed himself to the rope and slid down it into the dinghy in a passable imitation of the man by her side. True, he descended with more speed and less caution than his predecessor, and he reached the dinghy in an undignified rush. The rowboat tipped alarmingly, and Lee caught her breath, but the boy hung on like a limpet and manoeuvred himself over the side, and into safety. He stopped there for a second or two, and she saw him hold up the palms of his hands and inspect them.

'That'll teach him not to grip hold of a rope so tightly when he slides down it.' The hint of a chuckle sounded in the stranger's voice, and Lee snapped,

'If you hadn't shown off by walking along the guard rail the way you did, the boy wouldn't have tried to copy you. His hands are probably rubbed sore by now,' she flared angrily.

'I don't expect to guard my every movement in case someone else's brat tries to copy it.' His tone was cold, and he turned on her a look where anger lurked. 'If people have children they should be prepared to look after them. And if his hands are sore, it's nothing to what his seat is going to be, any minute now.'

Before Lee could divine his intention, he turned and strode back across the harbour wall, and ran down the steps to the beach. He glanced once at the boy, who with commendable common sense, Lee thought, ignored the oar, which was three times his size anyway, and lay across the side of the dinghy and used his short legs as a means of propulsion away from the high side of the fishing smack. With a hefty double kick, he sent his transport skimming shorewards.

Unlike the man, he forgot that the painter would snap tight at the end of the tether, and the resulting jerk tumbled him into the bottom of the dinghy, but he had achieved his objective, and with a grin of triumph on his freckled face he jumped out on to the beach. His legs were too short to span the shallows, and he waded the last couple of feet through the water with happy enjoyment. He did not notice the tawny-haired man waiting for him at the water's edge.

'He'll tick him off, good and proper, I expect.' Betty sounded awestruck, and automatically Lee followed her to the edge of the harbour wall. She could not hear what the man said to the boy, the distance between them was too far for more than a murmur of his voice to reach them, but she saw him point sternly towards the rowboat, and the boy's grin vanished. With lightning speed, he twisted away from the retribution that he evidently guessed was about to fall upon him, but he had not gone two steps before firm fingers reached out and grasped his brightly coloured tee-shirt by the slack, and hauled him back again. Instantly, a small, soaking wet sandal lashed out. The kick missed, the length of the man's arm was twice that of the boy's leg, but a stream of sandy water splattered down his immaculate cream slacks.

'He'll get his bottom smacked for that, for sure,' Betty prophesied as the man pulled the boy towards him with a sharp, angry movement, and Lee cried out,

'Don't you dare to touch him! Leave him alone, he's only a child.' She drew in a shaky breath. 'The big bully!' she muttered, in a furious aside to Betty. 'He should pick on someone his own size....'

Her words died in her throat as the man turned. Two cold, tawny eyes stared at her for a second or two, then without a word he deliberately crooked his knee, bent the boy across it, and administered two sharp slaps to the small denim-covered behind. The cracks of them, instantly followed by the boy's anguished wail, echoed across the harbour, and both Lee and Betty winced. Unconsciously Lee's hand felt the seat of her own denims, with urgent sympathy for the small victim, and she hastily pulled it away again as the stranger let the boy go and strode back towards the steps.

'What did you have to do that for?' she demanded

angrily as he reached the top. 'Didn't you ever do anything you shouldn't, at his age?' Her voice quivered with indignation, and her eyes snapped as she faced him.

'If he hadn't been checked, he'd have tried it again, and the next time he might not have been so lucky. There may not have been anybody there if he fell into the water. You may not have noticed, but there's no sign of his parents around,' he pointed out with sarcastic justification. Lee's face flamed. Her eyes told her he spoke the truth. The beach was practically deserted, and the boy was too young to be left to play about in the harbour on his own. The very fact that what the man said was reasonable only added fuel to the fire of her anger.

'Need you have been quite so brutal?' she asked him icily. 'Surely a scolding would have been enough for a child his age?'

'A child his age soon forgets a scolding. He won't forget a smacked seat.' His voice was as cold as her own. 'If nothing else, he'll have learned two lessons this morning.'

'And what might those be?' Lee could have kicked herself for asking. He led her into the question, and she walked into the trap like an innocent abroad, she thought furiously.

'He's learned not to grip a rope when he slides down it. And not to court death by walking across the guard rails of boats,' he returned evenly, no whit put out by her annoyance.

'They say things always go in threes.' Betty was determined to put her oar in and be noticed. 'That's another lesson he's got coming,' she simpered, in a way that made Lee want to smack her.

'He's probably learned his third lesson, too,' the stranger said grimly. 'That is if he's wise. He'll remember in future that it's dangerous to cross my path,' he added, and his eyes ignored Betty and sought and held Lee's, and in them there was anger, and a latent challenge. Instinctively she backed a step, and the tawny eyes fired as if with triumph, conscious of mastery. The look in them made Lee stop and draw herself up, and wish she was at least six inches taller. It had not seemed to matter before, but she did not like the feeling that this man towered above her, dwarfing her not only by his height but by the sheer force of his personality. Again she was reminded of a mountain lion, tensed, and ready to pounce.

'Pig!'

The shrill insult broke the tension between them. They both spun round and looked at the small urchin, one hand still nursing his smarting posterior, and his pink tongue stuck out rudely towards the stranger. Did the hint of a twitch show on the firm lips? Lee could not tell. If it had, it was gone as quickly as it came. The boy was a safe distance away, at the corner of the street, and well out of reach, she saw thankfully. The stranger took a quick step forward, but somehow Lee knew he did not intend to pursue the boy, although the youngster was evidently not prepared to take a chance.

'Pig!' he shrilled again, then spun about and vanished round the corner of the street at top speed.

'Betty, there's customers waiting.' Mr Dunn called his daughter's attention to business, and with a last wistful look at the stranger Betty reluctantly waddled back to the shop, and the mundane art of weighing potatoes and apples.

For a brief moment of time the stranger waited. Lee looked up at him uncertainly, disconcerted to find him still watching her. His expression was aloof and enigmatic, and something else that was unreadable. She turned abruptly towards the Mini van, and fumbled for her key.

'Allow me?'

How did he guess she had left the driving door unlocked? It was something Jon always grumbled at her about, and she knew it was silly to be so incautious, but she just forgot. Something of her guilt must have expressed itself in her face, for the stranger's lips quirked upwards for the second time, his grin reaching his eyes as he read her expression, which told him clearly she knew he had guessed her thoughts, and found it amusing to make her feel guilty.

'At least you know what the boy thinks about you,' she snapped ungraciously as she slid into the driving seat. 'And I agree with him. Entirely.' She slammed the door emphatically, and gave the ignition key a vicious twist. She would have liked to shout 'Pig!' at him herself. The male chauvinistic variety, she muttered through gritted teeth, but something in his look warned her not to say it out loud.

The engine spluttered into life, protesting at her unusually violent treatment, and she saw with satisfaction that the arrogant stranger had hurriedly made himself scarce out of her path and on to the safety of the pavement. Realised too late, from his mocking bow, that his haste was a sarcastic questioning of her driving ability, and with compressed lips, she turned the Mini round and headed with an angry toss of her head back in the direction of Polrewin.

'You look rattled.' Her brother looked at her curiously as she jerked to a halt in front of the house, and he emerged from one of the glasshouses with a stack of tomato trays in his arms. 'Simmer down,' he grinned, 'or you'll go off pop.' Jon had a milder temperament than Lee's. He had inherited it, along with brown hair and hazel eyes, from his father's side of the family, whereas Lee got her black hair and eyes, and fiery nature, from their Spanish grandmother.

'Oh, I've just had a brush with an idiot holidaymaker,' she shrugged off her irritation with difficulty. 'Some of the summer visitors we have around here make me sick!' she declared tempestuously. 'Here's Mr Dunn's tally.' She fished it out of her pocket, and her brother patiently put down his burden to take it. 'And he says he could do with the same delivery every day now that new caravan site has got going along the coast,' she added. 'Betty says the stuff's selling like hot cakes there.'

'Suits us fine.' Jon glanced at the tally and gave a whistle of satisfaction. 'At least it keeps us in the black with the bank until we've decided in which direction we want to go at Polrewin.' He glanced at the two big greenhouses with justifiable pride, and Lee saw his eyes wander across to the space where she knew he planned to put two more when finances permitted. 'By the way, talking of visitors,' he turned back to her impulsively, 'will it put you out much if we have one come to Polrewin?'

'Of course it won't.' Lee felt she would welcome company, it would make a pleasant change for both of them. 'I'm sure Nell won't mind,' she blessed the co-operative nature of the housekeeper they had taken on along with the flower farm, 'and with Mr Dunn's cheques coming in regularly like this we can afford to feed another mouth,' she said frankly. 'Do I know him? Or is it a her?' she asked mischievously.

'It's a him, and you don't,' her brother grinned back. 'At least, you know of him. It's Haydn Scott. We were at college together, but I don't think you ever met him, did you?'

'It was a bit too far for me to come,' Lee said drily, referring to the fact that she had been at finishing school in France at the time. 'I didn't know you still kept in touch with him?' Vaguely she remembered Jon talking of someone called Haydn, but it was too long ago to recall details.

'Only now and then.' Her brother heaved the tomato trays back into his arms again. 'But I knew he'd be interested to hear about Polrewin. I wrote and told him we'd inherited it from Uncle Bill and decided to make a go of it between us. It seems he's over here on a sort of working holiday himself, and thought he'd look us up. He rang from Tarmouth just before you came back.'

'How long will he be staying?' Much as she wanted Jon to enjoy his friend's visit, having to look after a guest would add to the workload outside. She would have to help Nell rather than lend an extra pair of hands for tomato picking.

'Only for supper.' Jon allayed her fears. 'I thought we might offer him a bed for the night if we got talking late, rather than give him the bother of going all the way back to the harbour afterwards.'

That meant he was probably staying at the Royal Anchor, Lee judged. Oh well, one night would make a pleasant break for them all, without unduly disrupting their busy routine.

'Haydn came to see me while I was managing Whitefields last year,' Jon went on, 'but you were away at the time. It was just before we heard that we'd inherited Polrewin. That's what made me write him, when we did.'

She was away in Scotland, Lee remembered, trying to sort out her feelings about Dennis. In a way, Polrewin helped her to make that particular decision. It meant a place of his own for Jon, even if it was a rundown one that resembled a jungle rather than a flower farm. He would be his own master here, which was better than managing an estate for someone else, however big, and his interest had always been in horticulture rather than agriculture, in that he took after their uncle. He lacked experience, but he was learning fast, and if they could manage to survive the first two years, Lee reckoned he would turn Polrewin into a viable holding. As for Dennis.... She was glad, now, she had the courage to break things off between them. She was fond of him, she always had been, from the time they were both little. Perhaps that was part of the trouble, she reflected; they knew one another too well. There was a vital spark missing from their relationship—something that Lee felt ought to be there, but Dennis seemed quite content to do without.

'I'm going in with Jon at Polrewin,' she told him, as gently as she could. 'With our joint savings, we can just about manage to start the business again. Uncle Bill must have had contacts there, he ran it as a flower farm once.'

'But your uncle hasn't run it as a business for years,' Dennis protested, very upset. 'His contacts will all be taken over by someone else before now, probably one of the big combines from the Channel Islands. And your savings—we were thinking of a mortgage....'

A mortgage on a semi. Perhaps eventually working towards a detached house of their own. Twenty-five years to pay, and their youth going while they trod a predictable middle path towards old age. Dennis was predictable, and to an increasingly restless Lee it was not enough.

'I'll go and tell Nell, and see what we can manage for supper,' she promised Jon. 'Come on, Bandy—Jet—come here!' Her tongue sharpened with sudden panic as the two dogs circled the tomato trays still on the ground, with an interested stalk. 'We really must teach those two that tomato trays can't be used as trees,' she wailed despairingly, and grabbed the shaggy off-white mongrel with the bandy legs, the result of a road accident that first brought it to Polrewin, and the liver-and-white spaniel, before the worst happened.

'You must admit there's a scarcity of trees around here,' Jon grinned. 'We'll just have to remember not to leave boxes of produce lying around, until they're trained.' He went off whistling, and Lee hauled the two animals indoors with her to impart her news to Nell.

'There's plenty of supper.' The homely, middle-aged woman was unperturbed by her news. 'It's good to cook for hungry mouths again,' she expressed her satisfaction at the present arrangements. After cooking for their elderly uncle, her delight at the opportunity to use her culinary prowess on young people with healthy appetites had not abated even after twelve months, and occasionally still made Jon groan at the amount of food she plied him with. 'There's only the pie to finish, and the sauce to make.'

'I'll do the sauce for you.' Lee sorted out a basin and saucepan and busied herself at the stove. 'It'll do Jon good to have a break,' she spoke her thoughts aloud, and Nell looked up from paring the pastry round the edge of the apple pie.

'It'll do you both good,' she said significantly. 'Too much work isn't good for anybody, and it'll give you a chance to get into something pretty for a change.' She gave an unenthusiastic look towards Lee's jeans and workmanlike top.

'The work hasn't hurt me, I'm not exactly a teenager,' Lee reminded her with a smile. She was twenty-five, and Jon three years older, indisputable facts even if Nell chose to ignore them, and mother them as if they were chicks round a broody hen. Just the same it would be nice to wear a dress for a change.

'It sounds as if your visitor's arrived,' Nell gave her a timely reminder as the two dogs set up a clamour and raced round to the front of the house.

'I've finished the sauce.' Lee poured it into a jug and set it on the stove top. 'I'll go upstairs and change before I say hello.' She had not heard the sound of a car in the yard, but perhaps it was because she had not been listening for it. She fled upstairs to her bedroom, thankful for once that there was a back stairway from the kitchen quarters. Jon could do the honours while she tidied herself up.

A glance at her watch told her she had three-quarters of

an hour yet before supper. After a moment's hesitation she decided on a shower first, and her hair curled damply in soft ringlets round her head as she towelled the drips away, and pulled a hurried brush and comb through it. By the time she was dressed it would be nearly dry. That was the advantage of short hair, she reflected as she opened her wardrobe and glanced through the possibilities for the evening. A casual invitation to supper did not merit anything special, but since they were going to enjoy a rare evening's relaxation, she might as well do the occasion justice.

She chose an acid yellow dress, sleeveless, with a scoop neckline and softly draped skirt, and a pair of scandals of the same colour. Yellow and white ringed bracelets gave a touch of coolness to the clear, astringent colour, which set off her dark hair and eyes and even tan to perfection. She knew she looked attractive, and it gave her added confidence as she pushed open the living room door and stepped inside to join the male voices she heard talking there. One, of course, belonged to Jon. There seemed something strangely familiar about the other.

'Meet my sister, Haydn. This is Haydn Scott, Lee. I can't think why you two never met.' Jon performed the introduction.

'But we have,' a lazy, amused drawl contradicted him, 'though I didn't immediately recognise the transformation.'

Lee turned, her colour flaring. She knew, now, with a sinking heart, what it was she recognised about the voice. The tawny-haired stranger from the harbour rose from where he lounged in the best easy chair, deliberately placed his glass back on the tray on top of the occasional table at his side, and looked down on Lee's discomfort from his annoyingly superior height with frank appreciation of the transformation. 'We met on the harbour wall this afternoon,' he answered Jon's surprised question with smooth ease, 'though of course I didn't know then you were related. You're not much alike.' He held out his hand—the hand that had so recently smacked the hapless child—and perforce Lee had to take it or appear unforgivably rude. She winced at its hard grip, which surely was just that bit harder, and held on for that much longer than was absolutely necessary in the cause of politeness. Perhaps he enjoyed inflicting pain on other people? Her eyes met his in mute, angry protest, and he released her.

'Have a sherry before supper, Lee?' Jon rescued her, and she turned and accepted the thin-stemmed glass from her brother with fingers that smarted, and suddenly trembled. Why, of all people, did the first guest they had entertained since they came to Polrewin have to be this hateful creature? she asked herself stormily. And to think they had got to be polite to him for the whole evening! Memory reminded her that he would probably stay the night as well. 'Rather than go all the way back to the harbour,' Jon had said. That explained it, she realised vexedly. She had assumed he would be staying at the Royal Anchor, but of course he was probably sleeping in his cabin cruiser, which meant he would not have a car.

'Haydn walked up,' Jon confirmed her guess. It was nearly three miles from the little town, but the picture of his long, easy stride between the two boats, and then again from the dinghy on to the dry pebbles of the beach, told her he would make short work of the distance. But no car probably meant no luggage, either. A quick glance round the room confirmed the absence of a case. Maybe that meant he would not stay the night. Sudden hope flared in her. He could not stay the night unless he had some nightclothes with him. Unless.... She glanced at him doubtfully over the rim of her glass. He looked quite capable of sleeping without them. Not in our sheets, she told herself firmly, and coloured furiously as a pair of amused, tawny eyes looked into her own, and read the thoughts that were going on inside her head, and laughed at them, not caring....

'We've got quite a lot to show you.' Jon broke into her defiant stare, unaware of the twin daggers of dislike and challenge that passed between his sister and his guest. 'Stay the night, if you've nothing better to do. We can talk over supper, and you can have a look round Polrewin in the morning. I can lend you some 'jamas,' he offered accommodatingly. 'We're about the same size.'

'Thanks, I'd be glad to,' his friend accepted calmly, at the same time glancing at Lee with a glint in his eyes which she did not know whether to interpret as meaning he did not have anything better to do, or he would be glad of the offer of pyjamas....

'Supper's ready, Miss Lee.' Nell knocked on the living room door and put an end to her confusion, but only for the moment. The table in the low-ceilinged dining room was small and round, and although it gave adequate room for half a dozen people by normal standards, their guest seemed to dwarf it, and the room. All through the iced melon, grown at Polrewin as an experiment, but purely for their own consumption as yet, followed by delicate young lamb and fresh picked peas, asparagus tips melted in butter, and ending with Nell's enormous apple pie, Lee could feel his eyes upon her, cool, assessing, and infinitely disturbing to her poise, to the point that she became clumsy and dropped her fork and her bread roll, and did not even think to scold the dogs for being in the dining room when they mopped up the unexpected titbit with relish.

'Have I got a smudge or something?' she asked at last, irritably, and he leaned back in his chair, with his head to one side, and to her increased annoyance paid an even keener attention to her face.

'Not that I can see,' he murmured consideringly. 'What makes you think...?'

'I just wondered what you were looking at, that's all,' she retorted sharply, and he smiled, with a slow, amused, upward lifting of his lips that mocked her discomfiture.

'I was merely thinking what a good photograph you would take. The contrast between dark hair and eyes, and that acid yellow colour of your dress would come out nicely.' Still he did not bother to take his eyes away from her face.

'Well!' She let out an angry breath, but before she could think of a suitable retort her brother butted in.

'Are you still interested in photography, Haydn? You were pretty keen on it when we were at college, I remember.'

'I use it professionally now,' the other answered. 'I've taken over the advertising side of the business.' He removed his eyes from her face at last, and Lee breathed an unconscious sigh of relief. 'It needed bringing up to date, with a bit of public relations stuff thrown in, and it seems to have paid off.'

Lee did not doubt that he had taken over whatever side of his firm he worked for. Wherever Haydn Scott happened to be, he would take over, and dominate, she thought resentfully. And the fact that his tactics paid off was evident, not only in his cabin cruiser, and the cut and quality of his clothes, but in his whole self-assured bearing. Watching him covertly as she poured coffee afterwards, while he discussed photography with her brother, she was aware of a slight tremor that felt disturbingly like fear.

'I just don't like him, that's all,' she dismissed the tremor robustly. She did not like self-assured men with spectacular good looks, who strolled across other people's boats as if the whole world belonged to them, spanked the first child they came across when they got ashore, and then came to supper and sat surveying their hostess with self-possessed, impersonal detachment, because she happened to be in a dress that might show up well in some advertising campaign they were interested in working on.

Except that the look in Haydn Scott's eyes, she remembered with a return of the tremor, had been neither detached nor impersonal.

CHAPTER TWO

SHE sorted out a suit of Jon's pyjamas, and put them aside while she closed the airing cupboard door.

'I hope they're too small, and stop him from sleeping,' she thought maliciously, then knew with horrid certainty that if they were in the slightest bit uncomfortable he would jettison them without a thought. Her cheeks warmed, and she grabbed the offending nightwear and made her way to the spare room.

'He shan't have Jon's new pair, anyway,' she determined. Not the blue silk pair she had recklessly bought her brother for Christmas, and she knew he had not worn yet. She regarded the pair over her arm with satisfaction. They were well worn, and faded, and she noticed there was a button missing from off the jacket. She had meant to sew it on, but somehow there had not been time since Nell did the ironing on Monday, and she had no intention of doing it now.

Taking a resolute grasp of her manners, she forced herself to do her duty towards their guest, and turned down the covers on the spare bed and laid her burden on top. She hesitated for a moment. The window had swung itself shut in the slight breeze off the sea, and the room felt hot.

'If he wants fresh air, he can open it for himself,' she thought rebelliously, and shut the door with a bang loud enough to drown her conscience. If Haydn was made too comfortable, he might want to stay for another night, and the thought was not to be borne.

She made her way downstairs on feet that dragged. There was no further excuse for her to stay away from the living room any longer. She had helped Nell with the clearing away and washing up after supper, despite the housekeeper's protest that she could manage for tonight on her own, and there was nothing further to do in the spare room.

'An attractively laid out catalogue makes a lot of difference,' Haydn was holding forth to an interested Jon when

Lee joined the two men. He gave a polite inclination of his head to acknowledge her presence as she entered the room, then carried on talking, and perversely Lee felt a flash of annoyance. She did not go along with the idea of silent, submissive womanhood in the presence of the all-important male, and she took the easy chair nearest to Jon with tightened lips. No sooner had she sat down than she realised that by sitting opposite Haydn she was right in the path of every glance he sent towards her brother as they talked, but it was either that or sit right by him. She gave an impatient wriggle and settled herself as far back in the cushions as she could. The dogs wandered over, and Bandy dropped his head on to her lap with a sigh, his pink tongue protruding in protest at the warm evening, and she rubbed his shaggy head sympathetically. The air was becoming oppressive, and it was not only Haydn's fault, she acknowledged with a slight inward grin. There was a storm brewing, and the atmosphere felt sticky. It would be even worse in Tarmouth, at least Polrewin was situated high on the cliffs, in a cleft that sheltered it from the worst of the winds, as well as kept it reasonably cool in the summer.

'I take photographs of anything that looks interesting during the year,' Haydn went on, and Lee wondered if that was why he had wanted to photograph her, then she remembered it was merely the contrast of her dress with her hair and eyes that had taken his attention. 'Then I use half a dozen of the best in the annual catalogue. One superb photograph splashed across the centre pages can turn an ordinary catalogue into a work of art,' he enthused, and Lee slanted a glance of dislike across at him. It was typical of the man, she thought sarcastically, that he would believe the photographs he took to be both superb, and works of art.

'People started sending for the catalogues for themselves,' Haydn continued. 'The Board didn't think much of it at the time, but when we had to have a second reprint they began to sit up and take notice. After that, they let me have my own way, and just awaited events.'

Oh yes, Haydn would have his own way, Lee thought. She did not doubt he would do so in whatever circumstance he happened to find himself, and she found her ears did not want to listen to him boasting to her brother about how much of a success his brilliant ideas had been. She and Jon had worked hard to bring Polrewin up to what it was now, and thanks to their efforts it was still afloat, but no doubt it looked a homespun sort of enterprise in comparison to whatever sophisticated business Haydn Scott was engaged in.

'What was the outcome?' Jon sounded enthralled, and Lee could have smacked him. For a moment of unease she hoped her brother would not become too interested, be perhaps dazzled by the picture of success that this man was painting in front of him, and maybe become drawn into the maw along with Haydn Scott, no doubt to do the jobs that the great man himself could not be bothered with, she thought worriedly. There was still a long way to go before Polrewin could be called successful, but Jon was a man who liked an open-air existence, and she doubted if he would be happy in a high-powered commercial atmosphere that probably Haydn revelled in.

'The outcome is a growing mail order business,' their guest continued. 'I'd seen the possibilities for years, but I bided my time until I'd learned the business, and then got my photography up to a sufficient level to use it commercially, before I broached my plans. Now I'm thinking of expanding that side of it. We aren't really geared up to deal with it on the scale I'm thinking of, and we shall need new premises.'

So he was capable of waiting, too, staying quietly on the sidelines until the right opportunity should present itself. Again she was reminded irresistibly of a mountain lion, crouching patiently, watching its prey. She wondered idly what sort of business he was engaged in. The rag trade, probably. He looked the sort who would have an eye for expensive clothes and furs.

'No doubt your pictures come in useful, for pin-ups,' she commented, and the bite in her voice made him look across at her directly, with a clear, level stare.

'I don't use models,' he told her coolly, immediately aware of her implication, 'the perfectly groomed, sophisiticated types wouldn't be right for our work.'

So it could not be the rag trade, Lee silently eliminated one possibility.

'The fresh, outdoor girl, with a hint of naïveté—the serene type—would be more the line I'd go for if I ever needed a girl for my work.'

But not if he needed a girl for himself. The thought came unbidden, and she felt a tide of pink flood across her cheeks as a sudden flare of laughter lit his eyes, and told her he guessed what was going through her mind. She bit her lip and dropped her eyes away from his, then felt furious with herself for having done so. She was behaving naïvely. She should have held his stare, as no doubt a sophisticated woman of the world would have done, and sent a cool retort back. Only she could not think of one, only of the angry, impatient words that surged through her mind and could not be spoken to a guest under their roof. Was that how he saw her? she wondered crossly. As a fresh, outdoor, country lass, rather simple.... A picture of Betty's vacuous stare flashed across her mind and she got up from her chair abruptly. At least he could not accuse her of being serene, she thought with satisfaction; she had only known him a few hours, and their meetings had been anything but.

'It's time I fed the dogs.' That was the truth, anyway. Enquiring noises were already beginning to come from Bandy and Jet, and she realised with compunction that it was half an hour later than they were normally fed. 'I thought you two were hungry,' she complained as she set two bowls of food on the scullery floor, only to have her efforts deserted in favour of chasing a cat that wailed suddenly from outside. 'Come on, you'll have made yourself twice as hot by now,' she scolded the hairy Bandy affectionately, as the errant pair rushed back with laughing tongues, having seen their adversary safely off the premises. 'As soon as you two have had your usual wander round, I can go to bed myself.'

She whiled away the time making a drink for herself. There was no need to make one for the men, they were quietly enjoying a glass of whisky each when she left them, and beyond a brief goodnight, which they equally briefly disturbed their conversation to answer, she thought with illogical pique, she turned towards her own bedroom with a feeling of relief that the evening was over.

She could not sleep. From downstairs came the murmur of voices. It seemed to go on and on. She glanced at her bedroom clock as footsteps sounded on the stairs at last, and discovered the illuminated hands had long since passed midnight. She thought guiltily of how hot Haydn's bedroom must be, and on the qualms of conscience eventually drifted into an uneasy doze, only to be awakened some time afterwards by a yapping clamour from the scullery. She roused herself to dazed wakefulness, and realised the caterwauling outside her window was the cause of the noise from inside the house.

'Psst! Shoo!' She leaned out of her bedroom window, but the cat was either deaf or uncaring, for the jungle singing continued, to a rising tide of indignation from the two dogs.

'Pests!' She referred impartially to feline and canine alike, and slid out of bed. There would be no sleep for anybody, herself included, unless the three were quietened, and she hurried downstairs without bothering to slip on either dressing gown or slippers. The storm was still hovering, and the air was oppressively hot. She dealt with the cause of the noise first. With a quick slip of the catch she opened the front door, grabbed up a handful of gravel from the path, and flung it in the general direction of the caterwauling. An abrupt cessation of feline song, and a startled scampering, told her her aim was not far out, and she turned into the scullery and subdued the two dogs, who slunk guiltily back into their baskets at her irate scolding.

'Now go to sleep, and let everybody else do the same,' she bade them sternly, and clicked off the light. She really had no need to switch it on in the first place, it was moonlight outside, even though the stormclouds blotted it out with increasing regularity; there was still enough illumination to see quite well. It told her she had not bolted the front door, and she stooped down to remedy the omission. The full skirt of her sprigged pink and white cotton nightdress ballooned out from the ruched waistline and got in her way, and she pulled it to one side with her other hand.

A stair creaked—the bottom stair, it always did—and she looked round sharply, suspecting that the dogs had disturbed Nell too. She gave a sigh of relief as she caught sight of faded striped pyjama legs above bare brown feet.

'It's you, Jon,' she exclaimed thankfully, 'I thought the dogs had awakened Nell. I—oh!' She dropped her nightdress skirt and stood upright, her dismayed glance rising above the faded stripes to a bare, teak-coloured chest and rippling shoulder muscles under a tousled tawny head that definitely did not belong to her brother.

'It isn't Jon, it's me,' Haydn said unnecessarily.

'I—I can see that.' A warm tide of colour rose from the base of her throat and flooded across her cheeks in a deep flush of rose. Confusedly she wished the moon would go behind another cloud. A shaft of clear white light glowed perversely through the top glass panel of the front door, and too late she regretted not stopping for the few seconds it would have taken to slip on her dressing gown. Thank goodness the heat of the night had made her abandon the filmy, transparent folds of coffee-coloured lace and nylon she had been wearing, in favour of a cooler cotton nightdress. Even so, she was uncomfortably conscious that the deep broderie anglaise neckline left a generous area of softly tanned shoulders for the moonlight to play with, and Haydn's appreciative look told her he was fully aware of the fact, and of her embarrassment, and she asked him sharply,

'Did the dogs disturb you too? I'm sorry,' she apologised stiffly.

'No.' He smiled slowly, not attempting to move from his stance on the bottom stair, and effectively blocking her only avenue of escape unless she went back through the scullery to the kitchen flight. Her temper rose as he continued to loll negligently against the newel post. 'I came down for a drink of water.' The tawny eyes gleamed in sudden laughter as he presented the age-old child's excuse for deserting his bed. 'My room was hot, the window had blown shut.' He continued to watch her, and Lee's colour deepened further still. It was her fault his room was hot. Her fault that he was leaning against the bottom of the stair now, watching her. Instinct told her that he was fully aware she knew about the closed window, maybe he thought she had closed it deliberately. That, at least, was not on her conscience.

'I'll get you a drink.' She spun away from him and opened the kitchen door, thankful to turn her back to him. She reached into the cupboard for a beaker and filled it from the tap, then promptly spilled half of it into the stone sink when he spoke from just behind her.

'I could have done it myself,' he told her mildly. She had not heard him follow her. Too late she remembered his feet, too, were bare, and moved as silently as her own across the quarry floor. The stone struck cold on to her soles, and she curled her toes and lifted one foot to ease it. Water dripped down the side of the beaker, and automatically she wiped it with a cloth and put it down on the table while she hung the towel back on the rail, using mundane things to hide her confusion.

'Is there anything else you want?' She regretted her question the second it was spoken, but it was too late to retract. A light of unholy amusement lit his face, and he stepped towards her, hemming her in between himself and the draining board of the sink. Without haste, he reached out and took her by her bare shoulders. She gave a startled gasp and strained backwards, her eyes wide and furious on his face, but the stainless steel sink behind her pressed like a knife into her back, and her strength was as nothing against the sheer male muscle power of his arms.

'Since you've asked,' he drawled softly, 'there is one thing....' He laughed down into her face as he pinioned her against him. 'I'd like a goodnight kiss.'

He took it.

He ignored her protest, and pressed hard lips against her own, effectively punishing her for leaving his window closed and allowing his room to resemble an oven. Punishing her for her rudeness after he had spanked the boy in the harbour, when common sense told her he had been in the right to do so. And then, with narrowed eyes watching her, he let her go and stepped back, with his catlike, silent tread, and picked up the beaker of water where she left it on the table.

'That's all I need—for tonight,' he said with soft emphasis. 'Thanks for the drink.' And he went out and closed the kitchen door behind him. Lee leaned back against the hardness of the draining board, fighting for composure. Her fingers went up to her bruised lips, and discovered she was trembling. Despite the storm-charged heat of the atmosphere, the steel behind her felt cold, and she shivered, and became conscious again of the chill of the quarry floor under her feet. They felt like blocks of ice, but they were as nothing to the ice-cold fury that possessed her at Haydn Scott's high-handed action.

The memory of Betty's starry-eyed stare crossed her mental vision, and she snorted scornfully. Betty could have him, she decided furiously. She had no use for cavemen tactics herself. But hadn't she found Dennis too predictable? She pushed the thought aside impatiently. There had to be a happy medium somewhere. And besides, the last thing she wanted at the moment was another entanglement. She wanted to see Polrewin on its feet first. That would have to be enough, for the next couple of years. She pushed herself away from the draining board and stepped towards the door on legs that felt curiously unsteady, then she stopped. There was no guarantee that Haydn was not still sitting on the stairs drinking his water. After a moment's pause she turned back and walked quietly through the kitchen into the scullery. She was being a coward, but she could not face him again tonight. The dogs stirred when she passed them, but they settled again when she spoke to them, and she ascended the back stairs and gained her own room in safety.

If he's waiting for me to come out of the kitchen and up the front stairs, he'll wait all night, she thought with malicious satisfaction, that brought some comfort back to her frozen toes as she curled up into a ball and dropped off to sleep almost immediately.

The storm broke just before daylight. It was brief, and fierce, as were most of the storms in that area, but after listening to it for a while Lee turned over and dozed off again, relaxed in the knowledge that the wind direction would miss the two big greenhouses, which were sheltered on that side by a particularly steep rise of the cliff. She spared a thought for the people in the harbour as she drifted back into unconsciousness. It would hit them full on, and give the boats moored there a rocky ride. Wistfully she was reminded that if their guest had not stayed overnight at Polrewin, he too would have had a rough time on his cabin cruiser, but unfortunately he was safely in bed in their spare room, and she was denied the satisfaction of thinking of him being storm-tossed in the harbour. He was the type who would enjoy the challenge of the elements in any case.

It was calm when she woke the next morning. The sun gleamed from a clear sky that showed no hint of its sullen anger of the night before. Defiantly she dressed in her working gear, the same jeans she had on the day before, and a clean blue shirt. It had got long sleeves, and she rolled them up past her elbows out of the way, presenting a workmanlike picture as she went downstairs to breakfast.

'I'll bring the coffee through in a minute, Miss Lee,' Nell called out to her as she passed the kitchen door. 'Mr Scott isn't down yet.'

'If he's not quick, we'll have our breakfast without him,' Lee muttered. There was the day's batch of tomatoes to pick, and the chores to do around the greenhouses, and if Haydn thought he could treat the place like an hotel he would shortly find his mistake, she thought ungraciously. She glowered out of the big, circular window that was like a porthole, and the only reminder of Polrewin's builder, an ex-naval captain who brought to his retirement a perpetual reminder of his career.

'Unusual shape for a window,' Haydn observed appearing silently at her side, and she hunched her shoulders at his cheerful 'good morning', and refused to look at him.

'It's a nuisance,' she said curtly. 'I like a windowsill I can lean my arms along, and there's no room for flower vases, either.'

'You seem to have found plenty of substitutes.' Her guest's glance round the room rested on sweetly perfumed vases filled with a variety of both wild and cultivated blooms that brightened the dark furniture, and betrayed Lee's weakness at the same time, and to her annoyance he ignored her ill humour.

'Here's your coffee, Miss Lee.' Nell bustled in with the aromatic brew, and added as she put it on the table, 'Mr Jon asked me to let you know he'd had his breakfast early and gone out into the glasshouses, so he can do the picking and be free to show you round later, sir.' She smiled at Haydn, and Lee smarted with silent chagrin. Even Nell seemed to have fallen for the man's charms, she thought cynically, aware that their guest had taken the trouble to seek out the housekeeper the evening before and congratulate her on their perfectly cooked supper. 'Miss Lee will look after you, though,' she beamed, and left them, and Lee looked up to meet his quizzically raised eyebrows.

'Aren't you going to ask me if there's anything I want this morning?' he asked her softly as they took their places opposite to one another at the table, and her colour rose with a rush.

'If you want anything, you can help yourself,' she snapped, and then her eyes widened as a dawning grin lit his face, and she gripped the edge of the table until her knuckles showed white when he pushed his chair back, preparatory to getting up. 'Any breakfast, I mean,' she added hurriedly, and was unable to contain a small sigh of relief as he settled back into his chair with an exaggerated air of disappointment. 'There's a grill under the hot dish, or cold if you'd prefer it here,' she indicated a plate of ham within his reach.

Confound Jon, she thought vexedly. I've got to stick it out now until he comes back, or Haydn finishes eating. From the leisurely way in which her companion tackled his breakfast, it looked as if he was going to go on all day. She fidgeted restlessly, crumbling her own sparse piece of toast into chips on her plate with sheer frustration while he helped himself to grilled bacon, mushrooms and kidneys, after first tasting Nell's hot creamy porridge, and then taking a second piece of toast and another cup of coffee, and all the while keeping up a steady flow of small talk. He questioned her about Polrewin, and what they intended to do there, until she could have screamed with impatience, but he seemed unaware of her reluctant response. Only the thought that he was her brother's invited guest kept her glued to her seat, and she answered in monosyllables, discouraging his searching questions as best she could.

'You seem unusually interested in Polrewin,' she said coldly at last, and he looked at her, as if surprised.

'Jon knew I would be, that's why he wrote me when he first inherited it,' Haydn retorted, and she flared.

'When *we* first inherited it,' she corrected him tersely.

'I stand corrected,' he acknowledged gravely, then added with a fine bite in his voice, 'I can see this morning that you must be a working partner.' His eyes flicked over her severely practical garb, and Lee bit her lip angrily.

'Feminine frills aren't much use when you're picking and sorting tomatoes and things,' she said bluntly, and scowled at the lazy smile that formed in his eyes even before it tilted the edges of his well cut lips.

'The feminine frills I saw looked becoming enough last night,' he reminded her softly, 'or was it in the early hours of this morning? I don't remember.' His grin taunted her.

'Sorry I couldn't join you for breakfast.' To her relief Jon came in and saved her from having to reply. 'But I'm free now for a bit, we can have a look round,' he invited Haydn, and seemed quite oblivious of the strained atmosphere that fairly crackled between his two companions.

'In that case, I'll....' Lee began, and pushed her chair against the table, prepared to make a hurried exit.

'Nell said she'd cope inside today, and leave you free as well,' Jon told her happily. 'If you come with us, you can fill Haydn in with the bits I forget,' he offered accommodatingly.

'It looks like being an interesting tour,' Haydn said smoothly, and held open the door for Lee to precede him, with a slight bow that brought a cheerful grin to Jon's face as he cast a glance at his sister, and a scowl to Lee's. Jon might think his friend gallant, but Lee caught the mocking glint in the amber gaze that challenged her to accompany them. Or challenged her to refuse? She gave an impatient sigh and walked on to the gravel outside, and took a couple of deep breaths to steady her, taking in the clear air that had been cooled wine-sharp by the storm of the night before.

'It's great, isn't it?' Haydn came to stand beside her, and she could see the movement as his rib cage expanded under the thin cream silk of his shirt.

'It'd be even better on your boat,' Lee suggested tautly, but her barbed hint did not even dent his calm self-possession.

'You must come down and put it to the test,' he retorted smoothly, 'both of you—I'll be staying around for a day or two in any case.'

'There's not much to see around Tarmouth,' Lee began inhospitably, and he interrupted her with a meaningful remark.

'I've got—er—an interest in the area,' he said obliquely, and turning to Jon made a comment about the greenhouses as they walked towards them, leaving Lee wondering what was behind his statement. She lagged behind the two men slightly, and puzzled over it. There was nothing around Tarmouth that might even remotely interest a man like Haydn. She watched his tall, flat-hipped figure striding out beside her brother with the same lithe ease that he had walked the guard rails of his boat the day before. He had mentioned he was thinking of expanding his mail order business, but Tarmouth was not a commercial town. Its main industries were fishing or flower farming, and the visitors and artists who flocked there during the summer months were an added bonus and an extra income for the residents, but that was all.

'Your vines look healthy.' Haydn reached out an interested hand and took a half ripe tomato. He rubbed it briefly with his handkerchief and bit into it.

'Cheek!' Lee muttered under her breath, and felt a momentary qualm as he slewed a glance at her, but he could not have heard what she said. I don't care if he did, she thought mutinously. It *was* cheek, to pick someone else's fruit without even asking permission first.

'Hmm, the flavour's good.'

So he was a connoisseur of food as well, was he? she thought sarcastically.

'A bit on the small side, though.' He gazed at the trusses on the rest of the vine with a critical eye.

'They suit the market they're intended for.' She could not keep silent and listen to such comments. 'They go like hot cakes,' she repeated Betty Dunn's words triumphantly.

'I'm sure they do.' He spoke indulgently, as if he was humouring her, and her anger mounted.

'We send all our stock to the local greengrocer, and he sells it to the caravan site. They prefer smaller tomatoes, because of the children,' Lee told him flatly. She could not think why it was because of the children, but she vaguely remembered Mr Dunn saying something of the kind. She found she could not think clearly anyway, with Haydn looking at her like that.

'Hmm.' He finished the fruit and chewed silently for a minute or two, then, 'Do you send all your stock to the one greengrocer, Jon?'

'At the moment, yes. His monthly cheque's been a godsend,' Jon said fervently. 'It's helped to keep us afloat.'

'Fine, but it might pay you to branch out a bit when you expand,' Haydn said seriously. 'If you think about it,' he thrust teak-coloured hands deep into the pockets of his beautifully tailored cream slacks. Lee noticed the leg that had been splattered with sand and water by the child's kick the day before showed no sign now of ill-use, which meant they were probably the expensive, stain-resistant as well as crease-resistant kind. 'You must admit, it's a closed sort of market,' Haydn went on. 'You've only got one outlet, and your man relies on purely seasonal trade, like caravans, for the bulk of his outlet.' He stopped significantly, and Jon nodded.

'I see what you mean,' he acknowledged, thoughtful in his turn.

'There's another thing,' Haydn went on, 'you've got a lot of wasted space in your glasshouses.'

'Wasted space?' Lee burst out indignantly, her glance ranging round the tightly packed beds. 'Where on earth could you find another inch to put plants, without overcrowding them?'

'In the roof,' Haydn answered imperturbably. 'You could have got a crop of strawberries from up there if you'd got stretchers, and an arrangement of ropes and pulleys. I'll show you when we get back to the house, and I can sketch it out on paper for you,' he offered.

'We can't possibly let Mr Dunn's contract go, Jon.' Lee turned to her brother anxiously, ignoring the strawberries. 'Where else could we sell our produce if we broke with the greengrocer?' Panic touched her at the thought of the loss of Mr Dunn's monthly cheque.

'Covent Garden?' Haydn suggested, and she turned on him angrily.

'Covent Garden!' she repeated, with withering scorn. 'From an outfit the size of Polrewin? You must be out of your mind!'

'He does know what he's talking about, Sis,' Jon began, taken aback at her outburst.

'Does he?' Lee shot back at him furiously. 'What does he know about this trade?' she demanded. 'His job is photography. He said so himself.'

The sheer effrontery of the man took her breath away. If Jon listened to his suggestions he might easily ruin their efforts. They had both worked hard to put Polrewin on a firm footing, but it was a foundation that was still vulnerable, and could crumble as easily if they had a severe setback. Her eyes filled with angry tears at the thought of losing Polrewin, because of this stranger's arrogant interference.

'Photography, yes, but it's all to do with his father's business,' Jon tried again, placatingly.

'And what is his father's business?' she asked stormily, in no way appeased.

'He's Haydn Scott, Lee....'

'I know, you introduced us,' she retorted crushingly, incensed by her brother's assumption that everyone ought to recognise the man's name.

'He's the son of the founder of Scott's, the nursery garden people on the Channel Islands. You must have seen their boxed produce,' Jon insisted, and his words stilled the angry rejoinder trembling on the tip of her tongue.

Haydn Scott . . . the Channel Islands. For a moment Lee felt her senses swim. Why had she not connected the two? The enormity of her faux pas began to dawn on her. This man came from people who were specialists—highly successful specialists. A vision of a perky little kilted figure, with bagpipes, and tartan ribbons flying, crossed her shocked mind. It was the trademark of the biggest chain of nursery gardens in the south.

'I—I—didn't connect the two.' She forced the words through tight lips. She did not want to look at Haydn, did not want to see the sarcastic smile that no doubt lit his face as humiliated colour flooded her cheeks, and the angry tears of a moment ago turned to tears of mortification that she refused to let fall in front of him. One crept unwillingly over her lashes, and she flicked at it angrily, pretending it was a fly.

'Why should you? Scott's a common enough name,' he asked her mildly, and she sent him a surprised stare, and found no sarcasm in his face, only a look of grave interest that must be occasioned by what he had seen in the glasshouses. She realised now the reason for his interest, it was a common one to them all.

'Mr Jon, can you spare a minute? I want to know what to do about this fertiliser.' Ben, their only male help, came into the glasshouse, and stopped nonplussed when he saw Haydn. 'Sorry, I didn't know you'd got someone with you,' he apologised.

'Never mind,' Jon told him goodhumouredly, 'I'll come and see to what you want, and join you later, Haydn, if you don't mind?' He turned back to his friend. 'Carry on showing him round, Lee, and I'll catch up with you.' And he turned and quitted the glasshouse, leaving Lee and Haydn alone.

'Shall we call a truce, and carry on the tour of inspection?' Haydn suggested gently, and his eyes smiled down at her, seemingly without guile. She took a deep breath and nodded; she could not speak, and the knowledge did nothing to help her poise. Something happened to her knees when Haydn looked at her like that.

It's because I've had no breakfast, she told herself hardily. She never went without breakfast unless she was sick, and that was such a rare occurrence it almost never happened. Until this morning.

'Let's go outside.' Suddenly the greenhouse seemed too small. Even the light from the high roof was darkened by Haydn's tall figure, and she felt a claustrophobic sense of suffocation that made her want to run blindly away from him.

'The ground stretches quite a way,' he commented after they had walked the length of one field in silence, and three more still stretched out in front of them before the edge of the cliff. 'It's quite a lot bigger than I imagined.'

'It's big enough for the two of us to handle.' She relaxed slightly. So far he had made no comment on her behaviour, which she was uncomfortably conscious had been less than perfect towards a guest under their roof, but then so had his towards her. Guests did not usually kiss their hostesses. At least, not in that way.... The memory of it brought the traitorous colour to her cheeks again, and she spoke hurriedly.

'We're thinking of having two more glasshouses when we can afford them.' She did not try to hide the fact that they were having to inch their way along at the moment, it must have been self-evident to Haydn in any case, she thought wearily.

'Before you buy them, Jon might like to come over to the Islands and have a look at the ones we've got,' he suggested. He did not invite her to go along as well, Lee noticed, but she made no comment other than a slight shrug, and he went on, 'We run several different kinds for the different types of produce.'

'As well as stretchers for strawberries,' she could not resist reminding him, and he gave her a keen look, and nodded.

'As well as stretchers for strawberries. We can't afford wasted space and heat any more than you can,' he pointed out reasonably.

'I thought Jon said you had a chain of gardens.' She

could not resist the thrust, and the glint returned to his eyes as he responded.

'So we have, but the larger the outfit the larger the loss if you allow space to go to waste.' It was logical, she knew, but somehow it still had the power to annoy her. The very sureness of the man made Polrewin look even smaller and shabbier than it had before. Or was she merely seeing it through a stranger's eyes for the first time?

'Jon might find it a help to see how our gardens work.' He spoke of gardens in the plural, casually, indifferently, and Lee felt her temper stir within her again. She and Jon did not want Haydn's patronage. They had done well enough so far on their own, and she fully intended that they should go on doing so. Without his interference. They would expand in their own good time, when they could afford to. Silently she determined not to let Haydn Scott hurry Jon into expanding too quickly. Too many businesses overreached themselves too soon, of that she was well aware, and the result was usually bankruptcy. The mere thought of it sent cold shivers down her spine.

'I doubt he'll have time, at least this year,' she told her companion firmly, and his lips tightened.

'That's for Jon to say,' he said evenly.

'Not entirely, I'm his partner,' she retorted, and she lifted her chin defiantly. The move brought her head back, so that she looked up and straight into his eyes, though she had to tilt her chin even higher to meet them when he straightened his shoulders. The move brought a subtle change to his expression, and her own was suddenly uncertain as his face hardened, and the familiar glint returned to his eyes.

'Then it's time he brought you under control,' he told her sternly, and with an impatient movement he pulled her to him. 'For two pins I'd treat you the same as I treated that lad on the beach yesterday. It's a lesson you both need,' he said grimly, and Lee gave a gasp as she remembered his words on the harbour wall, about the third lesson the boy should have learned.

'It's dangerous to cross my path....'

'D-don't you d-dare....' Instinctively her hands went

back to cover her seat. The sound of the smacks he administered yesterday still rang in her ears.

'I'm not going to spank you, though it's what you deserve,' he told her roughly. 'There are other ways of taming people.'

She tried to bring her hands up between them, to push him away, but he gave her no time. His grip pinioned her arms to her sides, and for the second time that morning his lips descended, hard and angry, on her own. His one hand cupped her head so that she could not pull it away, and his other clamped against her back, as immovable as a vice. She held herself stiff, trying to press away from him, feeling the bruising pressure on her lips that silenced her with deadly expertise, until against her will she felt herself responding, becoming pliant in his arms....

He released her, then. He loosed his hands and let her go with a mocking laugh that made her hate him, want to lash out at him, but he must have sensed her movement even before it materialised, because she felt her hands captured by his.

'You ... I'll....'

'You'll what? Slay me? Or tell Jon?'

He let go of her hands, daring her to strike him, laughing at her impotent fury because she knew if she tried he would merely catch her hands again, and prevent her. She gave a choking gasp and spun away from him, and almost sobbed with relief as Jon's voice came across the field, calling them,

'Haydn—Lee!' and the voices of the two dogs joined in. Lee turned towards the sound, almost hysterically thankful to feel the spaniel's big paws climb up her for a fuss, and she filled her arms with his silky coat and hugged him to her, using him to hide the rush of tears that she could not hold back any longer. She rubbed her face dry with the back of her wrist just in time as her brother joined them.

'I'm glad you hadn't gone far,' his face was creased with concern. 'Ben's just told me about the damage the storm caused in the harbour last night,' he said urgently. 'It seems some yachtsman ran for shelter in the teeth of it, instead of sitting it out. He was a bit of an amateur, from all accounts,' he told Haydn. 'He seems to have lost his head when he came into the harbour, and he damaged a couple of boats. One of them is quite badly holed, I believe. I hope it isn't yours, Haydn,' he finished unhappily. 'But if it is,' he brightened, 'you must stay here with us at Polrewin until it's seaworthy again,' he invited generously.

CHAPTER THREE

'I'D better get down there right away, I suppose.'

Haydn did not seem particularly concerned, thought Lee, at the possible wanton damage to his cabin cruiser. If the boat belonged to her she would have raised the roof. His comparatively calm reaction puzzled her, until she remembered that the bill for repairs would not unduly bother him.

'Lee will take you,' Jon offered immediately. 'There's no need for you to walk that far, and Nell's taking over in the house today anyway.' He took his sister's co-operation for granted.

'I've got to take the day's batch of tomatoes in any case.' Lee refused to let Haydn think she would only go because of him, and she stepped out briskly beside the two men towards the house. 'I'll run the van round. Will you help me to load it, Jon?'

'Yes. I'd take you in myself, Haydn, but I've got to wait for a delivery of fuel,' her brother said. 'The tanker's due—oh gosh! Here it comes,' he exclaimed as they neared the house and the rounded sides of a large tanker rose above the hedgerow tangle of the lane. 'I'll have to leave you to it,' he apologised, 'unless I back the driver in he can't turn to come through the gate, it's too narrow.'

'I'll pick you up in about ten minutes,' Lee told Haydn, and turned towards the garage. She heard him speak to Ben behind her, but she did not turn round, and when she braked to a halt outside the house it was to find the man missing, a pile of filled tomato trays stacked waiting for her to load, and Haydn stood beside them.

'I'll help you with these.'

'There's no need,' she told him shortly, 'I can manage.'

She swung the doors of the van wide, and turned to find Haydn behind her with an armful of tomato trays. For a moment she stood her ground resentfully, and he gave an impatient motion of his head for her to stand aside, away from the doors. When she did not immediately comply he deliberately tilted the tomato trays and to her dismay she saw the top one shift on the pile. Another half inch, and it would crash to the ground. She moved aside hurriedly, and with a sharp glance at her Haydn righted it by the simple expedient of flexing his body backwards until it tipped the other way. He had to bend his knees and stoop low to slide his burden on to the floor of the van. He pushed the first stack well in, and stooping carefully to avoid cracking his head when he emerged he backed clear and straightened to his full height.

'Thank you,' he said evenly, and Lee eased the stack of trays in her own arms, preparatory to sending them to join the others in the van.

'I can manage by myself. I always do,' she told him crushingly, and with easy dexterity slid her load next to his. She did not have to stoop so far, nor back out so carefully, her much shorter stature making the Mini van more her size than Haydn's, but nonetheless he picked up another armful of trays ready to take her place by the time she turned round again to the stack on the gravel. They finished loading the van in strained silence, and Lee waited until he slammed both doors shut, automatically giving them an experimental tug to make sure the lock had caught properly.

'I'm ready, if you are,' she said tonelessly, and at his nod she walked round the vehicle and slipped into the driving seat. She inserted the key in the ignition before she realised the door on the passenger side was still locked, and she reached across unhurriedly and slid up the knob to allow him to get in beside her, conscious of a small satisfaction that it was Haydn who had had to wait. Doubtless in his world it was the women who waited, she thought grimly as she watched him stow his long length into the seat beside her.

'It's roomier than it looks.' He sounded surprised, and she switched on the engine and cruised slowly along the drive to the gate before she replied.

'It does well enough at the moment for what we want.'

'You'd find it easier to load if you had a bigger vehicle.'

'I find this one easy enough as it is,' she answered shortly, and her chin set stubbornly. Haydn seemed to assume that because he belonged to a big concern it gave him the right to criticise and try to alter everything he saw at Polrewin. She had had the Mini before she came to Cornwall; it had just the right amount of carrying capacity for her equipment in her previous work as a domestic science demonstrator, as well as the added advantage of being small and nippy enough to pop into crowded car parks without too much of a struggle.

'Is the daisy motif on the roof going to be Polrewin's trade mark?' He asked politely enough, but Lee sensed a note of amusement in his voice, and she answered curtly.

'We haven't got as far as thinking about a trade mark yet. I put the transfer on for my own convenience, just after I bought the van.'

'Ah, your own personal motif,' he smiled in a superior manner, as if she was still a teenager dabbing transfers on everything, she thought crossly.

'No,' she contradicted him with dignity, 'I put it on for a purpose. The Mini happens to be a popular car, at least it is in the world I belonged to before I came here,' she added sarcastically. Doubtless Haydn's world was populated by Jaguars and Bentleys, but she had not progressed so far yet. 'In a city car park there are usually dozens of vehicles exactly alike, and it saves a lot of trouble walking about sorting out which one belongs to you, if you can spot it at a distance.' It happened to be a true explanation of the large white daisy transfer with the yellow centre she had in a moment of exasperation stuck on to the roof of the little van, after having forgotten the particular parking slot she was in, and found on her return some hours later that there were dozens of similar vehicles scattered about the huge car park, entailing half an hour's tramping she could ill afford before she eventually found her own.

'Logical,' he drawled, 'particularly if you've got a bad memory.' He put his finger unerringly on the true explanation, and her hands tightened on the steering wheel vexedly, but he went on before she could say anything, 'And do you intend to return to the world you came from, in time? Or will you remain at Polrewin, partnering Jon?' He sounded only mildly interested, as if he was making conversation to pass the time, and she answered him readily enough, thankful to get on to something like neutral ground between them.

'I wouldn't dream of leaving Jon until Polrewin is a going concern,' she told him, in a tone that said it should have been self-evident. 'I admit I enjoyed my job—I was a domestic science demonstrator,' she answered the unspoken question in his glance, 'but nothing—and nobody—can be more important than one's own family,' she said adamantly in a tone that questioned any other course of action was possible.

'Domestic science demonstrator?' He took up her comment with a different slant. 'You'll be the answer to some lucky man's dream, one day,' he smiled lazily, watching her face. 'Unless, of course, your skills are already spoken for?' he quizzed her softly.

'They're spoken for at Polrewin.' She resented his probing of her personal life, and showed it. 'And so far,' she assured him, ruthlessly suppressing the memory of Dennis, 'there hasn't been a man lucky enough, as you call it, to lay claim to my domestic science skills. Though it looks as if I might have to get in a bit of practice at home if your boat has been damaged,' she added slowly as she braked to a halt outside the greengrocer's shop in the harbour, and glanced across the water towards Haydn's cabin cruiser.

'Poor old *Sea Mist*! What a mess!' Haydn gave a groan, and spoke as if the boat was a personal friend.

'It was your boat that was holed....' Lee could not eradicate the dismay in her voice, which was occasioned by the memory of Jon's invitation to her companion to remain at Polrewin until his boat was seaworthy again, rather than at the plight of the cabin cruiser itself. And that, even to her inexperienced eyes, looked quite bad enough.

The tide was out, and in common with other craft of its kind, Haydn's cruiser lay on its side like a beached whale, waiting for the returning water to float it off again. And in its exposed side a large hole yawned like a gaping mouth—

or an open invitation for the rising tide to fill the boat.

'Go down and have a look, I can see to these.' Lee got out of the Mini and opened the back doors, smiling at Mr Dunn as he hurried from his shop to remove the trays of produce.

'You've seen the results of the storm, then?' he questioned her cheerfully. 'Whoever owns that craft will have a tidy bill, I'll warrant.'

'It's this gentleman as came off her yesterday, Dad.' Betty appeared out of the interior of the shop, and sent a dazed glance towards Haydn. 'They was looking for you everywhere, this morning,' she told him with ghoulish relish. 'Nobody knew where you'd gone to.'

'I'm staying at Polrewin,' Haydn answered her with a smile that brought a delighted sparkle to Betty's eyes.

'Well now, you never said you knew him,' she reproached Lee.

'I didn't, until yesterday,' Lee answered her shortly. 'Mr Scott is a friend of my brother.'

'Ooh, an' after what you said to him in the harbour!' Betty gave a gasp in which awe and envy fought for supremacy. Doubtless she imagined all sorts of dramatic scenes when they were introduced, Lee realised impatiently, wishing the girl would stop acting like the heroine of one of her favourite novels, and go and help her father bring in the trays of salads.

'What happened in the harbour?' Mr Dunn caught the end of her remark, and looked interested.

'Chaos, from the look of it.' Haydn deliberately misunderstood him, and gestured towards his crippled vessel. 'Have you any idea where I can find the person responsible?' His look boded ill for the yacht owner, and Mr Dunn became immediately helpful.

'The harbourmaster's got all the particulars, sir. Didn't Miss Ramsay say your name was Scott?' he added interestedly, and at Haydn's nod asked, 'You're not related to the Scotts from the Channel Islands, I suppose? You are? Well now, no wonder you're friends with the folk at Polrewin,' he chuckled, satisfied with his piece of detective work, 'you're both in the same line, so to speak. Though on different scales, of course,' he added meticulously. 'I've heard rumours you're intending to expand on the mainland, Mr Scott?' he probed chattily.

'I'm looking round for a base, yes, but only tentatively so far,' Haydn answered him in a disinterested tone. 'Come on, Lee, if you've finished, we'll go and look up the harbourmaster and get some details.' He waited with every evidence of impatience while she pocketed the greengrocer's tally, nodded to Mr Dunn and Betty, and took her arm in a firm grasp and stepped on to the pavement, determinedly steering her away from Mr Dunn's obvious desire to continue their chat.

'You carry on, I've got the van to lock up first.' Lee remembered the driving door and grabbed at the excuse to be on her own for a few minutes.

'I'll wait while you attend to it,' he insisted, and to her chagrin he remained glued to her side while she checked all the doors in the van and pocketed the ignition key. She cast him a puzzled glance, and he met it coolly.

'Your presence might act as a calming influence,' he told her, and grinned openly at the expression on her face. She had been anything but a calming influence on him up to now, she thought. 'You just might prevent me from drowning the nitwit responsible for this,' he gave a hiss of suppressed anger as she walked beside him, propelled by his fingers under her elbow, down the harbour steps and across the dry pebbles, to stand beside the crippel vessel.

Lee felt a surge of sympathy pass over her as they neared the *Sea Mist*, and the extent of the damage became more obvious, but it was for the cabin cruiser, not for its owner, she told herself firmly. It looked so helpless, lying there on its side. Pathetic, somehow, in its mute appeal for help.

'Where's the harbourmaster's office?' growled Haydn, after a silent inspection that Lee began to think would go on for ever.

'Along the hard—I'll show you.' She would have gone on in front and led the way, but he still held tight to her arm, his fingers curled round her wrist now, obliging her to walk beside him. Close beside him. Lee could almost feel Betty's interested eyes upon them as they remounted the harbour steps opposite the greengrocer's shop.

'I've got the owner's name and address here, Mr Scott,' the harbourmaster was helpful, and sympathetic. 'He was only a youngster, really, with his first boat. I think he panicked a bit, he could have sat out the storm safely enough, but he lost his nerve and ran for the harbour just when it was at its worst. He came in far too fast, he'd got no hope of checking his speed in the wild water, with the wind behind him. Your boat was the first thing he hit....'

'I'll have to see about getting her repaired,' Haydn began, and the official interrupted to say,

'I've already made some enquiries at the boatyard on the other side of the harbour, sir. They're an old established firm, and they can take it in and have it ready for you in about a week, if that suits you?' he said helpfully. 'If you like to get your things out of the cabin, I'll make all the arrangements for you. Just leave me your telephone number. By the way, where will you be staying?' he asked, with a glance in Lee's direction.

'At Polrewin,' Haydn answered. 'My friend heard of the accident, and offered me hospitality.' He said friend, not friends, and unaccountably the omission rankled, and Lee wondered why it should. Her one desire was for Haydn to pack his bags and go. Only he hadn't got any bags to pack, not at Polrewin.

'I'll have to get my luggage from the cabin, if you're willing to take it back with us?' She was surprised he asked permission, he seemed to take everything else for granted, she thought tartly.

'We might as well go and get it while we're here.' The boatbuilders' people would not want to be responsible for his personal possessions. She accompanied him back to his cruiser, and would have remained on the beach, but he jumped lightly on to the tilting deck and leaned down, offering her his hand.

'Come up and have a look around her,' he invited. 'There's no need to be afraid, I won't let you slip. She's not tilting all that badly.' His look challenged her to refuse and decided her to accept at the same time.

'I've got rubbers on, they grip well enough.' She grasped his hand reluctantly, but found she was glad of his help in spite of her rubber soles, as they negotiated the steeply sloping deck.

'Mind this patch.' He stepped across a broad, shiny band of something on the deck, and turned to lift Lee across in her turn. 'I spilled a tin of varnish on it, and I haven't had time to do anything about it yet. It's probably still tacky, and you won't want to take it away on your shoes.'

So that was why he had stepped up on to the guard rail when he came ashore yesterday, instead of walking across the deck. He wanted to avoid stepping in the wet varnish. Lee went hot as she remembered how she had accused him of showing off, but he gave no sign that he remembered what he said, and he helped her descent of the tilting steps into the day cabin with solicitous care.

'It's a four-berth boat,' he told her conversationally. 'I like a bit of room to move about when I'm living afloat.' He spoke as if he used it frequently. Lee would have liked more room in the Mini van, but she would not admit it after Haydn's suggestion that they should obtain another vehicle.

'It's nicely fitted out,' she commented.

It was beautifully fitted out, from the look of it regardless of cost, but she kept her voice deliberately casual, though she could not hide the appreciative sparkle in her eyes as they roamed across the furninshing of the day cabin. The upholstery was in tweed, in soft muted tones of brown and cream, picking up the plain brown of the carpet under her feet. The curtains at the windows matched the seats, and Lee wondered if they had come with the boat, or if Haydn had a hand in their choosing. If so, he had a good eye for tone, she acknowledged reluctantly. The decor was a perfect foil for his own amber colouring. Probably photography had taught him discernment, she thought.

'The other berths are in different shades.' He ducked through a door at the far end of the day cabin, and seemed to take it for granted that she would follow him, because he held it open for her, and after a moment's hesitation she joined him.

'There's an advantage in being tiny,' he told her wryly, 'you don't have to bend double to get through the door.'

He could stand upright in the cabin itself, she noticed, it was only the shorter door that foiled his extra inches. This cabin was just as pleasant as the other one, she silently approved the soft tones of sage green, and almost as roomy. Only the one bunk was made up for use, the other, parallel one was covered by a bright travel rug and soft cushions. It made a comfortable couch, and Haydn motioned her to sit down.

'I shan't be long.' He slid open a pair of doors underneath the other bunk, and revealed a bank of neatly filled shelves. With accustomed ease he jack-knifed his long frame into the space between the bunks and emptied the contents on to the cover.

'That's the lot.' He checked the empty shelves with a quick eye. 'Now for the suitcase.' He spun round on the balls of his feet without bothering to straighten up. 'Swing your legs up on to the bunk,' he bade her, and when she hesitated, added drily, 'There's no ulterior motive, I assure you. I simply want to get my suitcase out from the locker underneath where you're sitting, and your legs, pretty as they are, happen to be in the way.' Her colour rose at his amused tone, and she swung her feet out of the way and up on to the travel rug. The movement brought her out of balance with the tilt of the boat, and after a second during which her taut back muscles screamed for relief, she gave way and leaned back on her elbow, and watched him flick open the second lot of sliding doors.

He reached into the cupboard underneath the bunk and withdrew a lightweight travelling case. Lee noticed the motif of a famous maker discreetly adorning the lid, and with a precision and economy of movement that told her he was accustomed to doing his own packing, Haydn laid in small piles of clothing, and shaving tackle. He must have borrowed a razor from Jon this morning. Without thinking, she glanced at his chin. It was clean-shaven, as well as uncompromisingly square.

'Jon lent me his spare.' He saw her look and divined her thoughts, and a grin flicked his lips as she dropped her eyes hastily. 'Ready?' He brought them back to his face again as he added sweaters to the top of the pile in the case and clicked the lid shut. He left it on top of the other bunk, then turned round and stood looking down at her, and instinctively she tensed. His grin deepened, his eyes lighting with twin imps of laughter that mocked her embarrassment.

'I admit I'm sorely tempted,' he murmured, and his tone flicked the flags of colour to full mast in her already hot cheeks, 'but unfortunately the tide's due to turn, and I've no desire to be—er—distracted, and end up having to wade ashore. It would be too much of an anti-climax,' he grinned. 'You'll find it easier if you let me pull you up.' The truth of his words was self-evident when she tried to push herself upright against the tilt of the boat, and reluctantly she held out her hand, but he ignored it and putting both his hands round her waist he lifted her bodily and swung her to the floor, where he kept one hand on her to steady her until she got used to the tilt of the deck beneath her feet again. 'Let's get rid of this case,' he suggested. 'We can put it in the van, and then go and have some lunch.'

'Nell will have it ready when we get back home,' Lee protested, and he shook his head.

'Not for you and me, she won't,' he told her blandly. 'I told Jon I'd take you to the hotel to eat, and he said he'd warn Nell.'

'You might have told me,' she began hotly. 'I can't go to the Royal Anchor dressed like this!'

'Why not?' he asked her smoothly. 'They must be used to people in holiday garb strolling in off the boats for a meal. It would be different if it was evening. Anyhow, I've booked a table,' he told her with an air of finality.

He must have telephoned the Royal Anchor before they came away from Polrewin that morning. Lee's temper rose at his cool assumption that she would be willing to fall in with his plans. She glanced at her watch. It was almost lunch time now. A hollow feeling inside her confirmed the time, and she realised with mounting annoyance that it would be of little use defying him and returning home, if Nell had been warned they were to be out. She would have to make do on a scratch meal, and she had not eaten any breakfast.

'I hope you're not one of those people who lunch off a lettuce leaf.' Haydn settled her into a chair in a secluded corner of the large dining room at the Royal Anchor, and took his own seat opposite to her. The panoramic windows gave a perfect view of the harbour, but the sight of his crippled boat did nothing to diminish Haydn's appetite, because he promptly ordered a large lunch for both of them the moment the waiter came up.

'We'd better drink when we've eaten.' He refused the proffered wine while they were waiting. 'You had no breakfast this morning,' he stated flatly as the waiter departed.

Lee would have waited until she had some food inside her before having a drink anyway, but she resented Haydn assuming command of her actions. It made her feel like a schoolgirl being treated to lunch by an indulgent uncle, and she gave him a mutinous look.

'I'm not particularly bothered anyway, and I'm not very hungry, either.' She was. She had eaten nothing since supper the night before, and that was—she counted the hours silently—heavens! that was seventeen hours ago. No wonder her legs had felt wobbly when they came up the harbour steps. She felt quite relieved to realise that the state of her legs had nothing to do with the fact that Haydn held on to her arm and kept her close to him as they mounted to the top of the harbour wall. The relief cooled her resentment at the fact that he had ordered for her, without consulting her first, and a healthy appetite gave the lie to her denial that she was hungry. The iced melon was delicious.

'I know you like that, at least,' Haydn redeemed himself slightly. 'The one Nell served last night was a beauty, and I noticed you enjoyed yours.'

'Mmm, but we don't grow them for sale yet.'

It was good to be able to relax over the meal, without the thought of the dozens of jobs waiting to be done outside. For the first time Lee realised just how unremitting the work had been since they came to Polrewin, and had a moment's pang of conscience that Jon was not having the day off too, but it was shortlived when she remembered that it was her brother's guest she was spending it with.

She was not doing exactly as she would have liked, either. The tender chicken breasts and young vegetables, followed by a fresh fruit salad, successfully dulled the rest of her conscience, and she surfaced finally with a sigh of satisfaction.

'I enjoyed every minute of that.' She shook her head at his offer of wine. 'I'd rather not. We'll be going soon, and I don't want to feel sleepy when I'm driving. A coffee would be nice, though.'

'That'll suit me, too.' He looked round for the waiter, and turned in time to see a man at the far end of the room raise his hand in Lee's direction.

'A friend of yours?' he enquired, and Lee answered rather shortly,

'He's Vince Merrick, the proprietor's son.'

'He's coming over. Perhaps he'll take our order for coffee,' Haydn said coolly.

'For goodness' sake don't ask Vince to take it,' she told him, panic-stricken. Vince was very conscious of his own position in the hotel, and would not appreciate being used as a waiter.

She got no further. The tall, fair-haired man who had waved to her from the door of the local bank yesterday strolled across the room towards them.

'Is everything to your liking, Lee?' She hid a grin as he addressed her directly, and beyond a slight nod, ignored Haydn.

'Fine, thanks,' she smiled up at him sweetly. 'Congratulate your chef, Vince, we've just eaten the most splendid meal.' She managed to convey from her tone that she was more grateful to the chef than to Haydn who had provided it.

'We aim to do our best,' Vince smiled, including Haydn this time. 'Are you showing your friend the local attractions?' he quizzed, and Lee felt her cheeks grow warm at the underlying bite in his voice. As if she might be one of the attractions.... Vince was being altogether too proprietorial for her liking, she thought uncomfortably. True, she had danced with him once or twice recently at the local get-togethers, and she was aware of his interest, but that was as far as it went, and so far as she was concerned it was not reciprocated. It did not give him the right. . . .

'Haydn is Jon's friend.' And that was tit for tat, she thought, for Haydn's comment to the harbourmaster, only she doubted if her definition would rankle with Haydn as his had done with her. 'And it looks as if he might be staying for the main attraction in a week's time,' she added unwillingly. 'It was Haydn's boat that was holed in the harbour last night.'

'That big white cabin cruiser?' Vince's eyebrows rose, and the movement gave Lee a moment of satisfaction. Vince was nice enough, but there were times when he was altogether too conscious of being the son of the man who owned the Royal Anchor.

'She won't do much cruising until she's repaired,' Haydn clipped in shortly, anger at the *Sea Mist*'s plight still simmering beneath the surface of his voice. 'But what attraction is it that's coming in a week's time?'

'They're holding the floral dance through the town.' Vince did not wait for Lee to answer, and she felt a flash of annoyance. Suddenly, she wished he would leave them. He had done all that politeness demanded, by coming over to speak to a guest whom he knew personally, there was no need for him to remain to talk. She became uncomfortably aware of an undercurrent between the two men. Vince, standing beside the table, tall and straight, with fair good looks, but nevertheless not as tall as Haydn, she realised. If her lunch companion got to his feet he would dwarf Vince, who underneath the professional bonhomie emanate a silent challenge, instinctively resenting the stranger on his own ground. Lee glanced at Haydn. He was leaning back casually in his chair, completely relaxed, and looking coolly amused as he surveyed the other man's face.

'It's for the visitors' benefit, of course,' Vince went on, rather too heartily, and Haydn's smile broadened.

'Of course,' he agreed smoothly, and went on, ignoring the kindling anger in the other man's eyes, 'I expect the festival will make it extra busy at the hotel for you. Or do you take time off yourself to join in the dancing?' he enquired softly.

'I—er—well,' Vince had set a trap for his own feet, and walked right into it, 'I get out if I can. For the sake of our guests, you know.' Lee knew Vince had every intention of joining in the festivities in the streets, he had already asked her to partner him. She wondered now why she had refused. There was no reason for her to do so at the time. Just something that made her say no, and leave her options open.

'We'll be doing the catering, of course, for the dance in the evening.' Vince had had enough of Haydn, and showed it. He turned to Lee. 'I suppose you couldn't help us out with some decent sized tomatoes, could you, Lee? All that Dunn can offer is medium sized, and he can't promise anything different. They're not much good when the staff's having to prepare dozens of salad meals.' There was a faint hint of patronage in his tone, and Lee felt her hackles rise. She opened her mouth to tell Vince that Polrewin supplied Mr Dunn—she was going to emphasise the Mister—and they had only got medium sized tomatoes as well, but Haydn interrupted before she could speak.

'We can supply all you need.' Lee caught her breath at the 'we', anyone would think Haydn was a partner in Polrewin as well, but he silenced her with a look, and went on, 'Tell us how many, and when you'd like them.'

'I—er—we——' Vince was unprepared for such a direct question, and obviously did not know the answer. 'I'll give you a ring, and let you know.' He stepped back and almost fell over the waiter. 'Here's your coffee. I'll let you know,' he repeated, and Lee felt almost sorry for him as he took the first excuse that offered, and retreated in evident disorder.

'What did you have to do that for?' Somewhere she hazily remembered asking him the same question, it seemed a long time ago. She simmered in silence until the waiter was out of earshot. 'You know full well we can't supply Vince with the kind of tomatoes he wants.' Panic touched her as she stared across the table angrily. 'I'll have to go and tell him we can't....'

'You'll do no such thing.' Haydn's tone set her back on her chair.

'But....'

'Lesson number one, if you're going to be a success in business,' his glance silenced her for the second time, 'never say no to a customer. Take the order, and you'll manage to supply it somehow. And on time.' He spoke with the voice of experience, and Lee watched him with growing bewilderment.

'Tell me how,' she said at last, sarcastically. 'What do we do to the tomatoes in our greenhouses at Polrewin? Pump them up? Or drown them in fertiliser for the next week, and hope they'll grow to twice the size they're meant to?'

'Neither.' He stirred his coffee, unperturbed. 'Just leave it to me. I'll see you have a supply in plenty of time.'

'I'm not prepared to leave it to you,' she snapped ungraciously, grasping at the reins of control which she felt desperately were slipping from her fingers into this man's over-capable hands. 'I want to know exactly what's happening, and how. In case you need reminding, you're not in charge of Polrewin,' she told him tautly.

'I am aware, and I don't need reminding.' His tone was short now, to match her own. 'But if you're going to make a success of the business, as you say you want to, you'll have to learn to listen. Jon's prepared to, and you're his partner.'

'Take orders, you mean. . . .' She would be prepared to listen to anybody, but Haydn. She bit her lip angrily, but he ignored her comment and continued,

'Buy a supply from one of our gardens, and re-sell as your own to the Royal Anchor,' he suggested reasonably. 'One of our men is coming over with a delivery, I'll get him to put a few trays of tomatoes in the back of his vehicle for you, and hey presto! You'll have a satisfied customer on your hands, wanting more.' He leaned back in his chair with a smug look.

'What do you expect me to do now? Clap?' Lee asked him hardly. She drew in a deep breath and tried to take control of herself, aware that she had begun to shake. 'What happens when Vince comes to us for more, and we can't supply them? Where will the satisfied customer be then?' she asked through gritted teeth.

'Heading elsewhere, if you don't give him what he wants.' Haydn snapped upright in his chair. 'For goodness' sake, Lee,' he leaned across the table and covered her hand with his, gripping her forcefully in an effort to get through to her, 'don't let an opportunity like this go to the opposition. With a hotel of this size to supply, you'll have a winter outlet for your stock long after all the caravanners have gone home. They'll want flowers for ballroom decorations as well. Presumably they hold balls in this place in the winter?' He was sarcastic in his turn.

'We're not exactly the capital, but we do have a decent social life here,' she hit back at him, and he relaxed into his chair again and loosed her hand.

'Then use it for business as well as fun,' he urged her. 'If the floral dance is going to end up with a ball here, think of the opportunity for floral decorations. It would be a priceless advert for Polrewin, and more than likely lead to other orders. Presumably there'll be civic dignitaries, and all the VIPs here to see.'

'We already have the order for the floral decorations, and I'm bothered enough about how to get sufficient flowers to satisfy them, let alone promising tomatoes we haven't even got.' Suddenly Lee felt close to tears. 'We're committed to decorating a float to add to the procession as well.'

'Then decorate it,' Haydn told her forcefully. 'Use it as an advertisement for Polrewin. It's a golden opportunity.'

'How? I don't even know where we're going to get the flowers from,' she wailed, her worry of the last week surfacing suddenly. She had not even confided it to Jon.

'Surely you had some idea, when you agreed to decorate the float?' He looked at her with a puzzled frown.

'But I didn't agree, that's just the trouble. Vince is on the festival committee and he simply took it for granted, and put our name down on the list, and if we back out there'll be only thirteen floats instead of fourteen, and that's an unlucky number....' Her eyes were over-bright, and she looked away from Haydn and blinked hard. Vince had done it for her, as a favour. Or had he done it because he hoped to win her favour? A sort of subtle blackmail? Suddenly she did not feel sure of anything any more.

'It'll be unlucky for Polrewin if you let them down,' Haydn told her forcefully, and Lee had an odd feeling that he knew exactly why Vince had done this thing. 'I'll tell you what,' he reached out for her hand again, and this time his clasp felt strong and reassuring, 'why not use the daisy motif on top of your van as your trademark?'

'It looks silly.' She sniffed mournfully.

'No sillier than our little piper, with his kilt and his bagpipes,' Haydn said brusquely. 'It's just a play on our name. Have you thought what kind of float you're going to have?' he brought her back to the main question.

'There hasn't been time,' Lee admitted in a small voice. 'There always seems so much to do.'

'Then do something simple. Why not cover the float in daisies—white ones, with a bright yellow centre, like the one on the top of your van. Then in the middle of the float, on a dais, set a big, upright daisy, with an arch of the petals round a sort of chair—throne if you like—and you sit in the middle in that yellow dress and sandals you had on last night, and be the centre of the flower? How does that sound?' he asked triumphantly.

'Splendid!' For a moment even Lee was carried away by his enthusiasm. 'We could pick out the name of Polrewin in coloured petals round the side of the float,' she agreed eagerly, 'it would tell the world we're back in action again as a flower farm. But we'd need stacks of daisies.' Her face fell. 'We simply haven't got that many marguerites.' She came back to earth with a bump, and a sick feeling of disappointment. It had all sounded so wonderful. Just for a minute, she had hoped....

'The flowers will be no trouble. I know where I can lay my hands on all you're likely to need,' Haydn said confidently.

'But think of the expense.' Polrewin could not afford costly advertisements. Lee shook her head. 'We'll have to forget it for this year. I doubt Jon would agree, anyway.'

'I'll talk to Jon. A lot of our business is done on credit anyway, and I know his word is good,' he said obliquely. 'Stay and finish your coffee while I make a phone call. I'll be back in a moment.' And he was gone. And without his forceful presence at the table, all Lee's doubts returned with full force. What would Jon say? Just as they were getting their heads above water financially, and things were beginning to run more smoothly, it seemed little short of madness to put their bank balance in the red again over a one-day flower festival, even for the sake of the advertisement. Their produce should be advertisement enough, for the time being anyway. They supplied good quality, and regularly. But only to Mr Dunn, her conscience reminded her. Only to the one outlet. She shrugged the thought away impatiently. Haydn was beginning to brainwash her, as well as Jon.

'Having trouble with the boy-friend?'

She looked up and realised Vince had strolled across and was standing by her table again. Hurriedly she wiped the frown from her forehead, but it was too late to prevent him seeing her preoccupation.

'I told you, he's Jon's friend, not mine,' she said coldly. It was odd, she thought, her gaze suddenly critical, how she had thought Vince quite handsome until now. She tilted her head back and looked at him with new eyes, seeing, for the first time, not only the fair, wavy hair and bright blue eyes, but the spoilt, rather petulant mouth, that for some reason she had not noticed before. A spiteful mouth. The thought pricked her. She hoped he would not cancel the order for the tomatoes—and wondered what made her hope that, when a few minutes before she had been going to cancel it herself.

'I've decided we'll want about ten trays of tomatoes.' Vince was speaking, and she struggled out of the maze of her own thoughts to listen.

He's been to see the chef, and found out how many tomatoes they're likely to want, Lee thought unkindly. Vince was second in command at the hotel, under his father, and he should have known himself.

'The chef said he thought you supplied Dunn with all his stock. I didn't know you grew two types of tomatoes?' Vince's tone was suspicious, and Lee felt in a quandary. She did not want to lie, but....

'Polrewin grows all sorts of things.' Haydn saved her.

He returned to the table and jack-knifed himself back into his chair, and reached for his cup of coffee, which was by now turning cold. 'Pity about those melons,' he told Lee urbanely, 'if they weren't all committed I'd have liked to take a consignment back with me. Oh, nothing against your melon,' he turned to Vince as if only just realising he was there, and listening. 'I assure you it was delicious. Only these,' he gave a sort of dreamy smile, as if he was savouring something extra special, 'they're smaller, maybe,' he had the air of a connoisseur, Lee thought, amazed, 'but the quality of the flesh, and the flavour—it's out of this world.'

'We use melons here, you've just eaten one.' Vince scowled.

'Like I said, all Polrewin's supply is committed,' Haydn went on regretfully as if he had not spoken. 'Remember, I'm first in the queue when you have any to spare,' he told the bewildered Lee. 'Now, if you're ready?' He stood up, and perforce Vince had to back away to leave Lee room to do the same. 'Thanks for the meal,' Haydn said politely. 'A pity about the melon,' he added regretfully, 'but the imported ones are all much alike, aren't they?' and he ushered a dazed Lee out into the sunshine, and back along the harbour wall.

'What do you mean about our melons all being committed?' She walked beside him because she had no option, his hand was firmly over her arm, too firmly to pull away without an undignified struggle, but it allowed her enough freedom to twist round and face him. 'We've only got a few plants, to see if they'd grow well enough, and we're using the fruits ourselves.'

'That's what I mean,' Haydn said smoothly, 'they're all committed. But next season round, young Vince will remember, and want some. And you'll have a customer for melons as well.'

'You're impossible!' she gasped, torn between indignation and laughter. 'And anyway, he's not "young" Vince. He's as old as you are,' she hazarded a guess.

'Thirty next birthday?' Laughter lines creased round his eyes. 'Well, maybe,' he looked doubtful, and Lee could understand why. Vince was twenty-eight, which was only two years younger than the age Haydn admitted to, maybe less if he had only just had his birthday for this year, but setting the two men together Vince appeared immeasurably younger. Immature was the word that crossed her mind, and she stole a glance at her companion. Vince's jaw was soft and rounded. Indecisive, and already showing signs of running to fat. She caught her breath in surprise. It was something she had not noticed before. The lean, square, determined-looking jaw above her head was anything but indecisive, and there was not a hint of superfluous flesh blurring the firm outline, below the well cut lips.

'I've ordered the flowers,' the lips were speaking, and Lee grasped at her thoughts for the second time to force herself to listen. 'They'll be along with the tomatoes, in plenty of time for the festival.'

Between Haydn and Vince, she thought dazedly, she felt as if she was being pushed along on a tidal wave, and helpless to swim against it. 'What about the bill?' she asked weakly, and he squeezed her hand in a reassuring grip.

'I'll see Jon about that,' he said, as if that closed the matter.

It was only afterwards that she remembered, with a sick feeling of dismay, what he had said about credit.

'A lot of our business is done on credit anyway....'

So that meant she and Jon would be in debt to Haydn's firm. She shook her hand free from his on the pretext of searching for her ignition key, trying to fight off a suffocating feeling of claustrophobia. It was as if some giant grab was reaching out and taking hold of herself and Jon, and their beloved Polrewin, and dragging them into a crusher. And she felt helpless to do anything to prevent it.

CHAPTER FOUR

'WE'RE stuck with him now, for at least a week.' Lee sought out her brother the moment they returned to Polrewin.

'That's fine.' Jon showed not the least sign of distress. 'He'll be able to stay and join in the flower festival,' he said cheerfully. 'I'm sorry about his boat, of course, but at least it didn't sink, and Haydn's not likely to worry about the cost of the repairs.' He continued to grade tomatoes into trays with deft, automatic movements that swiftly reduced the pile in front of him.

'It's us that'll be worrying about the cost,' Lee pointed out ungrammatically, and he turned then, and gave her his full attention.

'We can afford to feed him, surely?' Jon protested. 'We're in the black with the bank now, for the first time,' he reminded her.

'We shall soon be right back in the red again,' she told him grimly. 'Jon, I'm worried.' It all came out in a flood—all about Vince, and the float for the festival. The tomatoes, and the daisies, and doing business on credit. 'Haydn just took over. Like a—a—sort of steamroller,' she finished unhappily, 'and when I asked him about the bill he said he'd discuss it with you.' Her lips trembled. She could not help it.

'Whatever Haydn's doing will be fine with me.' Jon was not in the least perturbed. 'I'll have a word with him when I've finished in here.'

'Well, it's not fine by me!' Angry colour stained Lee's cheeks, and her lips set in a thin line. 'Just as we're out of debt and independent again, we're going right back to where we started, and all to please a casual visitor.'

'He's not exactly a casual visitor, Lee. Haydn does know what he's doing in his trade,' Jon pointed out reasonably. 'Better than we do, you know that.'

'Not when what he's doing is going to put us back into

debt again, and to him of all people,' Lee argued stormily, and her brother burst out laughing.

'Simmer down,' he grinned. 'Because you two got off on the wrong foot, there's no need to carry on a vendetta against him. You make him sound as if he's got horns and a tail! As for being in debt, I'd just as soon owe Haydn money as the bank,' he said seriously.

'You won't owe me much. Not anything, in fact, when the hotel pays up.' Haydn strolled through the glasshouse door and joined them. 'I've been doing some figuring here,' he produced a sheet of paper from his pocket. 'Lee told you about the tomatoes?' and at Jon's nod, 'You can have ten trays from us at this,' he ran his finger along a line to a figure at the end, 'if you let the Royal Anchor have them for this,' he pointed to another figure, 'that'll leave you with a nice profit, and there'll be no transport costs because our man's coming to the mainland anyway.'

'We don't want charity,' Lee snapped, and he turned and surveyed her with a cool stare.

'I'm not offering you charity,' he stated flatly. 'So far as I'm concerned, this is purely a business arrangement. It wouldn't pay us to bring small amounts of produce to the mainland, not even for a flower festival, we should have to charge an uneconomic price to get the business, but you're already here, and there could be several outlets through Polrewin, which would make it profitable for all of us, the customer included.'

'You mean use Polrewin as a sort of distribution centre?' Jon asked with obvious interest. 'It makes sense, if you supply what we can't.'

'We could both give something to the other,' Haydn pushed his advantage, talking to Jon and ignoring Lee, and her fury rose at his calm dismissal. She was an equal partner with her brother.... 'It would give you a ready supply until you can get your own glasshouses into full production. You said you wanted to expand the area under glass.'

'We do, we want at least two more houses,' Jon agreed, 'more if it looks like paying well, but we'll have to wait until we've enough pennies for those,' he admitted ruefully.

'You'll get the pennies quicker with a broader market,' Haydn insisted, and Jon nodded agreement.

'And put ourselves hopelessly in debt—in your debt—at the same time,' Lee ground out. 'And what happens when we've got our glasshouses going?' she persisted. 'You'll still want to distribute your crops, which will leave ours a glut on the market.'

'Hardly, from a place the size of Polrewin.' She did not know whether Haydn was being offensive, or patronising, or both, she thought angrily. 'And as for our produce, we could easily divert the small amount you take to one of the other markets,' he added easily, as if the total quantity Polrewin could take was merely a drop in the ocean to a supplier the size of Scotts. Honesty bade Lee admit that it probably was, but she was in no mood to be honest about anything Haydn said, just now.

'Jon and I will have to discuss it, before we come to any decisions,' she told him flatly, obliquely reminding him that even if he chose to ignore it, she was still her brother's partner, and neither one could do anything without the other's agreement.

'Naturally,' Haydn returned smoothly, and Lee bit her lip, taken aback by his sudden agreement, where she expected opposition. She stifled the defensive words that were already on her lips.

'I'm going to help Nell.' She turned swiftly and left the two men alone. If she remained in Haydn's vicinity for much longer, she thought wrathfully, she would explode. There was nothing predictable about the man, except that he could always be relied on to do the unexpected.

'There isn't anything to do in here, Miss Lee.' Nell shooed her determinedly out of the kitchen. 'I've done all the baking for the next day or two. You go off and have the rest of the day to yourself. It's high time you had a break.'

'I'll see if the dogs want my company.' Nobody else seemed to, she thought crossly, and wandered disconsolately outside and sat on the doorstep. It was hot underneath her from the sun, and she leaned back against the warmth of the house wall behind her. It felt strange, having nothing to do. The last few months had been too busy even for hobbies, and at night she was usually so tired she was glad to simply eat her supper and drop into bed. It was unexpectedly difficult to have nothing to do at a moment's notice. The hours until the evening meal stretched alarmingly long, and empty. She reached out her hand and rubbed Bandy's ears, and the shaggy little mongrel thumped his tail on the gravel and panted a welcome.

'A swim would cool you down.'

The idea took root. Lee was almost as hot as the dogs, and it was an ideal opportunity. She ran upstairs to her bedroom and popped on a brief white bathing costume under her slacks, then ran down the back stairs buttoning her shirt. She did not want to bump into Haydn and Jon and explain where she was going. She did not want them to come with her. Suddenly—urgently—she wanted to be on her own.

'Don't swim out too far.' Nell came through the door and her sharp eyes took in the white bra top of the bathing suit.

'I won't,' Lee promised, and hastily did up the last button of her shirt to cover up in case she met the men, and it betrayed her destination. 'I'm taking the dogs with me. Come on, you two.' At least they did not need a second invitation, she thought, dodging their excited cavorting. 'Hush! Not so much noise.' She quietened their exuberance, and feeling a bit like a conspirator she slipped through the wicket gate furthest from the greenhouses, and dropped into the steep narrow lane that ran to the nearest cove. Her lack of inches ensured that she was hidden by the wealth of tangled hedgerow, and she paused for a moment to pluck a sprig of honeysuckle from the riot of perfumed greenery above her before she ran on after the two dogs, glorying in her stolen freedom.

The cove was empty when she got to it. It was too far away from Tarmouth to be known, let alone popular, and it was unusual even at the height of the holiday season to find anybody there. Lee dropped on to a flat grey table of rock and kicked off her shoes. The dogs ran on, straight down to the water's edge, and she flung them a pebble to keep them happy until she could join them. With a quick shake she straightened her jeans and shirt and folded them over her shoes, and ran after them. The beach was sandy here, warm and dry under her toes, and the sun felt warm on her back. Petty irritations vanished. Irritations like Vince, and Hadyn. She paddled happily in the shallows, getting used to the temperature of the water. The dogs joined her, splashing wildly, and she splashed them back, and with a gay laugh she gave herself up to the water, and floated happily on her back, idly watching a drifting gull silver silhouetted against the arcing blue.

The dogs splashed out to join her, demanding she share their game, until their attention was distracted by a piece of driftwood, and they made a dive for it, and wrangled happily for possession, chasing one another in and out of the water with noisy enjoyment, until they flopped exhausted like two wet rag rugs on to the sand to think up something else to play with.

Lee did not remember when she lost the drifting seagull. She turned on her back again when the dogs left her, and floated lazily, and when she closed her eyes it was still there, its graceful soaring flight like silent music accompanying the caress of the waves. She opened her lids in protest when the sun went in, and frowned, puzzled, wondering where the shadow came from that lay across her, but not across the rest of the water. She righted herself with a quick flip, and looked up, seeking the cause. Her hair dripped in a wet cap flattened to her head, and she shook it back out of her eyes, sending a tiny shower of drops across her shoulder.

'Where did you come from?' she enquired coldly.

She had not heard him come. He must have walked through the shallows with the same silent, catlike tread he used to come ashore from his boat, and she saw to her chagrin that according to Haydn he was still standing in the shallows. The water, that reached nearly to her own shoulders, barely came up to his waist. She could clearly see the soft sage green of his swimming trunks not far below the surface. They were the same shade of green as the upholstery in his sleeping cabin, which confirmed her guess that he had had a hand in choosing the colour scheme.

'Nell told me you'd come for a swim.' His teeth flashed white in his brown face. 'Jon's already had one dip today, and he didn't want another, so I thought I'd come and keep you company.'

'I've got Bandy and Jet.' She told him without actually saying so that they were all the company she needed.

'They're busy playing tug-of-war with some seaweed.' He bent his knees and slipped full length into the water beside her, moving with the sinuous grace of controlled power, his brown body seal-like in its easy movement that betrayed the water as his second element.

She turned on her face away from him, uneasily conscious of his closeness, of his lithe strength, restrained, as a rider restrains a high-mettled horse, to keep an easy pace beside her as she swam. The distorting effect of the water accentuated the length and slimness of his body, moving alongside her, and his tawny mane, like her own hair, lay wet and flat against his head, giving it a clear-cut, sculptured look. She glanced sideways at him as she swam, thinking that this must have been how the old legends of seal man and seal maid had begun. Aware of him, as she did not want to be aware....

'Race you to the point.' He would easily outstrip her, she knew, but his speed would remove him from her side and give her time to bring under control the sudden hard beating of her heart, that had nothing to do with the exercise, as the tingling of her skin had nothing to do with either the sun or the salt water. It was as if her every nerve end saw him there, even when her eyes were turned the other way, and she ducked under the surface and swam submerged for a space. She could not hide under the water for ever. She had to come up for breath, and when she surfaced Haydn was ahead of her, swimming strongly towards the point about fifty yards distant.

The water seemed colder further out in the bay, reminding her that it was still only early summer; the green depths had not yet had time to warm like the sun-pierced shallows covering the sands. The coldness was pleasant at first, invigorating, lapping her body with a cool embrace that helped to calm her heightened nerves, and she kept a leisurely pace behind Haydn, unwilling to catch him up, even if she could. He swam with swift, sure strokes that cleft the water like an arrow, straight for the point of rock ahead.

She was about two thirds of the way there, idling along behind him, when a piercing pain knotted the muscles of her right leg. She gave a gasp of agony, and swallowed brine, choking on the cold, salty taste of it that took her breath away as much as the pain. She spluttered the water away, and for a brief, uncomprehending second stared downwards through the clear water, her eyes seeking jellyfish, then comprehension came as another surge of agony overtook her. Cramp! Her own enjoyment of the coolness of the water had been her undoing. Even before Haydn came to join her she had been in the sea for some time, mostly floating on her back, luxuriating in the sheer bliss of doing nothing, letting the tensions of the morning seep out of her. If she had joined in the games with the dogs, running in and out of the water, it would have kept the blood flowing. Lack of movement had allowed the cold to penetrate, and now, when it was too late, she realised just how numbed she really was.

'Haydn!'

She did not know if he heard her. For a brief second she caught sight of his green swimming trunks bright against the drab rock as he clambered out of the water at the point. It flashed through her mind that he had won—as he would probably always win. Then her screaming leg muscles doubled her in two, and her head went under. It could only have been a couple of seconds later that she surfaced again, but it seemed like a lifetime to Lee, an aeon of agony during which the alien element that supported her clung round her mouth and nostrils, blocking out the lifegiving air. Clung to her eyes and blinded her—she who normally saw well enough under water could not see now, and panic took her in a grip as cold as the sea itself.

'Haydn! Hel. . . .' Her shout for help was cut short. Strong arms reached down and plucked her back into the air, and the sunshine. A strong voice said, 'Cough it up,' and she found herself turned face downwards, and a hand slapped her hard on the back. She struggled, terrified, thrusting at the surface of the water to keep it away from her face, and the hands turned her the other way again so that she rested in his arms.

'Can you breathe now?' Haydn's face was above her, his arm supporting her under the shoulders. Unable to speak, she nodded her head.

'Then stop struggling and lie still, I'll tow you to the rocks.' He took her in an expert grip and struck towards the point, towing her with ease as if her weight was nothing to him. After what seemed an age she felt him shift his position. He pulled himself and then her upright in the water, then got to his own feet. He did not allow her to even try to find her own. He bent down and hoisted her high into his arms, and strode through the water to the rocks of the point. They loomed above her, grey and hard and infinitely reassuring, sunwarmed and safe. But not half so reassuring, or so safe, as the feel of his arms gripping and holding her, carrying her lightly as if she was no more than a child.

His face was almost touching her own, his square jaw making it seem hatchet-shaped as she looked up at it. His body was burned the same teak colour as his hands and arms, and his tawny hair was darkened by the wet, and he looked like some ancient Norseman, striding ashore from the longboats, Lee thought hazily, watching him through half closed lids, while her ears took in the soothing sound of his voice without bothering to listen to the actual words. She felt the rumble of it through his chest where her ear met his shoulder, then he moved her away and hoisted her high to sit on the rocks, drawing himself up with a bound to sit beside her.

'Ooh!' She eased her leg to a more comfortable position, and grimaced as she tried unsuccessfully to straighten it. Pincers of red-hot fire ran through her muscles at the movement, and the grimace turned into an involuntary gasp.

'Lie back and relax, and I'll undo the knots in it for you.' Slim brown fingers closed over her shoulder and pressed her down on to the rocks, then transferred themselves to her leg. She felt them probe the tight muscle, starting at her ankle, unravelling the knots as he promised he would, and leaving behind blessed relief from the spears of pain. She let out a sigh of pure bliss as she straightened her leg at last. The muscle still felt sore, but it was soft now, and pliable. She wriggled her toes experimentally, and they worked. They felt warm, too. She sat up suddenly, and her cheeks felt the same. Haydn still worked industriously, massaging, rubbing.... His face was bent over his task, the top of his tawny head, and the uncompromising outline of his jaw, was all she could see. He had got as far as her knee already.

'Er—that's far enough, it was only the calf muscle that hurt.'

He looked at her then, squinting against the sun, and she could not see whether it was the bright dazzle from the water or a sudden imp of mischief that glinted in the depths of his eyes that stared into hers for a long second before he said,

'Stand on it, then, and see if you can walk easily.'

He loosed her leg and took hold of her hands instead, pulling her upright against him, holding on to support her in case her leg did not. His hold was meant to be reassuring, but instead it made her other leg feel as weak as the first one, and this time it was not caused by cramp. She moved away from him hastily, and forgot her feet were bare. A sharp point of rock punished her lack of caution, and she stumbled, and instantly his arms closed round her, drawing her close against him.

'My leg's all right, it was the rock,' she stammered, and looked up into his eyes, protesting not for the sake of her leg but for her quickened breathing, accelerated by the agitated beating of her heart. The expression she found there did not help to calm it. It had not been entirely the glint from the sun, she saw now, but twin devils of mischief that lit them with an impish gleam, and reflected in the upward curve of his lips as he said softly.

'It's a good job I happened to be along, you might easily have drowned out there, from the cramp.'

His style did not suffer from the same affliction, was her

last wild thought as he bent his head unhurriedly, and his lips, still smiling, closed on hers. This kiss did not punish her, as his first one had done. His lips explored hers, seeking, demanding a response. His rebuke about drowning had been unnecessary. She was drowning now, in a tidal wave of emotion triggered off by the feel of his arms, of his lips, of his closeness that caught her completely unaware and threatened to engulf her more surely than the cold, clear waters of the bay.

With a strange detachment she felt her own lips part beneath the pressure, responding to his demand as if they had a life and will of their own, divorced from her command, and her arms rose to allow her hands to clasp the back of his head and draw it down to her own. His hair felt unexpectedly silky beneath her finger ends—not harsh, like the coat of a mountain lion would be harsh.

What on earth had come over her? She grasped ineffectually at her reeling senses. She had never felt like this before, not even when she was engaged to Dennis. A small voice from somewhere deep in the already forgotten recesses of the memory of her engagement burbled derisively, 'Dennis!' Nothing in her ex-fiancé's chaste embrace had ever had the power to rouse her like this. His kisses did not have the vital spark in them that fired this man's caress, a spark that burned and seared, and aroused in her emotions she had not known she possessed, and could not name them, even if she wanted to.

'My old nanny always used to kiss it better.'

'K-kiss what b-better?' She did not know how appealing she looked, slender as a boy in her brief white costume, her hair already beginning to dry, and curl back away from her forehead, and her wide, dark, startled eyes.

'Anything that hurts. Your leg,' he reminded her, smiling.

Lee had forgotten her leg. That wasn't the part of her that hurt the most, now. And no amount of massage would help to ease the ache that the feel of his lips had left behind. Her own felt bruised, burning. . . . She put her fingers up to them, and then drew them hastily away.

'It's time we went back.' A high-pitched yelping from the

beach rounded up the last of her scattered wits and brought her attention back to her surroundings, and the fact that the dogs had begun to miss her, and were probably searching for her.

'Not across the bay.' Haydn's fingers reached out and gripped her arm, and checked her move to slide down the rocks and into the sea again. 'It's too risky, your leg might give again. It'll get it working properly if we walk back across the cliffs. I'll carry you over the rough bits,' he promised as he saw her hesitate, and his eyes crinkled into laughter lines, sensing her dilemma, perhaps sensing, too, her sudden mutinous urge to defy him, although common sense told her it would be madness to swim back now, and if she did engage in battle with him over the issue, he would undoubtedly win—again.

She shrugged, pretending to be indifferent to whatever route they took back to the beach, as if, now she she was separated from his arms, she did not feel a surge of anger at her own weakness, a self-contempt as strong, almost, as the nameless emotions that gripped her before, and left her feeling drained and spent. What was it he had said? She frowned as the memory of his words came back to torment her.

'If ever I need a girl for my work—the fresh, outdoor type, with a hint of naïveté. . . .'

Her cheeks burned at the memory. Haydn must think her naïve. Her own reaction to his unexpected behaviour had been that of an ignorant country lass to a society Don Juan. She flogged herself with unmerciful scorn. It helped to keep at bay the uncomfortable awareness of him, scrambling with her across the rocky headland, helping her across the water-worn rocks as if he was indifferent himself to the sharpness of the rougher patches, as if he frequently lived without shoes and his feet were hardened, as they probably were if he lived much on his boat, she realised, wincing as she stepped warily in his wake.

'Allow me.' He noticed her flinch, and turned back, and before she was aware of his intention he scooped her up in his arms and strode across the rocks, depositing her on the beach, on a patch of soft sand, to the unrestrained joy of the two dogs, who behaved as if she was lost to their sight for ever. As she might have been, she thought, if Haydn had not been there to rescue her. But if Haydn had not been there, she would not have tried to swim to the point. She succumbed to the four-footed blandishments for a moment or two, thankful to have something to take her attention, and hide her face from Haydn's keen look, and she turned to search out her jeans and shirt with her poise more or less restored to normal. The man-made fibre of her swimsuit was nearly dry by now, and she dragged on her clothes, her confidence coming back with her normal attire. She gave her feet a quick rub to clean them free from sand, and slipped on her shoes. Haydn must have no further excuse to pick her up. Obscurely she resented it, wishing not for the first time since she had known him that her height was more equal to his own. She did not like being treated as if she was a child, to be indulged, restrained, but not to be taken seriously.

'Your honeysuckle has wilted.' He picked up the sprig she had plucked on her way to the bay.

'I'll get some more on the way back. I want a bunch for my room, anyway.' She did not intend Haydn to pick it for her. Though he would probably forget it as they reached the narrow lane leading back to Polrewin, he passed the first display of it without a second glance, but he paused when they reached the mass of perfumed hedge from which Lee had picked her first spray, and reached down one of the topmost sprigs.

'The top flowers seem to be the nicest.'

They always were, Lee thought ruefully, but she had not got the height to reach up to them, and she could not quite restrain the sparkle of delight as he gathered her a generous bunch, which was dimmed somewhat by the mockery in his glance as he handed it to her with a slight bow.

'They're lovely.' She buried her face in his offering. There was no reason for her to feel confused. No reason for the sudden attack of shyness that made her hide her face in the flowers, the heady sweetness of which pervaded her room as minutes later she left Haydn on the path and escaped upstairs to her room to slip them into a brown pottery jug, and rest them on her dressing table so that she could enjoy the double beauty of the flowers themselves, and their reflection in her mirror.

Her own face looked back at her from beside them, and she stared at it as if it belonged to a stranger. Her eyes held a glow she had never seen in them before, and her lips parted in wonder. Lips Haydn had kissed.... She raised her fingers to them for the second time, touching them, as if they might feel differently now, then she turned startled as his voice came from below her open window. He was talking to Jon.

'She had a pretty bad attack of cramp half way across to the point,' he was saying. 'Luckily I was there, and saw her go under. I guessed what had happened, of course, the water was cold farther out, and I was able to reach her in plenty of time.'

Oh, the conceit of the man! The glow vanished from Lee's eyes, and a snap of pure anger took its place, which was heightened to fury as he went on in a serious tone,

'If Lee's prone to cramp, Jon, it might be better if she didn't swim on her own, at least until the water's warmed up a bit later in the year.'

How dared he even suggest Jon should keep a check on her movements! He had no right.... Lee jumped to her feet, and her elbow caught the protruding handle of the jug with the flowers in it. She spun round and saved it from going over, then gave an exclamation of annoyance as some of the slopped water dripped off the shiny polished top of the dressing table and on to the glass tray underneath.

'Bother!' She grabbed for the towel hung beside her wash basin, and mopped up the mess. She would go down instantly, she determined, and tell Haydn to mind his own business. Anger put vigour into her efforts, and by the time she had refilled the jug and put it back where it belonged, her temper had cooled somewhat, but her resolve was as strong as ever. It was bad enough, she thought angrily, that Haydn had tried to assume control of Polrewin. It was insufferable of him to include herself in his dictatorial ways as well.

The sound of a car engine drew her to the window, and she caught sight of the top of a van negotiating the steep turn in to the gate. It attracted the attention of the two men on the gravel below her window, and she gave a small stamp of irritation. She would have to wait, now. Evidently Jon was taking delivery of something, and it would be impossible to give Haydn a piece of her mind in front of a van driver. She might just as well remain in her room and get changed. A gritty feeling inside her shoes was rapidly becoming uncomfortable, and she slipped out of her clothes and reached for some lightly perfumed soap and shampoo. She might as well stop and wash her hair as well. Sea water always made it feel sticky, and Jon and Haydn might be some time. Instead of exploding, as she felt like at the moment, she thought grimly, she would pick her own time and put their unwelcome visitor firmly in his place in a more dignified manner.

She showered and shampooed, and felt a good deal more human by the time she coated herself with a liberal dusting of her favourite talc to match her soap and slipped into a white sleeveless shift. She refused to wear the yellow dress again tonight. She did not want Haydn to think she would put it on again for his benefit. She clipped a narrow red belt around her waist, hunted out some red sandals to match, and left it at that. She glanced at her watch. Supper would be ready soon. She would just have time to slip outside and see what it was the van driver had delivered.

'Strawberries! Just look at the size of them, Sis!' Jon gazed exultantly at the shallow trays of berries at his feet. Lee counted them rapidly. There were four in all, and three trays of large tomatoes. Catering tomatoes, the sort Vince wanted.

'I didn't know you'd ordered them. Who brought them?' She knew already, of course. She had not caught more than a glimpse of the van roof as it came through the gate, but she knew with deadly certainty that somewhere along the side of the vehicle there would be painted the familiar kilted piper trademark, and the name of Scott.

'Haydn ordered them, not me. Apparently he phoned his place from the Royal Anchor while you were having lunch there, on the offchance of catching the delivery that was coming over on the ferry this morning. He was just lucky, as it happens. He told me about Vince and the tomatoes,' Jon grinned.

Lee did not return his smile. She said stonily,

'And what about the strawberries? There was nothing said about those.'

'They're a long shot, but I reckon it should come off.' Haydn joined them, and his eyes roved over her simple dress, lazily approving. His glance should have pleased her, but it only served to annoy her further. She did not want his approval.

'And if this long shot doesn't come off?' she asked icily. 'Who stands the loss? You—or Polrewin?'

'Oh, Sis, we can't expect Haydn to pay ...' Jon began protestingly.

'Why not?' She rounded on her brother angrily. 'We didn't order this fruit, and if Haydn wants to experiment on the local market, he can do it at his own expense, not ours.'

'They've been delivered on approval,' Haydn put in mildly. 'No order, no charge.' His casual manner stopped her angry utterance, and she choked the words back, feeling herself start to tremble. 'You must have noticed the size of those berries we had with our fruit salad at lunch time,' he turned to her as if for support, and in doing so put her at a disadvantage, she realised wrathfully. 'They were pitifully small. They looked, and tasted, more like tinned berries than fresh ones.' He wrinkled his nose fastidiously. Lee had thought the same, but one does not criticise the food when one is taken out to lunch. It had hardly been an invitation, more an order, she thought irritably, but even now she could not bring herself to admit she shared his feeling about the strawberries.

'And what do you intend to do with this lot?' She waved her hand at the admittedly magnificent berries, as if they were more fit to be consigned to the compost heap than be consumed. 'Vince didn't order them, he only ordered tomatoes. And if he doesn't want them, they won't be fit for sale in another twenty-four hours.' The greengrocer would take them, she had no doubt, but she did not intend to back down and admit it.

'We'll face that hurdle if we come to it.' His manner suggested that it was only a remote possibility, hardly worth considering, but in the unlikely event of the Royal Anchor not receiving his offering with open arms, he was more than capable of coping with the sale of several trays of highly perishable fruit. 'They've been picked under-ripe, they'll be just about right when you go down with your usual load of salads to the greengrocer in the morning. I'll come with you,' he stated, not asked, as if her agreement was a foregone conclusion.

'And what will you do when we get there?' she bit back. 'Walk up to Vince and tell him you've brought him fruit he didn't order, and in all probability doesn't want, and expect him to accept it, and pay up gracefully?'

'Nothing so blatant as that,' Haydn grinned, completely unperturbed by her sharpness. 'Something much more subtle,' he assured her. 'You'll see, when we get there to-morrow.' And with that she had to be content until the trays of tomatoes and strawberries had been loaded into the van along with the usual consignment for the green-grocer, the following morning.

'Mr Dunn might say he wants them.' Haydn remained silent the whole of the way from Polrewin, and Lee felt ready to burst by the time she pulled up outside the green-grocer's shop. She glanced surreptitiously at Haydn's face as she got out of the van, and scowled at the amused grin he shot in her direction.

'He won't be able to have them, will he?' he retorted blandly. 'It won't hurt him to see them, though, when he unloads his own produce.' He stopped her protest with a quick jerk of his head towards the shop. 'Shhh, here he comes. 'Morning, Mr Dunn,' he raised his voice, and Lee noticed he called the greengrocer Mister, not just Dunn, as Vince did.

''Morning, Mr Scott—Miss Ramsay. I'll soon have this lot out of your way.' He ducked into the rear of the van as Haydn obligingly opened the back doors to give him access.

'Yours are on this side.' Helpfully Haydn indicated the correct pile.

'Right you are—I say!' Mr Dunn's eyes widened as he surveyed the other trays carefully stacked so that both showed to advantage, Lee realised, coming round to join the men at the back of the van. She had not helped load it. Jon and Haydn completed the job while she went to answer the telephone, and by the time she had finally convinced the caller that Polrewin was a flower farm and not a health hydro, ten minutes was wasted, and the rear doors of the van were already closed when she got back. Her own eyes widened as much as the greengrocer's when she looked inside. The strawberry trays, and those containing the big tomatoes, were each neatly covered by one of Polrewin's paper 'hats' with a transparent window in it, showing clearly the superb quality of the fruit.

'These are the finest strawberries I've seen in many a long day,' Mr Dunn peered at them with avaricious eyes.

'They're not a bad strain.' Haydn was briskly business-like. 'I don't know if there'll be much call for them round here, though.'

'Call for them?' the greengrocer ejaculated. 'Why, with that caravan site further along the coast, I could sell all you bring me.' His hands reached out hopefully towards the other trays.

'They're spoken for, I'm afraid,' Haydn stopped him with apparent regret, and Lee stifled a gasp. They were nothing of the sort, and Haydn knew it. 'But if you feel you'd like to try some. . . .' He let his sentence trail away.

'Try some?' the trader exclaimed fervently. 'Just give me the chance, Mr Scott!' He scribbled out a tally, and absentminedly held it out towards Haydn, and Lee galvanised into angry action.

'I'll take that,' she sharply reminded the greengrocer to whom it belonged.

'Naturally,' Haydn acknowledged her right to it, but he took it from the greengrocer just the same, with a smile and a polite nod, then handed the tally to Lee. She pocketed it with an angry thrust and turned on her heel towards the van.

'Where to now? The Royal Anchor, I suppose?'

'Right in one,' Haydn complimented her, and her lips tightened. 'I'm rather looking forward to this,' he admitted, and she shot him a suspicious glance. He had a look on his face like a cat about to steal cream, she thought, and his voice held a purr of satisfaction. 'Why, how fortuitous,' he drawled, as she drew to a halt beside the hotel steps, 'there's the boy-friend himself, taking the air.'

'Vince isn't my boy-friend,' Lee snapped, and could have kicked herself for rising to his bait.

'He'd like to be.' She could not deny that. 'Not that I blame him.' Haydn looked at her speculatively for a moment, and smiled at her furious glare. 'Ah well, let's join battle.' He said it as if he put pleasure aside at the call of duty, and Lee shrugged. She slid out of her seat, unsure of what he would say to Vince, but determined she would not allow him to commit Polrewin again to something they could not supply.

'Hello, what lucky chance brings you here at this time in the morning?' Vince's face lit up at the sight of Lee, and he ran eagerly down the hotel steps to meet her. His manner should have been a boost for her ego, if it did not also prove Haydn's guess about the hotel proprietor's son wanting to be her boy-friend....

'We were delivering in the town, and....' The words stuck. What could she tell him? That there were trays of tomatoes and strawberries in the back of the van they could not hope to get rid of, and would he pay for them? She did not doubt Vince would take them, but he would do it as a favour to her, and he would expect her to pay for his benevolence by partnering him in the dance at the festival. And she had already refused....

'We thought you might like a sample of those tomatoes we discussed yesterday. Just to see what they're like before you commit yourself to an order.' Haydn broke in and saved her from having to reply. Vince had already ordered the tomatoes. Haydn knew that, too, but Lee reluctantly had to admire his smooth handling of the situation, particularly in the face of Vince's obvious antagonism towards the other man. The look he gave Haydn, when he got out of the

Mini from beside Lee, was the reverse of friendly. 'Did you lock the back doors, Lee? Oh, no,' Haydn tried one, and it gave to his touch. 'Just as well, we needn't keep you from your duties any longer than is absolutely necessary.' He deliberately needled Vince, and Lee watched the two of them, intrigued despite herself. It seemed a strange way to do business, she thought, if Haydn wanted to sell his stock to the hotel, to go out of his way to antagonise the owner's son.

'Well, of course there's a lot to see to, when you're in charge of a place this size.' Vince responded to what his natural conceit looked upon as flattery, and Lee felt a quirk of laughter start inside her. Haydn was a better judge of human nature than she gave him credit for.

'Are these what your chef's looking for?' Haydn slid off one of the paper tops and picked up a couple of tomatoes. He held them out on the flat of his hand towards Vince, and Lee saw they were two of the most perfectly formed fruit in the trays. Had he deliberately engineered that these two should be on the top? She did not question that he was capable of it.

'Hmm.' Vince tried to look knowledgeable, and Lee bit back a smile. 'They'll do, I suppose.' Her smile turned to righteous indignation at Vince's indifferent attitude. She knew, and so must he, that they were top quality fruit, and must be the best on the market.

'Why not let your chef have a look?' Haydn asked casually. 'The staff like to feel they have a say in the matter, don't they? An involvement, so to speak.' He spoke man to man, and again Vince reacted as Haydn obviously knew he would. It was like watching a puppet on a string, Lee thought, fascinated.

'Arthur,' Vince turned and called to the hotel porter, 'fetch Weston, at once.' He did not say 'please', either, Lee noticed. She saw Haydn give him an oblique look, and wondered if he had noticed, too, then the chef came down the steps towards them. He smiled at Lee, and she smiled back. She had met him once or twice, and wondered at first how a man of his obvious skill came to work in a small place like Tarmouth. He was a Londoner, and could have had his choice of posts in the capital. Then he told her about his small daughter who suffered from asthma, and who doctors thought would benefit from living at the seaside, and she understood how it was that a man of his quality could endure taking orders from a man like Vince.

'Have a look at these, and tell me what you think of them.' Vince turned everything he said into an order; he did not seem to have the necessary tact to make it a request.

'They're prime quality, the best I've seen this season.' The chef took one of the tomatoes from Haydn's palm. 'We've had nothing like them here since I came.' He ignored the scowl on Vince's face and turned his attention to the back of the van. 'How many trays have you got?' He moved closer as Haydn obligingly stood back to make room for him, and caught sight of the trays of strawberries. 'I say, are these for us, too? Those we've been using up to now are the absolute limit,' he exclaimed disgustedly, and Lee saw Haydn's lips twitch. The scowl on Vince's face deepened, but curiosity made him poke his head into the van too, and he could not quite erase the impressed expression on his face as he withdrew it, and said in what he tried to make an indifferent tone,

'We'll take those off your hands as well if you like, perhaps they'll come in for the afternoon teas.'

'They're perfect.' The chef had no such inhibitions; he said what he thought. 'If we could only get hold of berries of this quality, I could go to town on the fancies for the festival.' There was no doubt about his enthusiasm, and Lee felt a flash of sympathy for the man. How he must long to practise his art among the banqueting halls where his skill belonged! Vince truly did not know his own luck. And probably would not appreciate it if he did, Lee thought shrewdly.

'They're spoken for, I'm afraid,' Haydn said regretfully. 'Although....' He rubbed his chin with a thoughtful thumb and finger. 'I know they're not actually wanted for use until tomorrow—that's why they've been picked fairly firm. We might be able to spare three of the trays, and use the next picking for our other customer. What do you think, Lee?' he appealed for her help.

'I—er—that would probably be all right.' She hoped to goodness Vince did not notice her bewilderment, but his attention was on the chef. With a grin of undisguised delight the man picked up the tomato trays and dumped them into Vince's arms before the latter could utter a protest, and cradled the top three trays of strawberries in his own.

'We'll take them.' He had no intention of allowing either Lee or Haydn to change their minds. 'If you can let us have a regular supply while the season lasts, I'll be able to turn out dishes that will really put this place on the map.' And he disappeared up the steps of the front entrance, giving the strawberries, Lee felt, the accolade they deservd.

'That's what's called softening up the market,' Haydn remarked into the pregnant silence as Lee turned the van round and headed back towards Polrewin, still with one tray of strawberries in the back. 'Come on,' he urged her, 'admit that it worked.'

'It worked,' she got out reluctantly. 'What about the other tray of berries?' They looked delicious, but she was not going to think about that.

'I thought we'd take those back home and eat them ourselves.' Haydn sat back in his seat with a satisfied sigh. 'I reckon we deserve them, don't you?'

'Nell will be able to make use of them.' Lee had been longing to try some, but stubbornly refused to ask, and suddenly, now she had the opportunity, she found she did not want them. Polrewin was her home—hers and Jon's—not Haydn's. She objected to the proprietorial way in which he seemed to be trying to take over the business at Polrewin, and use it simply as a distributing base for his own produce. He had won Jon over, she thought bitterly, but he would not find it so easy to win her own consent. Or—an unpleasant thought struck her—had he already started a softening up process, as he called it, with herself? By the admittedly generous gift of a tray of strawberries now being carried in the back of the van, and—worse—by his practised lovemaking only that morning on the rocky point of the bay? To which she had responded....

CHAPTER FIVE

'I'LL take the strawberries in to Nell.'

Haydn jumped out of the van and opened the back doors as soon as Lee drew to a halt on the gravel at Polrewin, and she did not offer to help him carry the tray. 'Would you like a quick taste?' he asked in a friendly manner as he passed her with it in his arms. She shook her head.

'No.' She did not add 'thank you'. She did not feel like thanking him, and eating his strawberries would probably give her indigestion in her present mood, she thought angrily.

'Are those for us?' Jon asked hopefully, and when Haydn nodded he gave Lee a beseeching look. 'Will that mean strawberry shortcake for supper tonight? You've got to taste Lee's strawberry shortcake to believe it,' he told Haydn, and licked his lips with greedy anticipation.

'I shan't have time to make shortcake,' Lee said stubbornly. 'There's the rest of the day's tomatoes to pick, and....'

'You won't have to bother with those any more,' Jon interrupted gleefully, 'Ben's coming full time from now on. We arranged it this morning, so the work will ease off quite a bit, especially where you're concerned,' he said with satisfaction.

'We can't afford to have Ben full time, you know that.' Lee was appalled.

'But Sis, that was the arrangement when he first came to us,' Jon expostulated.

'I know,' Lee conceded through tight lips, 'but the rest of the arrangement was, when we could afford it. And we can't, not yet,' she reminded him grimly.

'But now we're distributing Haydn's stuff as well as our own, we'll have a bit more elbow room in the exchequer, and we'll need another pair of hands to cope with the extra work,' Jon pointed out.

'We're not distributing Haydn's stuff yet,' Lee retorted sharply. 'For one thing I haven't agreed that we should.' She could see from her brother's face that he already had, and her anger rose, not against Jon, but against Haydn. He was manipulating Jon as he had manipulated Vince, and where in the latter's case it had amused her, she saw no humour in such manoeuvres where they affected Polrewin. 'And for another, unless and until we do, we shan't need an extra pair of hands. We simply can't afford them,' she emphasised. 'Haydn's figures look fine on paper, but I want to see tangible results before we begin to think about building on them, and expanding our operations.'

'We'll have to expand if we want to stay in business,' Jon said reasonably. 'We can't live off tomato profits for ever. Those were only to tide us over until we got the place going, in any case.'

'I know that.' Lee drew a deep breath, and clutched at the shreds of her patience with both hands. 'But expanding from our point of view, and doing the same thing from Haydn's, are an entirely different matter. If Haydn expands he's got a big business concern behind him, and if his particular section fails the others will bolster him until he's on his feet again. If we fail, we go bankrupt,' she rubbed in the truth with uncompromising clarity.

'He'll give us credit until things begin to flow more evenly.'

'He's not going to give us any credit. We'll keep our books in the black, we've worked hard enough to get them that way,' Lee said mutinously. 'Can't you see,' she persisted urgently, 'if we expand too quickly, take credit from Haydn's firm and over-stretch ourselves, we could be out on a limb financially, and if anything goes wrong we'd be obliged to sell Polrewin whether we wanted to or not. And no doubt Haydn would be a ready bidder,' she added bitterly. 'We already know he's looking for a place on the mainland to extend his operations, he said so himself. What if he's decided Polrewin's an ideal spot? What would be easier for him than to put us in a position where we have to pull out of the business, and he simply walks in and takes over?' She remembered the haste with which

Haydn had steered her away from Mr Dunn's garrulous tongue, and his obvious desire to continue their conversation about Scotts expanding on the mainland. She had not thought anything about it at the time. Now, his move seemed to take on a sinister significance.

'Haydn's not like that, Sis.' Jon looked her straight in the eye. 'He's an honourable man. Remember, I've known him for years.'

'You knew him when you were students at College,' Lee answered flatly. 'When you were both a lot younger, impressionable, and full of high ideals. Haydn's probably lost most of his.' Jon had not, she thought thankfully, and loved him for it, while it exasperated her that he could not see the perfidy of the man who was now their guest. 'He's a business man now, with one aim and one only, and that's to get his business off the ground, and then make a profit. Remember that, and see where it leaves Polrewin in the eyes of your precious friend.'

'Simmer down a bit,' Jon warned her quickly, 'Ben's coming.'

'I'll do the tomatoes in this house first, Mister Jon.' Their helper beamed at Lee. 'I'm right glad of the chance to come here full time now,' he told her gratefully. 'My other part-time job was folding up, and I didn't want to travel to Tarmouth every day, this being so close handy to home.' He nodded in a cheerful fashion, and departed into the nearest glasshouse, and Lee watched him go in silence.

'I can't tell him to go back on half time now, can I?' Jon asked her helplessly, and Lee looked at him with a mixture of affection and impatience.

'So Haydn's got you doing two things for him,' she said wearily. 'Distributing his goods and taking the risks of the market, and hiring staff for which he doesn't have to pay. All highly profitable—for Haydn,' she said sarcastically. 'You said he was on a sort of working holiday, when he first came here. Well, he's getting both. His work done, and a holiday—both at our expense.'

Out of the corner of her eye she saw Haydn round the

end of the house from the kitchen quarters and head towards them.

'I'm going.' If she saw any more of him at the moment, there would be an open row, she thought furiously, and following Ben she took a short cut through the glasshouse and out at the other end. She did not look back. She strode through the wicket gate into the first of the flower fields, and skirting round it, headed away from the house. Away from Jon, and Haydn, and human beings generally, she thought miserably. Half way across the second field she became conscious that Bandy was at her heels, and felt slightly comforted. At least she did not have to be on her guard when she was with the dogs.

She felt suddenly tired, but she continued walking until she reached the end of the flower fields, before she dropped down on to an outcrop of rock overlooking the bay where she had swum the day before. Where she had got into difficulties, and been rescued from them by Haydn. She shook her head impatiently. She did not want to think about that, or its aftermath. She closed her eyes and leaned back. Haydn had spoken the truth when he said it was dangerous to cross his path. It had been disastrous for Polrewin. She felt a light thump beside her, and a rough little body leaned heavily against her legs, and she put her hand down to fondle the shaggy head.

'I wish we'd never set eyes on him, Bandy.'

A few weeks ago she had not, and life had been a hard-working but peaceful progression towards a set goal, which they were in sight of achieving, she thought with a sigh. Now, everything had been turned topsy-turvy, it seemed, overnight, and she no longer knew in which direction Polrewin was headed. Haydn probably knew. No doubt he had it already planned, she thought bitterly. Jon might possibly know—as much of his plans as Haydn thought fit to tell him. She herself did not know, she could only guess, and her guesswork took her on a journey of wild surmise that was distinctly unsettling.

'What is it?' Bandy's tail thumped on the ground, although he did not attempt to get up, or bark.

'It's me,' Haydn dropped lightly over the edge of the

rock and joined her on her eyrie. 'What a glorious view!' It encompassed the whole of the bay, and the snaking cliffs as far away as Tarmouth. 'Is this your secret hideaway?' he asked.

It was, but she had no intention of letting him know that she was hiding away from him. 'I come here now and then,' she answered non-committally. The spot had never failed to calm her before. Its magic worked, even now, although the deflation in her anger could have been partly the result of weariness, as well as the peace of their surroundings. Until Haydn joined her, that was. Reluctantly, she had to admit the sheer animal magnetism of the man. She glanced sideways at him. He would have succeeded in the rag trade, or in cosmetics, or hairdressing, she thought. Anything to do with women. Her lips curled as she remembered Betty Dunn's reaction at first sight of him. And then honesty made her admit she could not see him in any of those roles. The world of scented salons was not his forte. The world of business, yes, the challenge was there for him to meet and overcome. His strength would respond to challenge as it would to meat and drink.

'Jon didn't set Ben on full time at my instigation, Lee.' He spoke quietly, without looking at her, and Lee drew in her breath sharply, taken aback by his direct approach.

'The fact that Jon set him on full time at all is quite bad enough,' she retorted. 'He told him to come because he said we were doing your distributing for you,' she said accusingly. 'Distributing! Hah! Four trays of strawberries, and three trays of tomatoes....' Words failed her.

'Jon set him on because Ben asked him to.' Haydn turned his head then, and regarded Lee with serious eyes. 'The man was in difficulty, and he turned to Jon for help. And Jon took that way out because he knew he could accept my offer to distribute our stuff in the Tarmouth district any time he liked. Any time he and you liked,' he amended carefully, and Lee expelled her breath in a long sigh. Jon had not told her the background to his offer to Ben. With his usual enthusiasm for cutting corners, her brother had told her the fact without the details. And she had not asked, she just assumed.... Her assumption had put her in the wrong with Haydn, and she resented it.

'There's nothing we can do about it now,' she shrugged. 'The thing's done, and we'll have to find Ben's wages somehow.'

'You could easily accomplish that, if you took our produce for distribution.'

'I don't see. . . .' she began angrily, but he did not wait for her to continue.

'Jon deserves to succeed, Lee. He's put in a lot of hard work on this place.'

'So have I,' she reminded him tartly.

'And so have you,' he acknowledged indifferently. 'But where it's your livelihood, it's Jon's life. When it's successful, you'll probably go back and follow your own interests again, you suggested as much yourself,' he reminded her gravely as she opened her mouth to protest, and she closed it again, the words unsaid. She probably would pull out, once Jon was launched. But not until then.

'I'm only trying to help him to succeed,' Haydn pointed out.

'What as? The owner of Polrewin, or as one of your managers?' she flared angrily.

'I've got enough managers to contend with as it is,' Haydn answered her indirectly. That was the trouble, she thought furiously. He was too devious to pin down even to a direct answer to her question.

'There's another thing,' she put the matter of Ben aside and grasped the other nettle. 'Kindly remember that Jon is my brother, and not my keeper. And neither are you,' she added somewhat inarticulately. 'If I choose to swim in the bay, alone or in company, I shall do so, and I shan't ask your permission,' she finished in a rush.

'Ah, you heard me speak to Jon.'

'Since you were both standing right underneath my open bedroom window, I could hardly do anything but hear. I don't eavesdrop,' she snapped.

'No.' She did not know whether it was a statement or an insulting question. She decided to treat it as the former, and continued to look stonily out to sea. 'But since you seem prone to cramp, I felt I had to mention it to Jon,' he began, and she interrupted angrily.

'I should have reached the point safely enough, the cramp would have gone if you'd left me alone.'

'I would not.' He sat up then, and looked sternly into her face, and his own was set and angry. 'Don't ever run away with that idea and be tempted into foolishness because of it,' he warned her severely. 'I know what I'm talking about....'

'Do you?' she snapped back, and her chin came up stubbornly. 'I wonder....'

'I should do, I've lived on the coast all my life,' he retorted bitingly, 'I've seen the idiot tricks careless holidaymakers get up to, jeopardising their own lives and those of the people who try to rescue them. Jon's got quite enough on his plate trying to make a success of Polrewin, without you getting yourself drowned to add to his troubles.'

It did not seem to matter to him that she might be drowned, so long as she did not add to Jon's troubles. She simmered with silent resentment.

'I'm going back.' She jumped to her feet. She no longer found her hideout peaceful.

'It isn't supper time yet.' He consulted his watch.

'Supper's got to be prepared, and Nell will want some help.' Lee turned on her heel abruptly and left him sitting there, and it did not help her mood that Bandy elected to remain with Haydn instead of coming back to the house with her. Even the dog was on his side, she thought unjustly, and blinked back angry tears as she hurried back home.

The housekeeper did not need her help, but she accepted the welcome opportunity to chat when Lee presented herself in the kitchen, encased in a voluminous apron.

'Look at those headlines!' she waved towards the evening paper lying on the seat of her chair. 'You'd think folks would be more careful, wouldn't you?'

'Holidaymakers in difficulties. Council contemplating sterner measures against people who ignore warning notices. Hmm.' Lee surveyed the preparations for supper thoughtfully. There had been no warning notices in the bay near the point, the bathing there was perfectly safe, provided you did not take risks. As she had done, the voice of conscience reminded her.

'I've made the dry mix for some strawberry shortcake,' Nell pressed her into service after all. 'If you finish that, I can get on with the beans and potatoes.'

Doing the work she enjoyed most calmed her, and by the time she had slid the mixture into the oven to bake she was in a more rational frame of mind. The calf of her leg still felt sore from the cramp, it would probably be uncomfortable for another twenty-four hours, the attack had been a severe one. The headlines stared up at her from Nell's chair seat, silently reproachful, and perhaps it was their effect that made her chop nuts to fold into the stiffly whipped Cornish cream to garnish the shortcake.

'That looks more like Christmas!' Nell raised expressive eyebrows at her unusual extravagance, and she raised a flushed face from the bowl, and hoped the housekeeper would think it was whipping the cream that caused her heightened colour.

'The strawberries were free, so I felt I had to do my share.' That was true, but it did not entirely account for the turmoil of feelings that suddenly welled up inside her, making her feel confused and uncertain.

Had she misjudged Haydn? Were his motives in offering Polrewin a chance to expand as altruistic as Jon would have her believe? His concern for her brother's success seemed genuine. It did not extend to herself, but she did not care about that. Or did she? She did not know whether to believe him or not. While she was on the rocks of the point with him, folded in his arms, with his lips pressed down on her own, she would have believed anything he told her.... Her cheeks took on the hue of the strawberries at the thought, and she whipped and folded cream and nuts with a fierce concentration that drew a protest from Nell.

'You'll have that cream go back, if you set about it like that.'

So she desisted, and ran upstairs to change, and appeared at the supper table in her acid yellow dress and yellow sandals, with the yellow and white bangles on her arm, as a sort of half apology that Haydn could accept or not, just as he wished, she thought defiantly.

'D'you mean you've never tasted strawberry shortcake before?' Jon looked at his guest incredulously. 'You've never lived,' he sympathised.

'It's the first time, but I hope it won't be the last. I'll keep you supplied with prime berries if you promise to turn out dishes like this.' Haydn helped himself with undisguised relish to a second piece, and in spite of her defiance Lee could not help feeling a small glow of satisfaction that her cooking met with his approval. Every cook liked to have their efforts appreciated, she excused the glow, and allowed it to remain where it was and warm her through the rest of the supper time.

'With a bit of luck we'll be turning out our own berries next year,' Jon went on. 'I've given those sketches quite a lot of thought, and it should be a fairly easy matter to rig up some stretchers and sling them in the glasshouses ready for next season. When things slacken down a bit towards the back end of the year will be an ideal time. And Ben will help.' He slid Lee a glance of half apology. 'He was a ship's carpenter in his younger days, so he'll be just the man to turn his hand to making stretchers.'

'Sketches are all very well,' Haydn conceded, 'but it would be even better if you were to come over and see the real thing for yourself. Now is the ideal time, while the berries are growing. As soon as the *Sea Mist* is repaired, we could run over to the Channel Islands and back in the one day, if you'd be willing to come along? You could leave Ben in charge, now he's on full time,' he suggested, and Lee darted him a sharp glance. His offer was a sensible one, but.... She frowned. Everything seemed to fit in too well, somehow. Almost as if it was a preconceived plan. But however suspicious she might be, there could be nothing but good in Jon going to see for himself how the experts coped. And it would help him to grow his own berries for market —surely if Haydn merely wanted Polrewin as an outlet for berries from the islands, he would not be showing him how to grow his own? She shrugged and gave up the question, and turned her attention to her own supper. Evening was not the time to sort out conundrums, and it had been an eventful day.

'Just name the day,' her brother accepted the invitation eagerly. 'It'll be interesting to see how a big oufit copes.'

'In exactly the same way as a small one has to,' Haydn told him drily. 'We have to cost everything down to a fine degree, in just the same way as you do. Our costs are bigger, but then so are our expenses. What doesn't pay for itself has to go.'

The talk turned to technicalities, and as her brother's partner Lee should have listened, and joined in, but she found her attention wandering. There were enough strawberries left in the tray to make another batch of shortcake. Her love of cookery, which had taken her into the domestic science demonstration field in the first place, had not had much outlet since she came to Polrewin, and she realised for the first time how much she missed it. Now Ben was coming full time, perhaps....

'Sis! Haydn's asked you twice!'

She looked up and met the amused grins of the two men, and flushed. Whatever Haydn had asked her, she had certainly not heard him.

'She was wondering what sort of fancy cooking the chef at the Royal Anchor was going to conjure up with those strawberries, and maybe thinking she'd like to find out and try it for herself,' Haydn teased. His guess was so nearly accurate that Lee looked at him, startled, and he smiled. 'I thought so,' he chuckled, and she bit her lip vexedly. She must look very transparent, she thought, annoyed at his easy perception. 'Why not let's go there tomorrow and find out?' he suggested. 'I've got to go to the harbourmaster's office to see about the insurance details for the *Sea Mist*, and I might as well go to the boatyard at the same time and find out how the repairs are going, so that we can plan our trip home. What about it, Jon?'

'That's a great idea,' Jon said easily. 'I'll go along with whatever day you fix unless it's a Wednesday. Any deliveries we have, come then,' he explained, 'and since I don't know when your boat will be ready....'

'We'll make it convenient,' Haydn promised, 'but you haven't said whether you'll come along as well,' he reminded Lee.

'I didn't know I'd been asked.' He had not asked her, when he had first mentioned the trip just after he came to Polrewin. He had only suggested then that Jon should accompany him.

'You were daydreaming,' he smiled. 'Well, what about it?' There was a quiet persistence in him that pressed her for an answer, and for a moment she felt tempted to refuse, then she looked at Jon, saw the eager expression on his face, and had not the heart to spoil his trip. It would be an outing, if nothing else, and she could observe as well as her brother. Most of all, she thought warily, she could observe Haydn, and make sure he did not drag Jon into any further grandiose schemes that could bring about the downfall of Polrewin.

'I'll come,' she said. It was not exactly an effusive answer, but it was the only one she was prepared to give, and Haydn seemed cheerful enough when he came downstairs the following morning.

'You've accepted my invitation to lunch as well,' he guessed, giving her a quick, comprehensive glance.

'I'm not going to be caught out again going to the Royal Anchor in jeans and a shirt,' she retorted feelingly. Her white dress with the scarlet belt and sandals would do; it was plain enough to cope with a morning in Tarmouth, and still neat enough to enter the locally-select dining room and not feel out of place. She tried to sound matter-of-fact, but she could not still a feeling of anticipation at the expected lunch—not for the food, but to see what the chef had made of the delicacies they brought him. It would be an education to work with a man of his calibre, she thought wistfully, paying homage to a master of the art in which she herself, by comparison, was an amateur, although extremely good.

'You'd be stealing trade secrets.' Once again Haydn had read her mind. It was becoming a disconcerting habit, she realised uncomfortably.

'I won't,' she denied indignantly. 'Any more than Jon

will steal secrets from you, when he comes over to the Islands.'

'When you both come over to the Islands,' Haydn corrected her, 'or have you changed your mind?'

'No, of course not.' Unexpectedly she found she was looking forward to the trip. She did not feel inclined to let her eagerness show in such a transparent manner as Jon, but a trip on the cabin cruiser would be a pleasant experience. The child in Lee, never quite dormant in any except the most blasé of individuals, yearned to feel the powerful cruiser under her, set free in its own element.

'I've loaded the van for you, Miss Lee.' Ben stuck his head through the front door and called his usual good morning. 'It's ready when you are.'

'Thanks, Ben. We might as well go.' She turned to Haydn, and picked up her bag at the same time.

'Er—we're a bit early, aren't we?' For the first time since she had known him, Haydn looked mildly disconcerted. 'I'm waiting for a—ah, there it is.' The telephone in the hall gave an urgent summons, and he turned to the door.

'It might be for us,' Lee checked him sharply, and he paused. 'I'll take it, and see.'

He moved aside in silence, and let her pass. He could hardly do anything else, she thought indignantly. Whatever else he might be engineering for Polrewin, he had no right to answer the telephone calls that came to the house. His casual manner of treating the place as if it was his own home left her nerve ends ragged. She picked up the receiver with set lips.

'Polrewin.' She listened for a moment, then held the receiver out to him. 'It's for you.' The fact that he had been right again galled her as much as his cool assumption that he could direct calls to the cottage. He might have asked Jon first, of course, and if he had her brother would speedily give him permission. Jon would let him do whatever he liked, in the name of friendship, Lee thought tartly, but that did not mean Haydn should be allowed to impose. She lingered inside the dining room door, wondering what the call was about. It had been a woman's voice on the telephone.

'Right, thanks, Peggy. That'll be fine. Thanks for everything.' The receiver clicked back into place, and Lee turned sharply away from the door. Haydn had not bothered to lower his voice, so whoever Peggy was, it was not a particularly personal matter, but she did not want him to think she was listening, or even interested in what he was saying.

'That was the switchboard operator back at the nursery,' Haydn cheerfully imparted his news as soon as he returned. 'The foreman left a message for her to ring me by nine and tell me that there would be another few trays of berries and tomatoes coming with the morning consignment, and the van would be here by the time you were ready to set off. They weren't to know you'd be early for once,' he said accusingly.

'Vince didn't order them.' She felt her anger rise again at his cool command of their marketing arrangements.

'No, but he'll take them when he sees what his chef has done with the others,' Haydn prophesied. 'That man had every intention of going to town on those berries. It's my guess he's left the lunch today to the underlings, and the sweet trolley will be his own masterpiece,' he predicted. 'Now's the time to follow up with another supply. Not too big, just four trays this time, enough to whet their appetites for more. Strike while the iron's hot,' he advised her solemnly, and Lee winced. 'I know,' a grin brightened his face, 'but whoever invented that particular cliché had got the right idea, he—that sounds like the van coming, now.'

He broke off and peered out of the window, and Lee followed him in time to see a gaily tartaned figure of a piper on the side of the delivery van pulling to a halt on the gravel, and the name of Scott scrawled in larger copperplate diagonally across the doors. A smartly uniformed driver slid open the side door, and Lee's eyes widened at the sight of the purpose-fitted racks inside, each containing a carefully paper-capped tray, except for the nearest stack. The tops of those trays were bare.

'Here you are, Mr Haydn,' the man saluted his recognition as Haydn strode out of the front door to meet him, 'four of tomatoes and four of berries, like you said. Shall I make it a standing order now, until you tell me otherwise?' he asked briskly.

'Please, Tom, it'd be a great help if you would.'

'Consider it done, sir.' The man nodded to Haydn cheerfully, inclined his head in a friendly fashion to Lee, and was on his way again, leaving the trays as Haydn directed on the gravel beside the Mini van. What a difference in Haydn's handling of his staff! The thought flashed through Lee's mind. There seemed to be friendly co-operation on both sides, and no lack of respect on either. That was something Vince would not understand, even if it was pointed out to him.

'All we've got to do now is to cap these eight trays and load them. Ben said he'd put some paper covers in the van, ready.' Haydn opened the back door of the Mini, and Lee scowled. He had evidently told Ben, but he had not thought fit to tell her. She wondered if he had even condescended to mention it to Jon. He ducked inside the van and picked up a small pile of tray covers, and began to slide them over the newly delivered fruit.

'I suppose you think those ought to be altered as well,' Lee could not resist the thrust, and he glanced up at her from where he stooped over the trays.

'No, why should they?' he asked mildly. 'It might be a good idea to have coloured ones, if you're going to have a white daisy with a yellow centre as the Polrewin trademark.' He put his head on one side, considering the matter. 'A yellow paper would be distinctive, and show up the white daisy. The same as the yellow van roof shows up the daisy transfer on top,' he pointed out the obvious.

'I haven't decided whether we'll have a trademark yet.' She set her lips stubbornly. She refused to be hurried into doing anything, by Haydn. The idea of a distinctive trademark was a good one, and she liked the idea of a daisy. Somehow it seemed to fit Polrewin, and its stark simplicity appealed to her. But she would not be chivvied into anything, particularly by Haydn.

'You'll have to make up your mind before the festival,' he pointed out reasonably. 'If you're going to decorate the float with your trademark, it'll be useless having lots of daisies if you decide to do the same as we have, and make a play on the name.

The kilted piper was an excellent idea, neat and noticeable, but, 'How could we make a play on the name of Polrewin?' It did not lend itself very well to anything.

'You couldn't,' he remarked drily, 'unless you decided to be funny, and use the picture of a parrot clutching a bottle of gin. Not a good idea.' He paused to allow the significance to sink in, then added softly, 'I'd much rather have a daisy. Somehow, it suits you.' The significance of that did not sink in until they were half way to Tarmouth, and then Lee remembered he had said 'suits you', and not 'suits Polrewin'. A simple white daisy. Suited to a naïve girl?

'There you are, Miss Ramsay.' Mr Dunn handed her the tally direct this time, and she put it in her pocket and drove on to the Royal Anchor, where she dropped the tomatoes and strawberries with the delighted chef, then ran the van into a parking slot on the harbour wall.

'I thought it might be nice to walk across to the harbourmaster's place from here, it'll save you from having to drive round the bollards and so on along the jetty,' Haydn remarked, and Lee hesitated. She did not want to go with him. She felt edgy, and on the point of quarrelling with him if he should try to push her about the trademark, and she did not want to spoil Jon's trip to the Channel Islands. She would rather wander round the shops by herself until lunchtime, then meet him at the Royal Anchor, by which time she might feel in a better humour. She looked up, saw Vince strolling down the hotel steps, and made up her mind on the instant. She did not want Vince's company, either. He might press her to partner him at the dancing....

'That's a good idea.' She turned along the harbour wall, but not before she had seen Haydn follow her glance towards the hotel steps.

'Mind that lobster pot.' It was big enough for anyone to see, but Haydn put his arm protectively round her waist and ostentatiously steered her round it. She glanced up at him, puzzled, and met his grin, and remembered that Vince would be looking on.... Her glance turned into a glare, his grin widened, and he dropped his arm to let her walk free, but not, she noticed vexedly, until they had rounded some cars parked in the end slots and started to walk along the hard towards the harbourmaster's office, safely out of sight of Vince from the hotel steps.

'Here you are, Mr Scott, they're all ready for you.' The official saw them coming, and with commendable promptness opened out a sheaf of papers in front of Haydn. 'If you'll just put your signature here, that's all that's necessary, and I needn't bother you again.' He waited while Haydn read the contents of the paper with cautious thoroughness before he signed.

'We're going over to the boatyard now,' he commented, 'just to see how the repairs are progressing.'

'Pretty well, I imagine.' The harbourmaster sounded encouraging. 'They haven't got much work in at the moment, and I know they were working on it the last time I passed. I suppose you wouldn't like to row across, would you?' he offered obligingly. 'I've got one of their boats here, and I promised to let them have it back.' He looked lovingly at his motor-cycle parked outside his office, and his preference in transport was plain.

'It'll make a pleasant change,' Haydn said accommodatingly. 'Come on, Lee, I'll drive for once.' He took her arm, not giving her time to object. The stone steps were steep and wet from the slopping tide, and the rowboat looked remarkably small from where they stood on top of the harbour wall, but encouraged by his hand under her elbow she negotiated them gingerly, and stopped on the last dry step.

'I'll go first,' he told her. 'Stay where you are until I'm settled.' He stepped into the skiff with catlike grace; she could not but admire his perfect balance, the boat scarcely moved under him, as he stood astride and held out his arms. 'Let yourself go,' he said, 'you'll be quite safe.' Safe from a wetting, no doubt. The thought crossed her mind with the memory of their swim to the point. She shut her eyes as she felt his hands grasp her and swing her away from the firm harbour steps, into space. She tensed, expecting the boat to tip, expecting to fall, then dry boards were under her sandals, and she opened her eyes, and Haydn's face laughed into her own as he said,

'Talk about wasted opportunities!' For a moment he held her close to him, as he had held her on the rocks of the point. 'If only this was as steady as the deck of the *Sea Mist*,' he mourned, and the devils lit his eyes again as the colour rose through her throat to her face, 'but there, we might both tip into the harbour,' he added regretfully, 'and that would be a pity, since you're all dressed up to go to the Royal Anchor.'

Carefully he let her go, sat her down in the centre of the skiff, and took up the oars, facing her. Lee wished desperately that he did not face her. It would be much better if he turned his back and looked the other way. If that was the way his thoughts were running, she was glad they were not on the *Sea Mist*.... Or was she? Confused thoughts raced after one another round her head, and she put her hand up to her eyes to try and brush them away, but the boat rocked at her movement and she put it hurriedly back again and held on to the flimsy seat, wishing they were walking back along the safe, steady harbour wall.

'Good exercise, rowing,' Haydn murmured mischievously, seeing her movement, and she gritted her teeth and tried not to notice the rhythmic smoothness of muscles in perfect trim moving under teak-coloured arms to the steady pull, swing, that drove the small skiff with precision and deceptive speed through the water towards the opposite side of the harbour. She turned her eyes away, uneasily conscious of his closeness, and even more conscious of her own inability to do anything about it.

'That speedboat—look, it's coming staright for us!' Her voice came out in a gasp of fear, and the noisy boat, with a grinning youth at the wheel, swung away from them at the very last minute and headed out of the harbour. They caught the full sideways wash, as the inconsiderate driver intended they should, and their small craft lurched alarmingly. Lee screwed her eyes tight shut and gripped the sides of the seat with terrified fingers, and she did not feel Haydn move, but the next second he was on the seat beside her, his arm round her, and his voice in her ear. An angry voice this time, with no amusement in it.

'That's the last time the young fool will do that in this harbour!' he grated furiously, then his tone changed. 'We're not going to tip over, don't worry. There's nothing to be afraid of.'

She felt the tension leave her. Her fingers eased their grip on the seat, and she leaned against him, trembling. 'You know,' he rebuked her lightly, 'someone who can swim as well as you can shouldn't be afraid of a ducking.'

'I'm not used to swimming in a tight dress.' She felt ashamed of her sudden panic, now. She kept her face turned into his arm, waiting for the trembling to go. Very faintly she could smell the freshness of his aftershave lotion, and she lay limp against him for a moment or two, her breath released in a long sigh. 'I thought he was going to run us down—that he hadn't seen us.'

'From now on he'll have his activities curtailed,' Haydn promised, and Lee knew he would carry out his threat, although she did not know how. She remembered the small boy he spanked on his arrival at Tarmouth, and momentarily felt sorry for the speedboater, then she told herself resolutely that it was his own fault, and he deserved whatever Haydn intended to mete out.

'Better now?' He tipped her face up towards him, his finger firm under her chin so that she could not look away.

'Almost.' The fright was nearly gone, although her heartbeat was not as steady as it should be, which was not entirely the fault of the speedboat owner.

'Then let's make it quite,' he said calmly. 'Remember my old nanny's prescription?' and he bent down and kissed her firmly on the mouth.

And only after all her thoughts of the speedboat had been effectively driven out of her head, and his old nurse's prescription had worked its charm, did Lee remember that from their position in the middle of the harbour, they were in full view of Vince from the hotel steps. And Haydn must have known that, too.

CHAPTER SIX

For the rest of the way across the harbour Lee sat very still.

It had not been necessary for Haydn to use her to score off Vince. He did not need to score off the other man, there was nothing between herself and Vince, any more than there was between herself and Haydn. Honesty made her admit that Vince's scarcely veiled antagonism when the two men met in the hotel had invited retaliation, but Haydn need not have been quite so blatant about it. She simmered with silent resentment, and resolutely kept her face turned shorewards. It was almost as if Haydn was openly staking his claim on her, and she had given him no cause to think he had the right. Or perhaps it was simply male aggressiveness, the one taking what he knew the other one wanted. That thought was even less palatable than the first one, and she breathed a sigh of relief as they bumped to a halt at the bottom of the stone steps on the other side of the harbour.

'Sit still for a moment.' Haydn gained the steps with a surefooted leap.

'Don't loose the rope!' Panic returned as the rope ran through his fingers, and slowly but inexorably the boat started to drift away from the side of the steps. Already a foot of water was showing between it and the harbour wall.

'Don't panic, I'll pull you back.' And he did, and took his time about doing it, Lee thought with asperity. She rose from the board seat, anticipating his move to help her ashore, and stubbornly determined not to accept it, then the boat bumped on the side of the steps and she sat down again abruptly.

'I told you to sit still,' he reminded her mildly—and infuriatingly—and did not wait for her to grasp his outstretched hands. He reached down and grabbed her, and with an effortless pull he swung her on to the steps beside him, then bent down to tie the rope to an iron ring with a dexterous twist.

'Now for the boatyard, and a look at the *Sea Mist*.' He straightened up and took hold of her hand again, although he had no need to now, Vince would not be able to see them from this distance.

'Slow down!' She could not keep up with his long strides, and he obligingly slackened his pace.

'I'm too keen to see my boat, I suppose,' he excused his haste.

'She'll be ready for you in another twenty-four hours, Mr Scott.' The owner of the boatyard strolled across to meet them. 'The damage wasn't so bad as it looked once we got down to it. All the real work's already been done. Come and look.' He led the way to where the *Sea Mist* stood in the boat shed, looking curiously vulnerable out of her natural element, like a bird without its flight feathers. 'A lick of paint is all that's needed now.'

'You've got quite a big outfit here.' Haydn sounded impressed, and he gazed about him with knowledgeable eyes. 'By the way, the harbourmaster asked us to bring your skiff back. It's tied up at the bottom of the steps.'

'I'll have it fetched up later.' The man nodded his thanks. 'As for the yard, here, it's not really big enough now,' he responded to Haydn's obvious interest. 'Our trade's increased by leaps and bounds over the last couple of years.'

'It's a nice little anchorage.' Haydn looked out appreciatively across the harbour.

'That's what the boating fraternity is beginning to discover,' the man said in a satisfied tone. 'The bigger anchorages further along the coast get crowded. This one's smaller, and of course so is the town, there's not so much entertainment going on, but the folk who like it a bit quiet keep coming back, and bringing more with them. They find there's more room for their boats and for them, and of course they bring the work with them. We're going to have to expand.'

Someone else with expansion on the brain, Lee thought irritably, and subsided on to a bollard with bored resignation while the two men talked. The hole had disappeared from the side of the *Sea Mist*. Apart from the lack of paint, it was impossible to see where it had been. Twenty-four hours, the boatyard owner had said it would take before it was finished. That meant the day after tomorrow they would be able to go to the Channel Islands. What should she wear?

'We'll be moving into a new yard at the end of the season.' Snatches of conversation reached her ears in between wondering what to put on when Haydn took them to his home nursery, and she listened in a desultory fashion, more intent on the respective merits of a smart outfit or a warm one for the journey.

'What will you do with these premises, after you've moved?' It was Haydn speaking.

'Sell them to finance the new place,' the boatyard owner said promptly. 'They would be ideal for someone who wants warehouse space with a good anchorage alongside, though we wouldn't want a rival boatbuilder to have them, of course,' the man laughed.

'The competition would be too close for comfort,' Haydn agreed cheerfully. 'When can I come and collect the *Sea Mist*?' he returned to the business in hand.

'About this time tomorrow morning?' the man suggested. 'We can go out on a trial run then, and if you're satisfied we'd anchor her in the harbour ready for you to take off any time you wanted.'

'We'll be here,' Haydn promised, and Lee wondered if he meant herself or Jon as the other part of the 'we'. No doubt he was relying on her to bring him to Tarmouth with the morning delivery of salads to the greengrocers.

'You looked miles away.' Haydn disturbed her from her seat on the bollard. 'It's lunch time,' he reminded her unnecessarily. 'What were you dreaming about? The chef's pastries?'

'No, I was wondering whether to wear something warm or smart when we visit your nurseries,' she told him frankly, and he smiled.

'Dress in layers that you can peel off, if necessary,' he advised. 'It'll be cool going over on the water, and hot when we get to the Islands, particularly if you stay with Jon and me and go through the glasshouses. Of course, you could make the bottom layer that fetching white swimsuit you had on the other day,' he suggested slyly, and she pulled a face at him.

'Keep your mind on the chef's pastries,' she told him, suddenly lighthearted, and laughed with him as they ran up the steps of the Royal Anchor and bumped straight into Vince, who confronted them just inside the door. Had he seen them coming, and deliberately waited for them? Lee's smile faded, but the one on Haydn's face, if anything, grew broader. He positively exuded bonhomie.

'You two look happy.' Vince looked just the reverse.

'We've just been talking about Lee's swimsuit. You know, that nifty little white number she wears?'

Vince patently did not know, and his scowl showed it.

'Haydn! For heaven's sake!'

'I forgot you were hungry.' He assumed contrition, which did not suit him Lee thought angrily, but there was nothing she could do about it, and she hurried after the head waiter who led them to the table they had occupied before, by the window overlooking the harbour.

'Something light, I think, today.' Haydn settled back in his chair and confided in the waiter. 'The chef promised he'd do something special with those strawberries we brought in, and we're longing to taste the results. Hmm,' he studied the menu, 'I think two omelettes will do nicely. We won't bother with the melon.' His look condemned the melon, and Lee turned on him in exasperation the moment they were alone again.

'Do you have to be so aggravating?' she whispered furiously.

'Why, what have I done?' Haydn's expression managed to convey a mixture of hurt and puzzlement, which might have deceived Lee except for the merry gleam in his eyes.

'You know very well,' she retorted crossly. 'Each time you meet Vince, you go out of your way to antagonise him.'

'I only tried to be polite. He might have thought we were laughing about him, otherwise, so I told him about your swimsuit,' Haydn grinned. 'He didn't look as if he'd seen it?'

'He hasn't—oh, eat your omelette!' She attacked her

own with an angry prod, which was cavalier treatment that the fluffy concoction did not deserve, and she thought nothing of it when she saw the head waiter give an unobtrusive signal towards the serving hatch when they finished eating, until the chef himself appeared, wheeling the sweet trolley. He made straight for their table.

'I guessed you'd come,' he greeted them, 'and I wanted you to see what'd I'd made before it's split up into servings. My wife tells me you were in the domestic science field yourself, Miss Ramsay?'

'I was,' Lee admitted, 'but my work didn't aspire to these heights.' It was a signal honour for the chef to come to them personally like this, and her eyes sparked as she regarded his handiwork.

'Nevertheless we have a common interest,' he told her courteously. 'You'll see I remembered your trademark.' He stepped aside and revealed the results of his efforts, and Lee gave a gasp of delight.

'It must have taken you hours!' She gazed incredulously at the shining white daisy spread across the entire top of the trolley, mounted on what must have been the biggest base she had ever seen. Meringue glistened like snow crystals, outlining each petal, which was placed on the base separately so as to represent one serving, and each petal cradled in its heart one of the perfect, ripened strawberries they had brought the day before. A dish of the berries, frosted with sugar, made the centre of the daisy. It was one of the most perfect examples of the culinary art Lee had ever seen—a masterpiece, created by a craftsman.

'It would be sheer vandalism to eat it!'

'But you must try it,' the chef insisted. 'Your strawberries helped to create it.' He slid a deft scoop under two of the petals, transferred them and some extra strawberries from the centre on to two dishes, and put them in front of Lee and Haydn with a flourish. 'And when you go, I want you to take this,' he produced a flat cake box from the lower tray of the trolley. 'It's something I made specially for you to take home and enjoy. As a thank you, for bringing such fine berries,' he smiled. 'No man likes working with inferior materials....' He broke off as Vince appeared behind him, and with a bow withdrew kitchenwards, and Lee hoped Vince had not heard what the man said. He would take it as a personal insult, and he was quite capable of venting his spite on the chef as a result, she realised unhappily. She glanced up at his face apprehensively, and knew with a sinking heart that he must have heard every word.

'This looks delicious,' she stammered, not knowing what to say. 'It would make a wonderful centrepiece for the table at the festival ball.'

'I've planned something special for that night.' Vince spoke offhandedly, as if the daisy were an everyday offering at the Royal Anchor. 'That's only a foretaste,' he said loftily. 'And that,' he waved to the cake box which the chef had left on a corner of the table, 'that comes with my compliments.' Lee felt sure this was the first Vince knew of it, but he rose to the occasion nobly and took the credit himself.

'Last round goes to Vince,' Haydn murmured wickedly as the other man turned on his heel and went to greet another batch of diners, and Lee looked after him with troubled eyes.

'I hope he doesn't take it out on the chef,' she murmured worriedly.

'The chef is more than capable of holding his own,' Haydn reassured her. 'Vince has got a goldmine in that man, and he's a fool if he doesn't realise it. Especially now he's seen what he's capable of achieving in this line. If I were in Vince's shoes, I'd be planning a speciality dinner dance at the hotel once a month throughout the winter season, and the speciality would be the chef's table centre. Folks would come from far and wide, just to see what his next offering would be.'

Lee looked at him from across the table. Haydn's mind was honed to a keen edge, and so was his enthusiasm. Beside him, Vince seemed like a pale shadow, and a sluggish one at that. She wondered how she had ever thought him attractive—and then wondered, uncomfortably, why she was bothering to contrast the two men, and in Haydn's favour....

'It's gorgeous!' It tastes as nice as it looks.' She covered her sudden confusion by dipping her fork into the daisy petal, and for a while there was silence as the two gave their offerings the attention they deserved. 'He's made us another daisy—look, a little one. Isn't that kind?' she felt touched by the chef's gesture, and slid the cake box over to Haydn to see.

'You'll have to use the daisy motif for you trademark now,' he said, and this time his eyes were serious. 'You can't reject a kindness like this.'

'No.' For once they were in accord, she thought. And once again Haydn had won. But this time it was through no effort of his own, and because of that it did not rankle. I'm mellowing, Lee thought, surprised, and said aloud, 'As soon as we're back from that trip to the Channel Islands, I'll have to buckle down again. There'll be that float to make and decorate....'

'I'll help you. If we work together, it won't take too long, and Ben can rig up the float for you.'

'But you won't....' She stopped. Haydn would not be with them, then. Once he had got the *Sea Mist* back, he would move out of Polrewin and live on his boat again. That was what they agreed, and that was what she wanted. The thought of him leaving brought with it an unexpected sense of loss, and she considered it abstractedly. It would make odd numbers in the house again. Just herself and Jon and Nell. Ben did not count, because he did not live in.

'Won't know how?' He misunderstood her, and she did not contradict him. 'Indeed I do, it's not the first float I've decorated, and I don't suppose it will be the last. And if the *Sea Mist* stands up to her trial tomorrow, we'll be able to bring the base materials like wire and stuff back with us. There's plenty at the nursery, it'll save you from having to buy, and I can take it back afterwards,' he offered casually.

'Mmm.' Lee hardly heard him. She was too busy examing the strange feeling of flatness—that was all it was, she told herself robustly—that being without Haydn at Polrewin would leave behind. Just because he'd kissed her once or twice.... She was unusually silent on the way home. She felt Haydn's glance rest on her, and once he started to say something, but he seemed to think better of it, and she managed to avoid him until supper time, although there was no reason why she should want to. They had not quarrelled today, for the first time since he had come to Polrewin.

'I'm glad your boat's mended.' Jon sat down at the supper table and listened to their news. 'I hope it doesn't mean you're going to desert us, though?' He put Lee's thoughts into words, and she gave a small intake of breath. Haydn looked up, straight at her, as if he might have heard it, though he would have to have unusually sharp hearing, she thought, and tried to look interested only in the contents of her plate, but all the time she was acutely conscious of his eyes upon her, and wondered what he was thinking. 'You promised to stay with us until after the festival, remember,' Jon went on, 'and I intend to keep you to that. It'll be a lot more fun if we can all go together.'

Lee tensed, waiting for Haydn's answer, but he did not speak. The silence seemed to stretch out of an aeon of time, and at last she raised her eyes to his, drawn by his compelling look that she could feel through the emptiness of no reply. He watched her, as if he waited for her to say something.

'You promised to help me with the float.' It was the best she could manage. Her mouth and throat felt dry, and her head felt curiously light, which was odd, she thought vaguely, considering the weight of confused thoughts that ran round inside it as she tried to read the strange expression in his eyes, and had to give up because it was unreadable, but not before it threw her mind into even greater confusion than before, making her heart race, and a strange, breathless feeling assail her, as if she had been running. Maybe it was cause and effect, she thought bemusedly. She felt she wanted to run, away from Haydn. And another, contrary part of her wanted to stay. Wanted him to stay at Polrewin. What was the matter with her? She took a mouthful of strawberry shortcake, and it might have been dust and ashes in her mouth.

'So I did. And I can't help build the float if I'm living on the *Sea Mist*, can I?'

She let out her breath, slowly, on a long sigh, and suddenly the strawberry shortcake tasted good again. Life seemed good. She felt like a prisoner under sentence who has just learned of a reprieve.

'Haydn said Ben could make the float,' she said happily, and was unaware of her brother's startled look, which passed from herself to Haydn and back again.

'Tell Ben what to do, and he'll do it,' Jon mumbled, and there was a grin on his face that might have been put there by his second helping of strawberry shortcake, and might not.

'Will the day after tomorrow suit you for the trip to our nurseries?' Haydn asked him. 'We've got to take the *Sea Mist* out on trial tomorrow, and if she's satisfactory there's no reason why we shouldn't go over to the Islands the day after.' Again he said 'we' and he seemed to take it for granted that Lee would accompany him on the trial the next morning after they had delivered the daily supply of salads to the greengrocer, and the strawberries and large tomatoes to the hotel, and afterwards sampled some more of the chef's superb preparations before returning to Polrewin, jubilant at the successful repair work that had been done on the cruiser.

'She's better than before—they gave her engine the once-over while they were about it, and generally did a good job. I'll take her in there for her yearly overhaul.' Haydn was pleased and showed it.

'The day after tomorrow will be fine by me,' Jon agreed easily. 'It'll give me time to warn Ben, and we can run the daily deliveries down on our way.' He settled the chores to his satisfaction. 'All that's needed now is the weather. It'd be a pity to meet up with a storm, and arrive at your nursery feeling seasick instead of interested.'

'It's got to be fine. The weather can't change now.' Lee felt quite shocked. Haydn had arranged the day out, hadn't he? And he always had his own way. The thought of bad weather had simply not occurred to her.

'I don't think you need worry,' Haydn smiled at her from across the table. 'The forecast's good, and it seems settled enough.'

He was right, of course. He always was, and the familiar exasperation at his rightness underrode her excitement as she got ready, but it was not enough to spoil it. She gave herself up to the enjoyment of the day, and determinedly forgot everything else. She surveyed her wardrobe, and thanked her lucky stars that her previous job as a demonstrator had made it both versatile and good. The need to appear before all sorts of people in all kinds of circumstances at a moment's notice had made her choose her clothes with care, and it served her in good stead now.

A well cut maize-coloured polyester trouser suit, and a white silk sweater, would serve to keep her cosy and neat, and she could peel the jacket off if it got too hot. The fact that Haydn liked her in yellow was just a coincidence, she told herself firmly. It was her own favourite colour, and the soft creamy gold was a shade she was particularly fond of. It also happened to set off her unusually dark hair and eyes, and golden tan to perfection. She rejected jewellery. Her watch would be sufficient for today, and a pair of flat-heeled maize-coloured slip-ons completed her simple outfit, which met both her requirements, being smart as well as warm.

She tucked a hanky in her pocket, and did not bother with a bag. She would not need money, and her short hairstyle was of the kind that obligingly keeps its appearance without attention unless it got wet. Briefly she remembered Haydn's teasing remark about putting on her swimsuit, and rejected that, too. The trip across to the Islands would take some time, and if they were to make a tour of Scott's nurseries there would not be time in one short day to go swimming as well. And swimming after dark, on the way back, was out so far as she was concerned. Her recent experience in the bay had frightened her more than she cared to admit, and Haydn's warning had not really been necessary. She closed her bedroom door, and felt oddly nervous as she went downstairs to join the men.

'I thought you were never coming,' Jon grumbled with brotherly candour.

'The wait was worth it.' Haydn took in her outfit, and there was a gleam of appreciation in his eyes which sent a shiver down her spine.

'Has the van been loaded?' She grasped at practicalities to cover the rising colour she felt in her cheeks, and knew to her chagrin that Haydn had recognised her move for what it was, and not for real interest. The glint in his eyes taunted her.

'Yes, it's complete with strawberries and everything,' Jon unwittingly saved her face, and turned eagerly towards the van. 'I'll drive. Can you manage in the back, Sis, among the boxes?'

'Shall I. . . .' Haydn began, and she shook her head.

'You're much too long,' she said emphatically. 'I can curl up in a smaller ball than you'd be able to.' She suited action to her words, and was soon comfortably ensconced with her knees drawn up to her chin and her arms round them, and trying not to look at the tray of luscious strawberries beside her. They were red, and ripe, and an open invitation, and she succumbed with a guilty look at Haydn in the passenger seat. His eyes gleamed at her through the driving mirror.

'Caught you!'

'I'm just sampling them to see if they're in good condition,' she retorted unrepentantly. 'Besides, I deserve payment for travelling in the back.'

'You could sit on my lap.'

'There's no room,' she threw back flippantly, and wondered why she suddenly wished the van was twice as big. Her thoughts were getting out of hand, she decided, and to Jon's surprise agreed meekly to wait for them on the quay while they delivered to the greengrocer and the hotel.

She was glad to quit the van and be by herself for a little while in the cool, early morning air, and attempt to regain some of her poise before the men returned. She sat down on a nearby bollard, and her eyes found the *Sea Mist*, riding at anchor on the full tide, where they had left her the day before. Her dinghy bobbed gently at the bottom of the harbour steps, waiting to take them to the cruiser. She hoped the speedboat owner would not try any more tricks while they were in the rowboat, and even as the thought struck her she saw the object of her aversion carefully easing his way out between the clutter of boats in the harbour, his own fast craft throttled down to a slow speed, and she smiled. Haydn must have made his wrath felt, and for the first time she felt glad of their guest's forcefulness. She suddenly wished, inconsequentially, that she and Haydn were going out together in the rowboat, instead of with Jon in the *Sea Mist*. Wished they were going somewhere where they could be on their own. Aghast at her own thoughts, she tried to stem them, but as useless to try and stem the tide. She knew, now, how King Canute must have felt, she thought with a wry attempt at humour that did not succeed.

Her thoughts rolled on, with the same inevitability that drove the waves with a regular beat against the bottom of the harbour wall. Hiss—boom—recede. Hiss—boom—recede. I—love—Haydn. I—love—Haydn. It had the steady rhythm of a heartbeat. Her own heart? The waves must be wrong. She did not love him; she could not love him. Panic took her and she tried ineffectually to wrestle with this strange, unexpected flood of emotion that could not possibly be real. She did not hear the two men return, did not see them, until Haydn stood over her.

'Daydreaming again! Those confections the chef made have really got hold of your imagination.' His voice reached her through a fog, probing, teasing, and she looked up at him, her vision clearing. He loomed above her, tawny-haired, tawny-eyed, with the same catlike virility of the mountain lion she first likened him to. He was indeed a lion of a man. His very presence made her heart feel weak inside her. As weak as her legs, whose sudden lack of strength chained her to her seat on top of the bollard.

'She doesn't like rowboats.' Haydn darted a smiling glance at Jon. 'We were nearly run down by a speedboat the other day, but don't worry,' he turned back to Lee reassuringly, 'he won't do that again.'

'I know. I've just seen him go out of the harbour—slowly.' Somehow she managed to force her voice to sound normal, though she had to clench her teeth to stem the great trembling that seized her, and threatened to show in her voice. Surely Jon and Haydn must hear it? With a great effort of self-control she slipped off the bollard, and waited for a moment to make sure her feet would support her. They felt distinctly uncertain.

'Come down the steps between Jon and me.' Haydn misinterpreted her hesitation, and went first, holding out his hand to guide her down, and when they got to the bottom one against the water he did the same as he had done before, stepped into the dinghy, and held out his arms and took her, then swung her down beside him and held her close to him until the boat stopped rocking. Lee clung to him, wanting the moment to go on for ever, then he put her down on to the middle seat, and the place where his arms had rested felt desolate, and she shut her eyes to blot out the feel of it, telling herself it did not matter, and only the boat tipping again told her Jon had joined them.

'You can open your eyes now, Sis, we're all safely in.' His voice came from a long distance, and she opened her eyes with an effort and met Haydn's grin. Unable to face the gleam in his eyes she lowered her own and watched the play of light and shadow on his face as he bent with rhythmic grace to the oars, the brown hollow of his throat moving slightly with the muscle pull under the cream, open-necked silk shirt that topped his chocolate brown trousers with pale elegance. Watching him thus did not help to resolve the battle between what her heart tried to tell her, and what her head said she could not do.... She was still in the same state of uncertainty when she felt the boat turn and bump lightly against the side of the cruiser, then circle it towards a gap in the rail above them.

'How ...?' She surveyed the deck, which seemed to loom miles above them.

'Up a ladder, it's quite easy. And safe.' Haydn reached for what Lee had taken to be a pile of rope, and now revealed itself as a pair of efficient grappling hooks attached to rope, but in the form of a rope ladder. She felt her scalp prickle.

'Don't look like that,' Haydn chuckled. 'We'll send Jon first, and if he falls in I promise we'll go back ashore at once.'

'I wish....' She did not know what she wished. She dared not voice the wish that was in her heart, not even to herself. Perhaps least of all to herself.

'Wish granted,' Haydn said promptly, and he could not know how her heart lurched at his easy words. 'You'll be on deck in two seconds. Just watch Jon, and when he gets to the top of the ladder, follow him up. I'll come right behind you.'

It was easier than she thought. At Haydn's instructions, she waited until the two boats rode high together on a wave, then reached over and grasped the rope ladder and found a foothold, and waited there until the boat swayed down and upwards again, and she started to climb. Physical activity, she found, helped to stem her thoughts, and she felt happier until she felt a tug on the rope below her, and looked down.

'It'll break!' she exclaimed. Haydn was climbing behind her. Climbing round her, she realised. He was only one step down, and his greater height made a backing for her, his arms reached round her body and made living guard rails through which she could not fall.

'It's made of nylon, and it's tested to stand the weight of a dozen like me.'

So she climbed, trusting him, and in a surprisingly short time she stood on the deck beside him, watched him go aft and untie the light rope from his belt that held the dinghy, and lash it on to the rail to be towed behind the cruiser. And then the boat's engine burbled into soft life, the sound not so obtrusive as she had thought it would be when it was opened up, and it made a pleasant background murmur which nevertheless had the sound of controlled power behind it, then they were nosing out of the harbour, leaving behind the anchored craft and the horshoe of shops that edged the harbour wall, and she knew a fleeting curiosity in case Vince was watching from the hotel steps. He would see them easily from there, and they were close enough for him to recognise them.

She forgot Vince in the new and exhilarating sensation coming from the deck under her feet as the boat responded to the stronger force of the water outside the sheltering arms of the harbour. It rose to its element like a live thing released from a cage, and Lee leaned against the rail and watched the hissing surge of water pass the side of the *Sea Mist* as the cruiser's bow cleft the waves like an arrow, their hypnotic effect gradually quietening the tumult in her mind, and allowing her to relax and look about her with more interest. For a while Haydn followed the coastline. They passed small bays, the one where they had swum, and saw Polrewin snuggled into the dip in the cliffs.

'There's the glasshouses, look. See how they shine in the sun.' They waved gaily in case Nell or Ben were looking, then they were nearing the lighthouse, and Haydn took a bearing from it and turned, heading out to sea and away from the familiar landmarks.

'I wouldn't mind a craft like this myself.' Jon eyed the controls with fascinated interest.

'You can take her for a bit if you like. Just keep her on the same compass bearing, and see what you think of the feel of her.' Haydn readily handed over the wheel, and joined Lee at the rail. 'How about a cup of coffee?' he asked.

'Not for me.' Jon wanted nothing more than to be left to enjoy the pleasure of the wheel.

'We'll bring you one up,' Haydn grinned, and Lee offered,

'I'll make it for you, if you tell me where the things are.' Suddenly she wanted to make coffee for Haydn.

'In here, look.' He led the way down to the day cabin, and opened a door and showed her a kitchen in miniature, complete with everything she needed.

'It's like a dolls house kitchen.'

'Galley,' he corrected her. 'You're at sea now.'

He opened a cupboard, and sorted out the dry ingredients.

'I forgot to bring milk.'

'There's plenty here.' It was tinned, but she was not disposed to be fussy about such things today.

'Mind when the coffee boils, she's a bit lively.' Lee staggered, unused to the movement of the boat, and stepped back on to Haydn's toe.

'I'm sorry,' she apologised hastily, and clutched at the end of the cupboard for support. She missed and staggered again as the boat tipped alarmingly, and Haydn laughed and put an arm round her, and drew her to him.

'Hang on to me instead, I'm softer to fall against.'

'I'll get used to it.' She felt breathless, suddenly.

'Used to what?' His arm tightened, and she looked up and found his face disconcertingly close to her own. There was a cleft in his chin. She had noticed it the last time he kissed her.... She did not know what to answer, and he saved her the bother. He kissed her again, lightly, laughingly, on her mouth and then again on the tip of her upturned nose, and she lifted her face eagerly, just as the coffee boiled over.

'We're not going to be allowed to get used to this,' he grinned. 'Pity....' He reached out a long arm and rescued the dark liquid, and poured it into a flat-bottomed jug. He poured the tin of milk into another, put three serviceable crock mugs into a tin tray, and said,

'I'll carry these up. You follow me,' and left her to climb the stairs after him, and blame the movement of the boat for the uncertainty in her legs, although in her heart she knew it was not the fault of the *Sea Mist* at all, even if it did put solid planking beneath her feet when she least expected it, and removed it when she most wanted it. In desperation she sat down on the deck and stretched both legs full length in front of her.

'You're a landlubber,' Haydn accused her, and she retorted mutinously,

'And proud of it. At least the land doesn't heave up and down like this.' She accepted her mug of coffee, and wondered why he watched her so keenly while she drank it.

'Another?'

'Please, that was lovely.' She surprised a look of relief on his face. 'What's the matter?'

'I wondered if you were feeling seasick, that's all.'

'Of course I'm not.' Heaven forbid! she thought, horrified. That would be the last straw. She wished he had not put the thought in her mind, then she forgot it when Haydn drew her to the rail and pointed out a school of porpoises on the other side of the *Sea Mist*, escorting the boat, and playing with happy abandon while they swam.

'I thought there'd be nothing to see, so far out as this,' she commented.

'There's always something to see.' He showed her different sea-birds busily fishing in the waters; laughed with her as they watched together while one swallowed a fish that seemed much too large and surely, Lee thought, must choke it, but it went down at last, and the bird dived for another, then the long dark streak of land that was the Channel Islands showed up like a pencil line on the horizon, and Haydn left her at the rail, and took over the wheel again from Jon.

'They're company, aren't they?' She followed him, unwilling to be left by herself, her mind still on the porpoises and the seabirds. What had Haydn called them? Comorants?

'I'm never lonely when I'm on the *Sea Mist*.'

He spoke abstractedly, his attention on the rapidly looming land, and Lee watched fascinated while the seemingly impregnable cliffs broke up into fissures that soon became small bays, with houses and people showing as they got closer in, and then they were heading towards a harbour that looked from where they were to be much like the one at Tarmouth, its friendly arms reaching out to welcome them, and they came to rest in quiet water again, and there was the business of descending the rope ladder, and getting into the dinghy and being rowed ashore, so that there was no time to think. People called out to Haydn as they passed, waving greetings across the water, for this was his home and these were his friends, and she and Jon were the strangers now.

At last the safe, solid feel of cobbles met her feet again on another harbour wall, and unlike the deck of the *Sea Mist* they did not heave up and down, until she remembered what Haydn had said, and the memory made them seem to waver before her eyes. 'I'm never lonely when I'm on the *Sea Mist*. . . .' Did that mean he, too, regarded the seabirds and porpoises as company? Or did he take with him other companions—human ones? It was a four-berth boat, and he said he liked room to move about when he was afloat. But two people on the *Sea Mist* would still leave plenty of room without feeling crowded. Perhaps he brought someone else with him sometimes, a friend. Maybe a woman friend?

'This way.' Haydn put his hand beneath her elbow, steering her in the right direction, and she went with him bemusedly, hardly hearing what it was he said.

For the first time in her life, Lee knew what it was like to feel jealous.

CHAPTER SEVEN

'I THOUGHT we'd look round the nursery first, then go home and have lunch with the family afterwards.' Haydn ushered them towards an open runabout waiting at the end of the harbour wall. Lee noticed the driver wore the same uniform as the van driver who had come to Polrewin, and he greeted Haydn with the same evidence of pleasure.

'Is it far?' Jon clambered in.

'About a couple of miles, and it's a steep climb away from the shore.'

Lee took her seat between the two men in silence. She had not taken into account the fact that she might meet Haydn's family. For some reason, the possibility had not occurred to her. She had looked upon the visit purely as a business trip, and found the sudden, more personal aspect of it disconcerting. She had concentrated so hard on keeping an eye on her brother, for fear his enthusiasm might run him into another grandiose scheme that they could not afford, that no other possibility had seriously entered her head. It was natural for Haydn to wish to visit his family while he was on the island, it had just not occurred to her, that was all. And now she was here, dressed in a trouser suit and a plain sweater—suitable for the sea trip and a day round the nursery gardens, but not for lunch with strangers, and Haydn's family at that. She felt as vexed, and as vulnerable, as she had on the occasion of their first lunch at the Royal Anchor.

Her first sight of the nurseries themselves did nothing to reassure her. The vehicle climbed steadily, following the coast, and giving them a breathtaking view of the harbour as they drove, and then it was cut off by a bend in the road, and the terrain flattened out, and what seemed like acres of glasshouses confronted them. Lee caught her breath. She knew Scotts was a big nursery, but she did not realise it was quite so large. The road ran alongside it for some time, and then they turned in at a manned gatehouse, with a striped barrier across the path, on top of which sat the familiar, kilted piper. It lifted at the behest of the gate security man, and with scarcely a pause they swept along clean gravel paths and drew to a halt beside a low, square, brick building with a thatched roof. A fair-haired girl with a clipboard of papers in her hand came out of the door, and stopped when she saw Haydn.

'The driver phoned from the harbour to say you were on the way, Mr Haydn,' she smiled in a friendly fashion at Lee. 'Coffee's on its way to your studio.'

'Thanks, Brenda, it'll be very welcome.' Haydn jumped on to the gravel and held out his hand to help Lee down. 'Follow me,' he told them. 'We'll have our coffee first, then start on our trip round the glasshouses.'

Lee followed him. She stole a glance at her brother's face. Jon looked dazed, and her heart sank. In his present mood he would be open to any suggestions Haydn might make.

'This is our office block.' Their host waved his hand at the whole thatched building, and once inside, the cottagy look vanished. Glass-fronted offices showed busy staff, in superb working conditions, Lee had to admit, and one long room where two white-coated people, a man and a woman, worked with looks of absorbed concentration on their faces.

'That's the lab,' Haydn explained casually. 'You'd find that interesting, Jon, they're setting out plants grown from frozen rose seeds.' He spoke directly to her brother, and Lee stiffened resentfully. 'They subject the seed pods to a very low temperature to simulate an artificial winter, then when they're planted they grow quickly.'

'Baby rose bushes!' Lee forgot her anger at being ignored, and peered eagerly through the glass, her nose pressed close against it with undisguised interest. The girl inside the transparent panels looked up and smiled, the same friendly, happy response of the other staff, and Lee knew a moment of quick envy. It would be good to work in an atmosphere like this. Haydn seemed to draw the same response from everybody, she thought. Everybody, that was, except herself. He must find her as prickly as a hedgehog. She shrugged the thought away. Whatever the message the waves tried to tell her as they drummed against the harbour wall, the need to protect Polrewin's interests still remained paramount in her mind.

'I didn't know you experimented.' Jon lingered beside the glass-fronted laboratory.

'We're experimenting all the time,' Haydn retorted. 'We have to, to keep abreast of the market. In a way, my own contribution is an experiment,' he admitted. 'We haven't tried a mail order business before, and there are quite a number of snags to be ironed out. A distribution centre on the mainland is an urgent priority that must be dealt with before the next season starts.'

Polrewin!

Lee's guard slid back into place with an almost audible click. It must have been a rare piece of good fortune for Haydn, she thought bitterly, when Jon invited him to stay with them, to find not only the place he was looking for, but a man he knew he could trust, and who would be willing—or gullible enough—to take on his distribution for him. Not if I can help it! she thought grimly, as she moved away from the laboratory window and followed Haydn along the corridor.

'My studio's through here.' He opened a door at the end and stood aside for Lee to enter. She stepped through, curious to see where he worked. She liked his quarters on the *Sea Mist*. She was in accord with his choice of colours, but they were surprisingly bare of any personal adornment. She had not seen any photographs or books lying around on the boat, or any of the paraphernalia one would expect its owner to personalise his possession with. His studio might reveal more of the man himself, and she looked around her interestedly. The conditions his staff worked under were unusually good, and as he was the son of the owner his own quarters here might be expected to show some opulence. She had seen Vince's office, once, at the Royal Anchor, and it was the last word in luxury.

Compared to Vince's office—even compared to the conditions of the general offices they had passed through outside—Haydn's studio was spartan. Plain parquet flooring met her feet in place of the expected carpet, and instead of a desk, a wide, flat-topped bench-like structure took up the entire length of one wall, under half of which filing drawers bore neat labels.

'They hold all my negatives.'

Strangely, there were no photographs adorning the walls. Lee looked round, hoping to see some evidence of Haydn's work, but the walls were bare. A picture window took up the wall opposite to the table, and gave on to a view of part of the harbour and coastline. Beyond that, the plain emulsioned walls held an almost monastic appearance.

'They make ideal backcloths for throwing up shots of any photographs I take,' Haydn explained, interpreting her look. 'If you put a slide through a projector, it shows up any imperfections instantly. Here's my darkroom.' He opened a further door into a room which had a scrubbed quarry floor. 'But we're letting our coffee get cold.' He drew forward two plain wooden chairs with horseshoe-shaped arms, devoid even of a cushion, which Lee found to her surprise when she sat down were extraordinarily comfortable. She snuggled back and found the back and arms fitted perfectly where she most needed support.

'I'll introduce you later to the man who made these for me,' Haydn answered Jon's outspoken appreciation of his own seat. 'He does all our carpentry for us. He made the table, too, it's solid walnut.' The natural shape of the log had been left as it was, and the wood held the glow of loving polish. 'Shall I pour out, or will you?'

'I'd like to.' Lee was not just being polite. The Royal Doulton service on a silver tray was the only touch of luxury in the room.

'It's my one extravagance,' Haydn admitted, reading the sparkle in Lee's eyes and the rapt look on her face as she handled the fine, delicately patterned china with a reverence that betrayed her own addiction. That at least was something they had in common, she thought; on everything else they seemed to be at cross purposes.

'I suppose you don't call the *Sea Mist* an extravagance,'

scoffed Jon, and Haydn answered him with perfect sincerity,

'No, and you wouldn't either if you lived on a comparatively small island. I told you, we do a lot of trade with the Continent, and Dad's been glad to use me as a leg man during the last year or two, the trekking backwards and forwards is getting a bit beyond him now.' He accepted his coffee from Lee, and went on, 'In time saving alone the boat will pay for itself over a period of a few years. Waiting for scheduled services wastes days at a time, and with the *Sea Mist*'s draft I can take her right into the heart of the Continent on the canals and rivers. A boat is fast, it makes an ideal mobile office, I can discuss business without having to bother to entertain, and come and go as I please.'

So that was why the cabin looked so bare, Lee thought.

'Well thought out,' Jon applauded, and Lee butted in before he could go any further.

'For Haydn, yes, but not for us.' She stressed the 'us'. 'We don't live on a small island, we don't trade with the Continent, and our business talks at the moment are confined to asking Mr Dunn how many trays of tomatoes he's likely to want next week,' she stated baldly. The possibility of Haydn talking Jon into buying a boat made her blanch. The strawberries and tomatoes they had already accepted from the big nurseries were bad enough, and there were the daisies for the festival float still to come. They were already in debt to Scotts to an extent that disturbed her sleep at night.

'I know that,' Jon protested, stung by her tone. 'I wasn't suggesting we dash out and buy a boat. It's a bit beyond us, yet,' he admitted wistfully.

'It's way beyond us, for a long time to come,' she snapped back. 'Our sole purpose in coming here is for you to see how to make the stretchers to hold strawberry plants for next season. Don't count your berries until they're grown and picked,' she misquoted darkly. 'We haven't even got the plants yet, let alone the fruit.'

'We could supply you with those,' Haydn offered mildly, and then before Lee had a chance to reply added, 'but as you say, you're here now to see how the stretchers are made. If you've finished your coffee?'

All Lee's doubts returned as she followed him towards the door. Haydn had manoeuvred Jon into a position where Polrewin would be a handy market outlet for plants, as well as a distributing centre for his mail order business, and bitter resentment welled up inside her at his unscrupulous manipulation.

'Polrewin's too small to be of any interest as a market to a place like Scotts,' she put in firmly, and Haydn paused at the bite in her voice, and eyed her strangely.

'The bulk of our trade is done through comparatively small outlets,' he said at last—almost, Lee thought irascibly, as if he was explaining the ABC to a particularly obtuse child. 'It eliminates the middleman's profit and allows us to sell at a more reasonable rate, and it also helps to maintain our reputation for supplying goods in mint-fresh condition, without the time lag of going through the bigger markets.'

The trouble was, Lee thought helplessly, it all sounded so reasonable. His arguments were perfectly logical, and if Polrewin had been a viable concern she would probably have been as ready to listen as her brother. But it was not. It would be another two seasons before they would be secure enough to consider launching out, and in the meantime their joint savings were at risk. Lee deliberately placed herself between the two men. If Haydn had any intention of putting more wild theories into her brother's mind, she intended to be there to field them, and mitigate some of the damage.

'Here's the block of glasshouses where we grow the strawberries.'

She had never seen a glasshouse packed to such capacity. There was scarcely an inch of wasted space from the floor to the roof, and it made Polrewin's two glasshouses, Lee realised uncomfortably, look like the work of an amateur.

'I say!' Jon was impressed, and showed it. Lee was equally impressed, and determined not to show it. 'Are you sure there's room for us?' Jon asked with heavy irony, and Haydn grinned.

'Plenty, so long as you keep to the walkways. You can see now what I meant when I said use all your space,' he went on conversationally. 'The same amount of heat keeps all this lot going.' He paused to speak to a man in overalls who wheeled a light trolley full of containers along the walkway towards them. Some of them, Lee noticed, were already full of strawberries. He must be picking the morning crop.

'Will it upset your count if I take one?' Haydn asked him, and the man smiled.

'No, I've got a few extra in case there's a split punnet.' He handed one over, and Lee looked on curiously. She could not imagine Vince asking permission from one of his own staff. He would be more likely to take what he wanted, and blame the staff for being one short afterwards.

'I'm just going to let this stretcher down and pick it, if you want a few berries for the young lady, Mr Haydn.' The man's friendly smile embraced Lee, and she felt her cheeks go pink, but Haydn merely said easily,

'That was the general idea. This gentleman,' he indicated Jon, 'is more interested in how the stretchers work. He's a grower on the mainland.' Again he overlooked, deliberately or otherwise, the fact that Lee was Jon's partner.

'A rival, eh?' The man eyed Jon shrewdly.

'A friend of mine,' Haydn corrected him quietly. 'Step back a moment, Lee, the stretcher's coming down.' He raised one hand and helped adjust it to a comfortable picking level while he kept his other on Lee's elbow, drawing her to him safely out of the way of the descending load. Her eyes widened as she surveyed what it contained.

'They're less trouble grown this way, the berries hang down and automatically stay clean.' Haydn let go of her elbow and started to fill the punnet in his hand. The berries were huge, replicas of those which had delighted the chef at the Royal Anchor, and Haydn handed her the filled punnet.

'These will keep you happy while Jon and I talk technicalities.'

'Any business discussions you have with Jon must include me.' She would not be thrust aside in this manner, she thought furiously, and with difficulty restrained a desire to hurl his strawberries back at him. He treated her as if she was a no-account child, to be given a bag of sweets to keep her quiet while the grown-ups talked.

'It's hardly a business discussion,' he retorted drily. 'Jon simply wants to see how the stretchers are made, so that he can instruct Ben when he gets back. Unless you're interested in carpentry, of course?' She was not, and he must know it, and he turned back to Jon. 'They're little more than stout slats, really, so that the air and the heat can get through....'

Lee bit into a strawberry angrily, aware of the curious gaze of the man in overalls. She felt deflated, and if Haydn's reply was meant to defuse her anger it had not succeeded. What would be the outcome of this trip? she wondered worriedly, and wished fervently that they had never come. If it came to listening to either herself or Haydn, Jon would certainly take Haydn's advice, regardless of what she said. A sick feeling of helplessness assailed her, and she surreptitiously slid the punnet of strawberries back on to the trolley. She did not want any more. She felt another berry would choke her.

'I'll take you to see Alan Walker, he's in charge of all the maintenance round here, and he's a master carpenter.' The two men finished their inspection of the stretcher and straightened up.

'He's working at the end of the glasshouse, Mr Haydn,' the man in overalls put in. 'Here he comes, now,' he indicated his colleague in a brown smock walking slowly towards them, his eyes searching overhead, as if he might be on a daily checking round.

'You've come at just the right time,' Haydn greeted him, and made the necessary instructions. 'Mr Ramsay wants to investigate the possibilities of using something similar in his own glasshouses on the mainland.'

'We've got some new stretchers made in the carpenter's shop, if you like to come and have a look at them.' The man was all friendly co-operation.

'If there's one spare, we could take it back with us,' Haydn suggested. 'Ben could see then for himself just what was needed.'

'Provided you add it on to our account.' Lee was determined that Jon should not accept anything they did not pay for.

'Oh, I will.' Haydn turned to her with a swift movement and looked straight into her eyes. 'Indeed I will,' he added softly, and there was a wealth of meaning in his voice that raised Lee's eyes to his with startled questioning, to meet the hard, impatient anger in his look, so that she dropped her gaze, and felt a shiver of apprehension run through her. Had she gone too far?

No! she denied to herself fiercely. You could not go too far to retain your own independence. What Polrewin received from Scotts nurseries, they would pay for. And Haydn's look confirmed that she would pay. She—and not Polrewin.... Suddenly subdued, she took refuge in silence while her brother and the maintenance man talked, and she shook her head emphatically when Jon asked,

'D'you want to come to the carpenter's shop with us, Lee?' She did not. She would much rather continue to wander round the glasshouses on her own. It would give her time to collect her wits before she faced another verbal sparring match with Haydn. For once, Jon must get by on his own, and if Haydn led him into any extravagance she would simply veto it. She had the right, as his partner.

'You go along with Alan, then, Jon, and we'll join up with you later.' Haydn neatly circumvented her move, and she bit her lip angrily. 'I've got something to show Lee that won't be of much interest to you.'

There was nothing Haydn could show her that would not also interest Jon, as her business partner. She opened her mouth to tell him so, and then shut it again, the words unsaid, because the maintenance man and the strawberry picker were watching and listening.

'This way, it's outside.' Wordlessly she followed him. Her feet dragged, and she wished she had elected to go with Jon to the carpenter's shop after all. She had thought Haydn would remain with Jon....

He did not speak as he led the way through the glasshouse and out into the open air. He paused then for a moment or two, and took a deep breath, and Lee found herself doing the same. Perhaps they both needed a breather, she thought humourlessly, but if Haydn thought she would agree to anything he suggested just because he had brought them out for the day, he had yet to find his mistake. She walked slowly, determined not to be the first to break the silence, and he led her away from the administrative building towards flat, cultivated fields which beckoned with strips of brilliant colour. A short windbreak of trees protected one side, and Haydn led her through it and out at the other side, where he stopped and leaned against a handy trunk, and broke the silence.

'There are your daisies,' he told her quietly. 'You can have all those to decorate your float with.'

A broad strip of white, nodding heads with bright yellow centres ran down the entire length of the field confronting them, and Lee knew a moment of quick jubilation. There were all the daisies she needed, and more. It faded almost as soon as it came. Picking, packaging and transport would be costly. And already Polrewin's debt to Scotts nurseries was mounting steadily. Her lips set in a determined line.

'We'll have only what we can afford.'

His face whitened. She watched the colour recede, and felt a quick prick of fear, but he held himself in check with iron self-control, and only betrayed what he felt by a quick gesture of exasperation.

'I'm offering them to you. As a gift. For my keep, if you like, while I've been staying with you at Polrewin. If you *must* be so damned independent....'

'We don't take paying guests.' She faced him with dignity. 'Any produce we have from here must go on to our account, and be paid for.'

She got no further. Haydn gave an exclamation of anger, and reaching out pulled her roughly towards him. She tried to turn away, but his hands held on to her shoulders with steel strength, and she was helpless in his grasp.

'If you won't accept them, then you can pay something on account now,' he growled furiously, and his lips came down hard on her own. She struggled, but his one hand rose and cupped the back of her head, holding her still. His body was hard against her, hurting her, as unyielding in his anger as the tree trunks among which they stood, and she moaned and tried to beat against him with her fists, but her arms were pinioned to her sides. He held her in a searing, devastating embrace, afire with suppressed fury. She could not draw away, and she could not breathe. Her heart beat with hard, heavy thuds, like the waves against the harbour wall at Tarmouth. She felt her senses begin to slip, and if he did not soon let her go, her resistance would do the same.... Fear that she might yield and respond as she had responded when he kissed her on the rocks of the point gave her last remaining strength the impetus of desperation, and she arched her back and pushed away from him. He let her go, then, thrust her from him, and the force of his thrust and her own push combined made her stagger backwards. She came up hard against one of the tree trunks, and reached behind her to grasp at it for support, trembling in every limb.

'I hate you!'

Her lips felt stiff. They throbbed from the angry pressure he had put upon them, and the inside of them felt bruised where they had been mercilessly crushed against her teeth. She faced him like a wild thing at bay, her black eyes enormous in her white face, and her breath came in sobbing gasps.

'I hate you!'

If she repeated it often enough, she would believe it. She loathed him! She detested him for his arrogant, domineering ways. If he had never come to Polrewin, she would never have experienced this violent upsurge of feeling that destroyed her peace of mind, and would soon destroy her too.... It was like being a human tug of war, attracted and repelled at the same time. But the attraction is only physical, her mind cried to her heart, and she despised herself for it. But her mind waited in vain for a reply. Her heart just cried....

'At least you've got something to hate me for, now,' Haydn ground through set teeth.

'Go away! Leave us alone,' she whispered frantically, and his head reared up and he glared at her with angry eyes.

'I only wish I could, but I promised Jon I'd help him, and help him I will, no matter what you say. He's working like a slave to get his business off the ground, and he asked me to come along and steer him,' he reminded Lee grimly. 'Every time I make a suggestion, you block my way. You can't get a business afloat by just sitting back and letting things happen,' he snapped.

'No, you push potential rivals into a corner, get them hopelessly into debt, and then take them over for your own purposes,' Lee hit back, stung into retaliation by the contempt in his tone.

'Purposes such as—what?' He stilled then, with a taut, alert stillness, like a mountain cat about to spring, she thought numbly, but it was too late now, she had to go on.

'Such as having a ready-made distribution centre for your mail order business,' she flung at him, and saw his face go paler still beneath his tan.

'So that's what you think,' he breathed softly. He held her eyes with a long, cold, considering look. There were no lights in the amber orbs now, they looked like quartz, and about as hard.

'What else am I to think?' To her chagrin her own eyes filled with angry tears, and she brushed them away with an impatient flick of her hand. 'We'd just got out of debt with the bank when you came on the scene, and then you tempted Jon to buy this and buy that, and got us back into debt again. First it was the tomatoes and the strawberries, now it's the wooden stretchers and the daisies, and this morning you put the idea of a boat into his head....' Despair choked her utterance, and she shivered to a halt. His face wavered in front of her eyes, and she blinked, but it did not clear her vision, and out of the mists she heard him say,

'You can forget the charge for the daisies, you're having them whether you want them or not. Jon needs the advertisement for Polrewin, and if you don't want to be a part of it, that's up to you.'

'That's fine by me,' she flung back defiantly. 'As far as I'm concerned you....'

'Mr Haydn!'

She stopped abruptly as a voice called through the trees, and the fair-haired girl Lee had seen earlier with the clipboard in her hand hurried towards them. Lee averted her face. She did not feel like facing another woman's intuitive glance just yet.

'Mrs Scott phoned through to say your lunch would be ready in half an hour, and that was ten minutes ago,' the girl warned Haydn with a smile.

'We'll be there,' he promised. 'We'll go and collect Mr Ramsay from the carpenter's shop first.'

'He's already waiting by the car,' the girl told him, and turned to go back the way she had come.

'In that case we'll come back with you.'

He turned, and took Lee's arm, and perforce she had to walk alongside him. Once she put her hand up to her lips, to her forehead. Her head ached now, too. She felt him glance down at her, and she withdrew it, and carried on walking, conscious of a heavy listlessness that made each step an effort. It seemed a hundred miles before she sa[illegible] the thatched roof of the office block again, and sl[illegible] how managed to respond to the girl's cheerful, [illegible] good day,' and walked towards the car pulled up [illegible] gravel. Jon was already sitting in the back. Haydn [illegible] for a moment to speak to the girl, she did not hear w[illegible] said, only the girl's cheerful, 'Leave it to me, Mr H[illegible] and she clambered into the car beside Jon, unwilling t[illegible] in case Haydn tried to help her in. She shrank from his touch, her arms already felt bruised where his fingers had gripped her.

'Those stretchers are an ideal thing.'

Jon noticed nothing amiss, and his enthusiasm bubbled over the moment Haydn appeared. The driver started off as soon as they were safely aboard, and while they drove Lee tried surreptitiously to scrub her face with her handkerchief. The tiny, lace-edged square was hopelessly inadequate, and with a shrug she desisted. She felt past caring how she looked. It was Haydn's fault for bringing them back to lunch, but the reflection did not make her feel any better.

She felt even worse when the car pulled up after about a couple of miles at a low, red brick house on the edge of a village. Sheltered by trees on the one side, it was girded by a garden that was a necklace of brilliance under the warm sunshine, evidence that the owner's livelihood was also his hobby. Roses of every description lent perfumed sweetness to the approach, and Haydn led them through a cool, panelled hall, scented with bowls of the same blooms, to a long, low-ceilinged room where an elderly man and woman sat waiting for them by open french windows.

'Meet my mother and father. Lee, and Jon,' Haydn introduced them, and Lee took an instant liking to the tall, white-haired woman with twinkling blue eyes, and the upright man with the pepper and salt hair and tawny eyes, who was a mould of what Haydn would probably be at his age. And she felt a surge of relief that her trouser suit would do. Moira Scott was dressed in plain, unadorned linen, mint green to cool the warmth of the day, and Haydn's father was in the same casual attire as the two younger men.

'You young people must be hungry.' Moira Scott's voice was warmed by friendliness and a faint hint of a Highland accent that gave an added significance to the nursery trademark. And confronted by snowy linen and silver cutlery, and china as fine as that from which they had partaken of coffee earlier, Lee found to her surprise that she was. Her nervousness vanished under the unassuming friendliness of the older couple, and by the time the meal was over she felt relaxed and completely at her ease.

'I did enjoy that.' She sank back into her chair with a contented sigh.

'You've just paid Mother the ultimate compliment,' Haydn told her, and seeing Lee's look of surprise he added, 'She does all the cooking herself. It's her main hobby. You two have a lot in common—you should taste Lee's strawberry shortcake,' he enthused.

'You must let me have the recipe,' their hostess began, and her husband smiled.

'So that's why you wanted those strawberries in such a hurry. I thought there must be an ulterior motive!'

There was, but it was not strawberry shortcake. Lee's after-lunch euphoria dimmed at the edges.

'She'll have a bigger variety to choose from when we get

our own soft fruit area going properly.' Jon could not forget his main interest for long.

'Soft fruit? For yourself, or for trade?' Haydn asked, and Jon replied,

'For both, but mostly for trade, of course. Why, don't you think it's a good idea?' he asked, as Haydn slowly shook his head.

'Not really, it's too cost-intensive,' he said, and Lee felt her temper rise. Whatever she or Jon suggested, it was wrong in Haydn's view.

'We're going to plant black and red currants, gooseberries and raspberry canes,' she stated firmly, and felt Haydn's look lance across the room at her.

'Plant what you like for yourself, but they're no good for trade,' he insisted.

'They'll be good for Polrewin's trade,' she was equally firm, and determined to hold her own. They had planned soft fruit bushes, and soft fruit bushes she intended to have.

'Not in a town like Tarmouth,' Haydn retorted just as firmly. 'You're placed very much like us, in a way, with a small resident population, and a big dose of holidaymakers for a short time every summer.' He turned to Jon as if seeking male reasonableness, and Lee flushed angrily. 'Leave that sort of thing to the inland farms,' he urged her brother. 'They've got the room and the populations of the large towns to draw on, and they can advertise "pick your own" and eliminate the labour charges. That way, they can keep costs down and still make a reasonable profit. On the coast as we are,' he included them all in his gesture, 'the resident population isn't large enough to make it worthwhile, and holidaymakers aren't going to pick a lot of perishable stuff to take home with them, when they can have a day out later on for the same purpose, nearer home.'

'We're a bossy lot, aren't we?' It came with a chuckle from Haydn's father, and Lee looked across and met the twinkle in his eyes, and became uncomfortably conscious that he must have been watching her, reading her expression.

'We made the same mistakes when we started up,' he glanced affectionately at his wife, 'one or two of our good ideas very nearly sent us bankrupt, and you might as well profit from our experience.'

Again, all the arguments seemed immensely reasonable. Lee sighed. She seemed to be wallowing in a morass from which there was no escape.

'Haydn tells me you were in the domestic science field yourself?' Did Moira Scott notice her sigh, or was she simply being polite? 'Don't you miss it? I should,' she said kindly.

'I do, but until Polrewin's safely in orbit, I'll have to get along without it,' Lee said frankly. 'In the meantime I'm learning a lot from a chef at the local hotel.' Because she felt she had remained silent for too long, she launched into a description of the daisy confection the chef had made in their honour. At first she spoke merely to make a polite contribution to the conversation, but when she found she was talking to a fellow enthusiast she warmed to her subject, and before she knew what had happened it all came out, the strawberries, the tomatoes, the daisies.... 'We've got to decorate the float when we get home.'

'And you're going to be the middle of the daisy? What a charming idea. I'd like to come over and see it for myself,' Moira said wistfully, 'but we've got a similar function to attend here, and we can't do both in one day, it's too far.'

'I'll take some photographs and send them over to you, so you can have the best of both worlds,' Haydn promised, and once again Lee felt trapped. The Scott family were impossible, she thought with helpless frustration. After Haydn's attitude about the daisies, she had almost decided not to sit on the festival float herself, and now, because he had promised to send photographs of it to his mother, she could not very well back out. It would be churlish to refuse, after accepting their hospitality.

'Better still, bring them yourself and we can all have another day together,' Haydn's father suggested hospitably. 'Jon can have a look at how we change the glasshouses over for the winter crops, and Lee and your mother can talk cookery to their hearts' content.' He, too, discounted Lee's involvement in practical matters at Polrewin, and Lee shrugged resignedly.

'I'll give you the recipe before we go,' she prevaricated, and Moira Scott got up.

'Come with me now and freshen up before you go back, and you can see my hobby room,' she offered, and Lee left the men behind with a feeling of relief. She wanted to see Jon launched at Polrewin, but increasingly she had to admit that her own interest lay more in her brother's success than her own personal involvement in the nursery. Had Haydn sensed this, even before she admitted it to herself?

'This is my own little retreat,' said Moira, and Lee voiced frank envy.

'This is just what I'd like. When we get the nursery on its feet,' she added with unconscious wistfulness.

'Don't give up everything for the nursery,' Moira advised her, suddenly serious. 'Keep something of yourself alive, you'll need it to fall back on when things are running smoothly, and your help's no longer needed. At least, not in that way,' she added.

'There's so little time. But I'll keep this in mind.' Lee looked about her appreciatively, her eyes lingering on the blue and grey embossed carpet, the soft grey, tweed-upholstered chairs, and the fresh-looking shadow cretonne curtains that picked up the colours of both, and added a warm rose tint of their own, at the same time reflecting something of the occupant of the room. Was it from his mother Haydn inherited his eye for colour? she wondered.

'Haydn didn't show us any of his photographs,' she realised aloud. She had been surprised that there was no evidence of his work anywhere about the nursery. Perhaps his photography was not of the standard he would like them to believe, but as he was the son of the owner it was tolerated, and he was allowed to go his own way.

'Haydn's too modest about his work, but this is one.' Moira swept aside a curtain where it had blown across part of the wall with the brisk breeze coming through the window, and took down a plainly framed picture. It showed a perfect rosebud, with the dew still on it, and just starting to open shaded pink petals to the sun. It was a superb picture, there was no doubt of the quality of the photography here. Lee took it from her hand. She could almost smell the perfume. 'But this is my favourite.' Moira reached another down, and Lee could not restrain her pleasure as she exchanged them.

'This is lovely! He must have waited hours to get a picture like this.'

It was a fieldmouse, busily engaged in making a meal of tiny, wild strawberries. One of the miniature berries was clutched in both front paws, and the little creature was in the act of beginning to nibble. Enough of the rough herbage showed to bring out the essential wildness of its surroundings, and turn the picture into a perfect wildlife still.

'He's got infinite patience,' Moira agreed, 'he spends hours along the cliffs with his camera. He'll wait for weeks, sometimes, until something is just right before he takes a photograph of it.'

The patience of a mountain lion, watching, waiting, until the time was ripe. Was he waiting like this for Polrewin to fall into his hands? Lee handed the photograph back, suddenly repelled. Moira took it from her and hung it back on the wall, as if sensing her withdrawal, but she said nothing, and they rejoined the men shortly afterwards and waved their host and hostess goodbye to echoes of 'Come again as soon as you can,' and Lee wondered, as they sped back towards the harbour and the *Sea Mist*, whether she would ever return. Jon would, in all probability. But not herself. Unconsciously she shook her head, not realising what she was doing until she heard Haydn say,

'Don't you want it, after all?'

'Want what?' She came back to the present with a start, and the realisation that their driver was holding out something towards her. Something she had not noticed was in the vehicle when it returned them to the harbour.

'It's a baby rose bush,' Haydn told her, and she took it automatically. 'One of our own, that we've grown from seed.'

Lee cupped it tenderly in her hands, enslaved from her first look at the miniature blooms, the minute buds that were beginning to burst into perfect flower.

'With the compliments of the nursery,' Haydn said gravely.

Her eyes rose from his gift to his expressionless face, and she could not help it if they were suddenly misty, any more than she could help the wild, irrational wish that it might have been Haydn's deliberate choice, rather than just coincidence, that the rose was a red one.

CHAPTER EIGHT

'IT'S a red one.'

'Yes.'

He did not say 'I know.' He did not give any indication that he might have had a hand in its choosing. He did not say anything, except just the monosyllabic reply that gave nothing away. Lee could not read anything from his face; he stood at the wheel of the *Sea Mist* and his expression was intent as he steered carefully out of the harbour, going slowly to avoid the clutter of small craft that slid about like water spiders on the sunlit surface, happy, carefree holiday-makers. Lee found herself envying them, with nothing more urgent on their minds than the hope that it would be fine tomorrow. They were not at war within themselves, as she was. And then they passed a boat with a couple in it who were not laughing and talking. The man was rowing, and the girl was looking away from him, frowning, towards the shore. Lee clutched her miniature rose bush to her and stayed thoughtfully silent. Maybe Haydn would hand the wheel over to Jon, as he had done coming out, and then perhaps he might talk. Perhaps tell her that he had chosen her rose himself....

'I'll keep the *Sea Mist* going back, it looks as if we might run into a storm.' Haydn dashed her hopes, and then her spirits with his next remark. 'If you're cold,' he told her formally, 'go and sit in the day cabin, you won't have to face the breeze there.'

She was not cold. The cockpit of the cruiser was well screened, so it probably meant he did not want her with them. Perhaps he wanted to talk to Jon, and he preferred her to be out of earshot. She hesitated for a moment, then gave in with a shrug.

'I'll make a cup of coffee as soon as we're out of the harbour.'

She left them and took her rose bush, and made herself

comfortable in the day cabin, and watched the harbour fade behind them, felt the stronger movement as the *Sea Mist* rose to the open sea. She put the rose bush on the table, but it slid about, and fearing it might get damaged she held it in her hands again. It gave her an odd sort of comfort, but it did not resolve the tug of war that was going on inside her, and which she seemed to have no power to stop. Haydn found her there when he came down, and she jumped to her feet guiltily.

'I'd forgotten the coffee.'

'Now will do,' he answered indifferently, and reached for his jacket which was lying across the other bench seat. He paused as he slipped it on. 'Can you manage on your own?'

'Yes.' She did not know whether she could manage or not. She only knew she did not want to. She wanted Haydn to stay with her, to hold her against the sway of the boat, to care whether she accidentally scalded herself with the coffee. She wanted him to.... She despised herself for wanting. She reached for the coffee things before her thoughts could go any further. 'I can manage.'

She burned her hand. The boat lurched, the hot coffee spilled and went over her fingers, but she gritted her teeth and said nothing. Somehow, she did not know how, she managed to get the filled mugs on to the deck without spilling too much of the contents, and whether they wanted her or not she remained in the cockpit with the two men while she drank her own. It was difficult, holding her mug with one hand and the rose bush with the other, and trying to brace herself against the movement of the boat at the same time, but she managed it, though not without drawing a comment from Haydn.

'Why don't you push the rose down? You'll find it easier with two hands free.'

'It might get damaged. It can't stand up either.'

'Have it your own way.' He handed back his empty mug and concentrated on his controls, as if he was not really interested. They were returning at a much greater speed than they had reached on the outward journey. 'The tide's behind us,' was all Haydn said when Lee commented on this, and she took the empty mugs and got them, herself and the rose bush back into the cabin again without encountering disaster. She swilled the mugs and replaced them in the cupboard, then after a moment's hesitation decided to remain in the cabin rather than go back to the cockpit. Indifference, she discovered, could hurt worse than anger. A hand on her shoulder shook her awake.

'My rose?'

'I've got it. Wake up, we're home.' It was Haydn. And he still called Polrewin 'home'.

'I don't want to go down that rope ladder again.' She rubbed balled fists into her eyes, willing herself back to consciousness, fighting against the awful drowsiness that still claimed half of her mind.

'You won't have to. The tide's right in, and we're anchored against the harbour steps. Come on.' He pulled her to her feet, but gently this time, not roughly as he had held her on the island. She shivered, suddenly cold, and he drew her to him, and the hard lean strength of him, and the closeness, brought her vividly awake, and she almost wished she was asleep again, and unaware, because being awake, and being aware, brought the tug of war back, and it hurt.

'I thought you said there was a storm?' The storm seemed to be inside her. It shook her with a ferocity which left her anchorless, and at its mercy, but there was no sign of the ordinary elements when she got on deck. She turned her face up to a clear sky.

'It passed off,' Haydn said, 'though there's a lot of electricity in the air still. Look at the masts.'

Lee looked, and wondered, as she had so often wondered before at the strange, faint glow surrounding the mastheads of the anchored boats. As if each mast tip had its own glowworm, working overtime to produce the weird, soft light.

'Static electricity,' Jon stated in a practical voice.

'St Elmo's fire,' Haydn contradicted him softly, and kept his hand on Lee's waist, so that they stood together on the deck, close together, watching it, each masthead like a subdued candle outlined against the dark sky, and the even darker outline of the buildings on the curve of the harbour wall.

'I wonder if....' Lee stretched out a tentative hand towards their own mast, to feel the bottom of it, then drew it away again, afraid to touch.

'It won't burn you.' Haydn looked into her face. 'It's only a glow. A nice warm one, but it lacks the spark of fire.' The vital spark. The one that he had, compared to Dennis, or Vince. She looked at the glow again. It was warming, comforting. And fire seared and burned, and the pain hurt unbearably. It hurt now, while he had his arm round her, and it would hurt even worse when he took it away. She sighed sharply, and he spoke.

'Come on, you're tired out. Home and bed now, tomorrow's another day. Here's your rose,' when she looked to see if he still held it, anxious not to leave it behind.

'It's a bonny little bush,' Nell admired it the next morning. 'By the way, Miss Lee, someone's delivered a trailer, the man said you'd know what it was, and he just left it and went away.'

'It's the float for the festival,' Lee identified it for her. 'The market are lending them for the purpose, we're going to drag it behind the Mini.'

'Why not make it into a flower train?' Haydn came downstairs and joined in the conversation. 'Turn the Mini into a little engine, and the trailer into a coach.'

'That's a wonderful idea,' Nell complimented him, and Lee wished she had thought of it herself. The flower train that travelled from Penzance daily, taking the produce of the local market gardens to the London markets, was a familiar part of everyday life in Tarmouth. It would be a popular display, one people would remember, and with it they would remember the name of Polrewin.

'I've been showing the stretcher to Ben.' Jon came in and gave brief approval to their idea before returning to his own immediate problems. 'It seems the boatyard are getting rid of quite a lot of wood, odd spars and things, and we can have what we want for next to nothing if we go down and sort it out today—they've even offered to send the long bits up on their lorry. It seems they're thinking of moving, and they want it out of their way. I know I said Ben could help with the float, but....' He eyed his sister doubtfully.

'Go ahead, we'll see to the float,' said Haydn, and Lee's lips tightened. He spoke as if he was giving Jon permission.

'I don't know whether I'll be able to manage this morning.' She was completely free, but she saw no reason why she should fall in with Haydn's plans.

'When you're ready will do,' Haydn shrugged. 'It's your float,' he reminded her drily, and Lee paused. 'If it isn't ready to put the daisies on as soon as they arrive, they'll be wasted,' he pressed his advantage, and once again his argument was unanswerable.

'If Jon will take the morning load into Tarmouth....' She gave in, as Haydn knew she would have to, and the submission galled her. It did not help her mood when she stood with him and surveyed the trailer after Jon and Ben had departed, and found she had no idea how to start on the job of turning the small-wheeled vehicle into a miniature railway carriage. There would have to be sides, and a roof. They would need wood.

'We'll have to wait and see what Jon brings back from the boatyard.' That would delay the proceedings for an hour or two, and maybe she could co-opt Ben's help, and it would release her from having to help Haydn. Maybe she and Ben could do it between them after all. The thought appealed to her. It would show Haydn once and for all that they were capable of standing on their own feet, without his interference.

'There's no need for that, I brought some stuff back with us yesterday, for the purpose.'

'I don't....' He stopped her protest with a look.

'If you're thinking of expense, forget it,' he said curtly. 'What I brought is a sort of glorified Meccano set, which we use for all display work. It can be put together and used, then dismantled and returned to the stores when it's finished with, so you won't owe us a penny.'

'I didn't see you bring it.'

'You were too sleepy when we got back last night to notice anything.' He slanted a look at her. 'Are you going to help hold things for me while I bolt them together, or not?'

If she said no, in his present mood he would probably leave her to it, she thought, and there would be no flower train, and no display at the festival. And no advertisement for Polrewin. She nodded, wordlessly.

'Then hold these, for a start.'

She took the bag of nuts and bolts and washers he thrust at her, then watched as he built a square outline of uprights and crosspieces on the four-wheeled wagon. It was already fitted with low sides, just enough to prevent boxes of produce from slipping off, so he had no need to fix the structure down to the base, and in spite of herself her interest grew as she watched the shape materialise.

'You've forgotten the window.' The words came out of their own accord. He must not forget the window....

'So I have.' He stepped back, and flashed her a glance in which laughter lurked. Once again, he knew he had won. Lee had been the first to break the silence. In spite of herself, her lips curved upwards in response, it was as if they worked of their own accord, but she felt better after that. She decided where the window should be, and how big, and helped Haydn set it into the structure. She altered it twice before she was finally satisfied, but he bore with her patiently, and at last she stepped back with a sigh of satisfaction.

'We'll make the back of the coach into a daisy, and sit you in the middle.' He looked pleased with their efforts so far. 'You can be the guard, if you like,' he grinned, 'it'll be drier for you if you sit outside. The inside of your coach is going to be pretty damp.'

'How will you fix the daisies?' To cover such a large area would take a lot of flowers, and Lee felt doubtful of their stability on a moving vehicle.

'Easily enough.' Haydn was not in the least disconcerted. He never was, thought Lee with asperity. He always felt sure of what he was doing. 'Come and help me to carry the material over, I've put it in the end greenhouse.' She went with him, curiosity overcoming her rebellion at his manner, and found herself gazing at a stack of what looked like thick sponge cake, cut into large squares.

'It's similar to the material florists use. If we fix it to the slats and put a wire background against it, it can't move, and it'll hold enough water to keep the flowers fresh for as long as they'd last in an ordinary vase.'

She helped him to carry it, found to her surprise that it was extraordinarily light in weight, and watching Haydn work she copied him, and soon became as dexterous as he was at fixing it against the wire.

'You'd make a good florist,' he encouraged her efforts.

'It's something I've always wanted to study, and never found the time.' She stood back and looked at their efforts so far. 'What about the daisy at the back? The one I'm supposed to be the centre of?' The sides of the coach would be easy, but the curved shape of the petals would not be. Once again Haydn had the answer.

'We'll keep the backing straight. Let's see, there's eight letters in Polrewin.' He counted again to make sure. 'If we outline nine petals with the daisies, we can put one letter of the name between each petal. And you as the centre,' he concluded. 'Stand up on the back of the float for a minute, and let me see how high the daisy has got to be to arc over your head.' He lifted her over the side impersonally, as if she was just another piece of the material he was working with, then made various marks on the structure with a piece of chalk, and a frown of concentration on his face. 'You can come down now.' He lifted her back beside him on to the gravel, and she said,

'If you're going to wet the backing the daisies are on, I shan't want to sit under an arch of the stuff. It'll drip all over me.'

'After the way you behaved yesterday, am I supposed to care?'

'After the way I behaved?' He said nothing about the way he had behaved himself, she thought furiously. Presumably that was different. 'What am I supposed to do?' she flung at him sarcastically, 'stand by in silence and watch you run Polrewin hopelessly into debt? Anyway,' she shrugged away the thought of yesterday, 'I refuse to be dripped on just to please you. If you want me to be the middle of the daisy....'

'Who said I want you to be the middle of anything?' he interrupted her grittily. 'I didn't....' He turned abruptly as tyres crunched on gravel. 'Here's Jon. I'll go and help him unload his wood.' He swung on his heel abruptly and strode away from her as if he had run out of patience, and Lee leaned miserably against the side of the trailer. He did not want her—he had made that perfectly clear. And it should not have mattered to her, but it did. Haydn did not want her—but she wanted him. Acknowledging it should have stilled the storm inside her, but it did not do that either. What she wanted for herself, and what she wanted for Polrewin, seemed to be at opposite ends of the tug of war, and she was in the middle, being pulled in two directions at once.

'Vince wants you to go down and get your instructions for the procession,' Jon called across to her, and Lee left her leaning post reluctantly and walked over to join him. Haydn did not look at her, he kept on talking to Ben as if she was not there, and she bit her lip. If he wanted to quarrel, let him, she thought rebelliously.

'I'll give Vince a ring, it's probably only to let us know what time to assemble in the market place.'

'It's more than that,' said Jon, 'the whole thing's being organised up to the hilt, from what I've heard, because of traffic congestion in the town. There's different starting times for each float, the speed you've got to keep to, and the exact route, because the Committee's hoping the festival will attract such a crowd there's an even chance the floats will lose sight of one another in the crush.'

'Oh well,' Lee shrugged, 'I've got to see to the flowers for the ballroom at the Royal Anchor, so I can do the two at once, and get it over with.' Her pleasure in the coming festival was dimmed anyway, and instead of looking forward to joining in the arrangements, they represented nothing more than an unwelcome chore now.

'As I'm driving the float, I think I'd better come and see Vince as well.' Haydn finished his leisurely chat with Ben, and took part in the conversation.

'I'm quite capable of remembering a few simple directions,' Lee told him coldly.

'You won't need to remember anything, except the colour you're given,' Jon told her. 'There'll be coloured route indicators, and you'll just have to follow the arrows, or something,' he said vaguely.

'That should be easier still,' Lee hailed the suggestion with relief. Surely even Haydn must acknowledge that she was capable of remembering a colour.

'If it's a colour you've got to follow, I'll need to come more than ever.' Unexpectedly he dashed her hopes. 'You don't seem able to differentiate between one shade and the next,' he told her seriously.

'What on earth are you talking about?' Lee felt flabbergasted. 'Of course I can tell one shade from another. How do you think I got on in the domestic science field?' Words failed her, and she lapsed into exasperated silence.

'Search me,' he shrugged. 'But you've been calling that liver-and-white spaniel Jet ever since I've been here....'

'That's short for Jetsam, it's got nothing whatever to do with his colour,' Lee snapped. 'We called him Jetsam because he swam ashore from a wrecked boat.'

'That's a relief,' Haydn grinned suddenly. 'I must confess I've been a bit worried now and then, sitting in the Mini with you driving, in case you couldn't tell which traffic light was which.'

'It didn't stop you from coming with me,' Lee shot back. He had used her morning delivery trip into Tarmouth as a free bus service ever since he had come to stay with them. And when she returned from collecting a pen and notepad from the house in case she had to write down any directions, he was already ensconced in the passenger seat of the Mini, waiting for her. Short of physical force, there was no way in which she could remove him. She accepted the inevitable with a resigned shrug, and could not help feeling some satisfaction that Vince pointedly talked to her and not to Haydn when she ran him to earth at the Royal Anchor just before lunchtime.

'I've allocated you the pink marker.' He leaned back in his armchair behind his big, leather-topped desk, and Lee knew a moment of sharp distaste. The contrast between

Vince's office and Haydn's studio was striking. She preferred Haydn's studio. Vince's room had an air of opulent stuffiness that belonged to its owner, and reminded her curiously of Dennis. She preferred uncluttered freedom, and good china....

'Pink doesn't suit her.'

He said it mildly. So quiet were his words that they did not register with Vince for a second or two, and he went on speaking. Then he stopped, and his face flushed an angry red.

'What did you say?' His voice rose with his colour. He would be fat when he was a few years older, and probably suffer from high blood pressure, Lee thought with detached interest. He showed signs of both now. His face took on a sunset hue, and he glared at Haydn with undisguised dislike.

'I said pink doesn't suit her. Yellow does. The acidy sort of shade,' Haydn said helpfully, and he darted a glance at Lee that suggested her temperament might be tinted with the same tartness. Her lips thinned, and she gripped the arms of her chair, determined not to be tempted into retaliation in front of Vince.

'Of course, if that's the best you can manage, I'm sure it will do,' Haydn went on politely. He held the coloured card of route directions between the tip of his finger and thumb, and eyed it critically. 'It's just a little crude, that's all.'

'Fluorescent colours are meant to show up.' Vince's face was rapidly turning purple, and Lee intervened hastily.

'It'll do beautifully, so long as we've got a colour to follow it doesn't matter what it is. Let's go and see the ballroom, Vince, then I'll know what to do about the flowers.' She held out her hand to him appealingly, and instantly mollified, he jumped to his feet and took it. Just as instantly Lee regretted her gesture. Her fingers were uncomfortably encased in plump, hot dampness, and she swallowed her aversion with difficulty.

'I must take my pad and pencil with me.' She chose the only escape route open to her, and ostentatiously kept her pad in one hand and her pencil in the other.

'There's the bandstand.' She made a note. She did not

need to, she already knew what she was going to put there. She felt Haydn's eyes on her. Briefly she looked up, and then looked hurriedly away again before the dancing mischief in the tawny orbs should spark off the bubbling laughter inside her that demanded an outlet. She crushed it firmly, and concentrated on the bandstand.

'That's the only place that needs decorating, surely,' Haydn put in. 'I imagine you'll have quite a crowd at the ball, and you won't want flowers in the way of the dancers.'

'There's the buffet room to do, on the side,' Vince said quickly, and turning his back on Haydn he spoke to Lee. 'We've got the leading citizens of three of the main towns along the coast coming.' He sounds pompous, Lee thought, and felt glad she had refused his invitation to partner him.

'You won't have much time for dancing yourself,' Haydn murmured sympathetically.

'I intend to take some time off during the evening,' Vince snapped. 'Don't forget you promised me some dances,' he reminded Lee. She pretended not to hear him, and snapped her book shut as if she had all the notes she needed.

'Did you?' Haydn asked casually, on their way back to Polrewin.

'Did I what?' Lee waited impatiently for the traffic lights to change. By the time she had managed to smooth Vince down, and then waited while Haydn went to the boatyard for some purpose which he did not divulge, they were later than she intended to be.

'Promise Vince some dances.'

'He asked me to partner him, and I refused.' Exasperation got the better of her, and she spoke the truth without a thought for the consequences.

'Just as well.' Haydn settled back into his seat with a satisfied look. 'It'll save you from having to break a promise.'

'Why should I break a promise to Vince?' Lee drew to a halt on the gravel outside the house, and fended off a vociferous welcome from the two dogs.

'Because you're partnering me,' Haydn told her blandly.

'I didn't say....' She staggered under the onslaught of eight legs and two wildly wagging tails. 'Get down, both of you!'

'There's no time to argue,' Haydn told her crisply as she disentangled herself and swung round to face him, ready to do battle. 'The daisies have arrived, and if you want the float to be ready in time ... There's the ballroom to do, as well,' he reminded her unnecessarily. 'As well as the buffet room.'

'We'll do the float first.' That, at least, Lee was determined to have her own way about. The argument about who should partner her at the festival must wait until later. Her mood softened, as it always did when she was handling flowers, and as soon as she opened the first of the stack of boxes piled against the trailer she forgot Vince, and almost forgot her antagonism towards Haydn.

'They're lovely.' It seemed a shame to shorten their stalks, the white petals, still in half open bud, looked like a newborn baby's fist, softly crumpled, but soon to open into full loveliness under the warm sun.

'We'll have to wet the backing first. Have you got a spray, or a hosepipe?'

'Use the hose with this gadget on the end.' She reached on to the top of a box just inside the door of the greenhouse, and fitted the sprayer dexterously on to the end of the hose. 'Will it do?'

'Famously.' Haydn ran the pipe straight. 'Turn on the tap and let's get to work.' He soaked the backing thoroughly on both sides, and the sponge-like texture of the material swelled with the water, fitting tightly to the spars that held it. 'Now for the daisies.'

She clipped and held them up to him as he worked from the top of a pair of high steps, and the time seemed to fly. Soon the top of the coach was covered in a deep layer of overlapping petals.

'We can work together now I've done the high bit.'

The daisies seemed to have a mellowing effect on Haydn, as well. We've both lowered our prickles, Lee thought with sudden amusement, and her smile must have shown because Haydn glanced down at her, and smiled back.

'I can't get this corner right, the strut's in the way.'

'Let me do it, my fingers are stronger than yours.' And he bent the strut back, moving it easily where she had struggled with no results, and filled the corner for her with daisy buds.

'I'll put the top ones in while you finish the corner.' She mounted the first two steps to complete the top of the window, which Haydn had left to do her corner.

'Mind, the steps aren't too steady.'

'They're safe enough for now.'

She felt them tip the moment she stood on the second step. She should have remembered he had slid them out of his way with the toe of his shoe when he finished the top of the coach, and they had not been properly set for climbing again. They gave a creak, and an ominous lurch, and the dogs scuttled from beneath them with undignified haste as Haydn called out urgently,

'Never mind the steps, let them fall. I'll catch you.'

He was even quicker than Bandy and Jet. He dropped his daisies and clippers, reached round and grasped her just as the steps disappeared from under her feet and landed on the gravel with a crash.

'What does it take to make you listen to common sense?' His friendliness vanished in a rush, and he gave her a shake. 'That might easily have been you instead of the ladder, sprawled on the gravel!' he shouted at her angrily.

'Why should you care?' she shouted back, shaken by her narrow escape.

'I don't,' he flung back at her angrily, 'but I'd have to find someone else to take your place on the float, and that would take time I haven't got. The procession takes place tomorrow,' he reminded her forcefully.

'You needn't drive, if you don't want to.'

'I promised Jon I'd take over for him, he's got to wait for the fresh supply of fuel to be unloaded, and then he's bringing Nell and Ben along, otherwise....' He paused as footsteps sounded on the gravel.

'I say, that's great!' Jon rounded the corner and stood back to admire their handiwork. 'You'll have to take that photograph you promised your mother before you start off, there won't be much opportunity when you're actually in the procession,' he reminded Haydn. 'I don't know enough about cameras to make a decent job of it for you.'

'We'll take it now,' Haydn decided, and Lee's face set mutinously.

'I'm not changed.'

'You can soon remedy that,' his look was unrelenting. 'I'll be a few minutes getting my camera, it won't take you all that long to slip into your dress.'

'Why not take a snap of us all?' Jon asked. 'It's Polrewin's first festival. It'll be a sort of landmark, really, won't it? I'll go and get Nell and Ben.'

He departed on his errand, and Haydn looked straight across at Lee, his tawny eyes gimlet-like, pinning her to the spot.

'Well?' he queried in a hard voice, and waited.

'I'll do it—but only to please Jon,' she said defensively.

'That's what I'm doing it for. Remember?' he taunted, then turned his back on her and strode into the house to get his camera.

Lee could not help being a long time changing. Her fingers trembled, and fumbled, and refused to undo buttons, and the zip on the back of her yellow dress caught on a thread of material, and her blurred vision could not sort out how to undo it. She could not fight any longer, she thought wretchedly, wondering if anyone else had ever felt as mixed up as she did now. She loved Haydn, and hated him at the same time. She had heard marriage described as a love–hate relationship, and now she knew what it meant. Only she was not married to Haydn, and was not likely to be; he had made his opinion of her perfectly clear. She hastily scrubbed a towel across her face and eyes. No matter how she felt, she must not let it show in front of him, or the camera. The thought that her feelings might come across on the photograph pinned a smile on her face as she went downstairs, and joined the others by the float which Jon had drawn up ready on the gravel, with the house and the glasshouses in the background. Even the two dogs were there.

'We've rigged up a chimney on the Mini.' It looked a passable imitation of a child's toy engine, and among the fantasy atmosphere of the carnival it would do well enough. 'What are you going to sit on up there?' Jon regarded the float with a doubtful eye. 'It'll have to be something fairly firm, remember you'll be moving.'

'I thought one of the kitchen chairs.' Haydn returned with his camera, and one of the chairs in question. 'The legs are fairly widely spaced, and they'll hold the chair steady, and we'll not be going at any great speed once we're actually in the procession.' He swung the chair up on to the float, shuffled it until he was satisfied it was in the right place, and said to Lee, 'Try it.' He left it to Jon to give her a helping hand on to the float, while he backed off, adjusting his camera and watching through the viewfinder.

'Let's try the one with all of you on it, first,' he suggested, and Lee sat back resignedly while her brother shepherded Nell and Ben and the two dogs into place, then discovered he was out of focus himself when he joined them. More shuffling took place, and Lee lost interest. One of the daisies over her head had become loose, and she blew at it experimentally. It swung, and loosened further still, and dropped lower, covering part of her face. She sat further back in the chair, and Haydn backed off again, peering through the viewfinder.

'Do you have to twiddle that daisy in front of you?' he asked, raising his head and glaring at Lee irritably.

'I'm not twiddling anything.' She sat virtuously with both hands clasped in her lap, and looked across at him serenely. 'It's come loose, I think. It's one you put in. . . .'

She stifled a desire to laugh as he lowered his camera and strode back towards the float. He reached up and plucked the daisy out with an impatient hand. 'Sit still,' he snapped. She did not know whether he spoke to herself or to Bandy, who showed an untimely desire to scratch one ear. The dog gave him a reproachful look from behind his shaggy curtain of hair, and obediently subsided.

'If he thinks I'm going to do the same, he's mistaken.' The dog's meek submissiveness sparked rebellion in Lee. First Jon did as Haydn said, then the dogs. . . . If he was much longer fiddling with his camera, she decided impatiently, she would get down off the float and leave him to it.

'That's just about right.' Did he sense his subjects were

beginning to fidget? He stopped backing away and turning levers, and looked up from the viewfinder. 'Ready?' He still had the daisy in his fingers. He looked down at it for a moment, as if reluctant to throw it away, but patently he did not want to hold it and operate the camera shutter at the same time, its presence would make the movement awkward, and could spoil the picture. He took the only alternative, and thrust it behind his ear.

Lee giggled—she could not help it. The delicate petals looked positively embarrassed at their unexpected siting. Her chuckle escaped before she could stop it, clear and uninhibited, and sympathetic grins spread across the faces of the others.

'That's fine, it should make a good picture.' Haydn looked up, and seeing the grins still in place he asked, puzzled, 'What's the matter?'

'The daisies look better on the float than on you,' Jon laughed. 'Well, if you've finished with getting our family picture, I've got some jobs to do. Coming, Ben?'

'Aye.' Ben cast a speculative look at the float. 'You'll be keeping them daisies wet, I expect? It looks like being hot again tomorrow.'

'The backing we've put them into holds water,' Haydn told him. 'I must try and remember to give them an extra spray first thing tomorrow morning.'

'I should if I were you,' Ben nodded. ' 'Twould be a pity to see them fade half way through the day, after all the trouble you've been to.'

'Sit where you are, I want one more, with just you sat in the back.' Haydn's look glinted up at Lee as she stirred in her chair. 'Keep a smile on your face,' he commanded her.

'That should be easy enough if you put the daisy back behind your ear,' she taunted him, and his lips tightened. I've made him angry now, she thought, but she did not care. He was getting a taste of his own medicine, and it served him right. But she smiled just the same as he clicked the shutter, so that his photograph should come out well.

'Perhaps it's as well you took the picture tonight, in case the daisies do fade before tomorrow,' she commented, and slid down from the trailer, ignoring his helping hand.

'I'll make sure they don't,' he retorted, and his eyes sparkled angrily, 'even if I have to soak them.' And he was gone before she realised if he did, indeed, soak them, she would have to endure a very damp ride on the following day.

CHAPTER NINE

LEE was up at the crack of dawn the next morning, but Haydn was before her. His eyes flicked over her jeans and shirt as she came downstairs.

'It isn't time to change yet,' she said defensively, before he could speak. 'The procession doesn't start until two, and I've got to decorate the ballroom at the Royal Anchor first, as well as see to the morning deliveries.'

'I know. I'm coming with you.'

'I don't....' She started to say 'I don't want you,' but the words died in her throat, because they weren't true. Perhaps he wanted to come with her so as to pay another visit to the boatyard. He had not said what he went there for the day before, but he obviously wanted them to do something else to the *Sea Mist*. The thought of his boat made her heart contract. It would take him away from Polrewin—away from herself, because once the festival was over there would be no need for him to remain. After that, his contact would be a purely business one, with her brother. Lee did not delude herself that Haydn would want to contact her. She had spent most of the previous night coming to terms with the knowledge, which was one of the reasons why she was up at the crack of dawn, with the decision formed in her mind that the instant Jon was able to cope with Polrewin singlehanded, she would go back to her own career. It would effectively remove her from any danger of bumping into Haydn accidentally if he should decide to pay a visit to her brother, whether socially or on business. The thought of continued contact with him, however casual, was more than she could bear.

'I don't expect the van's loaded yet,' she changed her words hastily.

'The tomatoes and salads are already in it, Jon ran the van out and loaded them straight away to save time. The strawberries and the big tomatoes are coming over on the early boat, so they'll be here any minute now.'

'We'll have to make the deliveries first, and come back for the flowers for the Royal Anchor.'

Haydn came with her on both journeys, but he did not go to the boatyard. He helped her cope with the early deliveries, then came back in the van without comment, and Lee refused to show her curiosity. There was too much to do, and the moment the van was parked back on the gravel at Polrewin she had the doors open ready to receive the consignment of gladioli, fuchsias, hydrangeas and cinerarias that she had planned for the display at the hotel.

'I didn't think we'd have enough.' She viewed the crowded rear of the van with something approaching dismay. 'There won't be room for the gladioli in here, they'll get crushed, and I didn't want to make another journey.'

'I'll hold them in the front, with me,' Haydn offered. 'You really need a bigger van,' he commented.

'For goodness' sake, don't make any more suggestions that cost money!' Lee lost patience. If he had stayed at Polrewin instead of coming with her, she could have tucked the boxes of gladioli in the front passenger seat, and her problems would have been solved.

'I don't mean right away,' Haydn said mildly. 'You need to plan long-term.'

'And don't preach, either,' Lee snapped. 'I'm not in the mood for it. It's too early in the morning.'

'And you haven't bothered to eat any breakfast,' Haydn prophesied correctly. 'It's enough to sour anyone's temper.'

'My temper's not sour!' Lee's voice rose, and she checked herself hastily. If she started like this, she would never get through the day, she thought desperately. 'Come on, if you're coming.' She slammed the driving door behind her and settled herself behind the wheel with an angry wriggle. 'The boatyard probably won't have the doors open yet, it isn't eight o'clock.'

'I don't want to go to the boatyard.'

'Then why....' She ground the gears in a way that made Haydn wince, and frightened her into silence. She could not afford expensive repairs to the Mini. With infinite care she slipped the gear lever over smoothly this time, and pointed the van out of the drive. If she was not careful her own bad mood would cost her more in the long run than any of Haydn's suggestions for improving Polrewin.

'You take the boxes of gladioli indoors, I'll follow with the rest,' Haydn told her when they drew to a halt outside the Royal Anchor. The other flowers were in the form of pot plants, and heavy, and she did not stop to argue. She should have thanked him, because she could not have managed them on her own, but she did not do that either. She did not feel she had got anything to thank Haydn for. He was responsible for her present unenviable state of mind. She was hopelessly in love with him, and irrationally she blamed him for it—blamed him for coming to Polrewin in the first place. If he had stayed away, she would have remained at peace with herself, and able to concentrate on the affairs of the flower farm without distraction.

She filled containers and placed the gladioli, then watched as Haydn slid tubs of fuchsias and hydrangeas into place. He seemed to have an instinctive sense of where they should go, and she placed her own containers among them, working with him without the need of words. Yellow against dark purple, pale pink against blue. She stepped back to admire the effect, and he paused with her.

'We'll mass the cinerarias in front to hide the containers, then we've finished.' He picked up a pot of the small daisy blooms, and Lee looked from it to him. The ginger-tan of the blooms was almost the same colour as his hair.

'We match.' He read her thoughts and grinned cheerfully, and her spirits lightened. If only they could stay civil to one another throughout the day.... 'We're well on time,' he consulted his watch. 'How about staying on at the hotel and eating some breakfast? One of the chef's omelettes would go down well.'

'I'll prepare them myself.' The chef popped his head round the door at that moment to see how the decorations were progressing, and decided for Lee, and she gave in with a shrug. She was hungry, it was a long time to lunch, and she had need of her energy today. Disregarding her workmanlike garb, she took her seat beside Haydn in the dining room, and did full justice to a substantial breakfast.

From somewhere the chef had conjured up small button mushrooms, grilled tomatoes, and curls of smoked bacon to go with the omelettes, and it tasted like nectar in the cool room, with the breeze blowing through the open window from the harbour. The *Sea Mist* rode easily on the rising tide, and Lee averted her eyes. She did not want to look at the thing that would shortly take Haydn away, and she felt relieved when their meal was over, and they were on their way back to Polrewin, and there were the last-minute jobs to see to, which gave her no time to think.

'You'd better be off upstairs, and change.' Nell hastened her on her way. 'It's gone one o'clock now, and you don't want to hurry in this heat.'

The temperature was rising to record heights, and her acid yellow dress felt cool and fresh. It was newly laundered and crisp, and in spite of her misgivings she felt a rising expectancy as she ran downstairs. Haydn gave her a nod that could have signified approval, but he did not actually say she looked nice, and she felt a sharp prick of disappointment.

'Let's go.' He gave a glance at his watch which could have been silent criticism, and she bridled.

'We're in good time,' she defended herself automatically.

'I didn't say we weren't.' He picked up the keys of the Mini. 'I'll drive, as we're pulling the float.'

Lee did not argue. She did not want to drive, because she had no experience of towing, and the thought of pulling the float through steep, narrow streets packed with a carnival crowd unnerved her. Almost as much as Haydn's aloof manner did, she thought ruefully. Since the disastrous episode beside the field of daisies, they had hardly exchanged a civil word to one another.

'Ride in the van with me, going down.' He steered her towards the passenger door of the Mini.

'I don't ...' he did not wait to hear the rest of her sentence, 'don't think we'll be late.' He frowned, and gave an impatient gesture with his hand.

'You never want to do what I suggest.'

That was because he had not suggested the right thing. If he suggested 'marry me' she would comply like a shot.

She hesitated momentarily, torn between a rebellious desire to defy him and mount the float whatever he said, or take the opportunity to ride with him in the front of the Mini, alone, for what would probably be the last time.

'For once, you'll do as I say. Get in.' He gestured towards the passenger door. 'We'll be travelling fast until we reach Tarmouth, and the float will rock at speed. It won't be safe for you to ride on.'

He held the door open for her and waited, openly impatient. And she got in. His tone, and his look, promised that if she did not, he would probably either put her there, or go without her.

She settled back and watched him manipulate the controls. His fingers were long, and brown, and slender. Not plump and hot and damp, like Vince's. And they slipped the gear lever into place and made a perfect take-off, despite the load they dragged behind them. Lee could not have done it so smoothly herself. She twisted round in her seat and had a look at the float. It seemed to be travelling lightly enough, and it did not rock all that much. There was no reason why she should not have travelled on it, if she had wanted to. Did he insist on her travelling in the front of the van merely to have his own way? She forgot the question when he spoke.

'The festival seems to have attracted a good crowd.'

'They all seem to have congregated in the one street we want to go up.' She meant 'up' literally. The cobbled lane leading to the market place where they were to assemble was steep, and packed with humanity. It looked more like a screen version of an Eastern market place than a side street in Tarmouth, and she regarded it in consternation.

'We'll never make it in time, if we've got to fight our way through this crush!'

'We shall.' He spoke confidently.

'How?' Even Haydn could not make a way through the solid block of people confronting them.

'Inch by inch, if necessary.'

As usual he was right. The crowd parted good-humouredly, and closed in behind them again, and they got through. Lee felt sure they would not have done so had she been driving, the task of keeping the Mini and trailer moving on the steep gradient without stalling the engine made her blanch. She kept the admission to herself, and waited until they were drawn into line with the other floats in the market place, and jumped down to inspect them.

'We might as well stretch our legs while we can.' Haydn led her away from their own float, along the line of the others. 'We're not due to start for a quarter of an hour, yet, we're sixth in the line.'

'A very creditable entry. All the floats are of a very high standard.'

Need Vince sound quite so condescending? Lee wondered, suddenly irritable. He was marshalling the floats, and she regarded him with a dislike almost as strong as Haydn's. And to think I nearly accepted his invitation to be his partner, she thought incredulously.

'There's a lot of talent around,' Haydn agreed blandly.

'It's almost time to go.' Lee grabbed Haydn's arm. She did not feel she could stand any more verbal warfare between the two men. Not now.

'Just follow the coloured arrows.' Vince was determined to have the last word.

'I know. The pink ones.' Haydn's expression showed clearly his opinion of fluorescent pink.

'Come *on*!' Lee almost dragged him to the Mini. Vince looked pointedly at her hand clutching Haydn's sleeve, but she did not care. She felt like a bone being wrangled over by two dogs, neither of which really wanted it. 'Get in and start the engine,' she implored him, and his lips twitched upwards as he complied. Not to please her, she felt certain.

'I'll help you on to the float.'

'I can get on by myself. For goodness' sake, stay where you are,' she said desperately. If he got out.... She could see Vince hovering, and she slipped round to the back of the float from the opposite side, pretending not to see him hasten towards her to help her up. She grabbed the struts that held the daisy in place and hauled herself on to the float. Haydn must have been watching through the mirror, because the moment she was safely installed he started the van moving before Vince could catch up. Lee breathed a sigh of relief. She did not want Vince to start asking her to partner him again.

The float gathered speed, and Vince did not try to catch it up—she guessed he was too out of condition to try. He just stood still and scowled after them, and she turned her attention to settling herself into place. The chair legs were widely spaced and held it steady, and she gave a sigh of relief. They were off at last. For the next hour, at least, she could sit down and be on her own. It seemed a silly thing to think, with all the crowds closing in around the floats, but with Haydn driving, and Vince organising, she would be isolated on the float with her thoughts, and be able to enjoy the spectacle in peace. They reached the exit from the market place, and turned into the street, where they were greeted with a cheer from the first of the crowds. Lee waved back to them, her spirits lifting, and prepared to enjoy herself. The chair beckoned, and she sat down—and immediately sprang to her feet with a furious exclamation.

'Of all the beastly, spiteful tricks!'

The back of her dress was soaked from the drips of water collected in the chair seat. She felt it seep wetly through her slip and pants, right to her skin. It must look unthinkable.... Hastily she turned her back into the daisy, and her face to the street. She would have to stand up; there was no help for it. Haydn must have got the hose and drenched the float just before they came away. Her eyes flashed angrily. He knew if he soaked it, the backing would drip all over her. No wonder he had insisted on her riding in the van with him on the way down, so that she would not find out, and refuse to ride on it. He steered her away from the float when they drew up in the market place, too, to make sure she remained ignorant of what was in store for her until it was too late to do anything about it. She could not jump off the float. It was not going very fast, but the speed was sufficient to make baling out hazardous.

'I'm not going to risk a broken ankle for Haydn, he's not worth it,' she fumed. There was no way of attracting his attention to demand he stop the van. It was not as if they were on a lorry, and the outfit was all in one piece, so to speak. The float was quite separate from the Mini, and he would probably ignore her anyway if she called out. It was unthinkable to ask for help from the crowd which greeted their arrival on the street. Her predicament would be one more amusement to add to the carnival so far as they were concerned. It might even end up in the local paper....

She gritted her teeth and forced a smile as the crowd began to throw coins. Belatedly she remembered the event was in aid of beleagured local charities, and added a wave to the smile. Some wag in the crowd chanted 'Daisy, daisy, give me your answer do,' and raised a general laugh, and on impulse Lee plucked a daisy from the float and flung it towards the singer. It was rewarded by a further shower of coins. She caught some, and scraped the others into a heap with her foot, muttering grimly,

'Haydn will get an answer from me when I see him!'

No doubt he thought it was a huge joke, soaking her through. She tossed her head angrily, and a splash landed on her curls. The float was awash with moisture. It was the longest tour round Tarmouth Lee could remember. They seemed to parade through every street in the town, and by the time they reached the front of the Royal Anchor where they were to park and remain on display until the next day, the boards of the float were slippery with wet, and she was afraid to stand upright without holding on to something. This made it difficult to collect the money being constantly tossed to her by the townsfolk, but she dared not sit down again and risk another soaking. She blessed the increasing heat, which made the man-made fibre of her dress and undies dry fairly rapidly. She gave an experimental wriggle. They already felt more comfortable. With a bit of luck by the time she got off the float, she would be able to turn her back on people with reasonable confidence.

The float slowed at last, and turned towards the harbour, and she could see Vince busy marshalling into line those floats in front of them as soon as they reached the front of the hotel. Soon it was their turn, but Haydn did not wait for Vince to guide him in, he followed the float in front of them, drew neatly in line alongside it, and braked to a halt. Lee saw Vince scowl at the move, but she had more on her mind now than keeping the peace with him. As soon as the float stopped she slipped to the ground and ran round to the driver's door. Haydn was just emerging.

'Phew, that was some ride!' he ejaculated feelingly. 'Poor old Mini, her engine's nearly boiling over.'

'And so is her owner!' Lee stormed, unable to contain the words any longer. They bubbled out of her the moment he shut the car door.

'Was it very hot on the back?' he asked. 'You should have ducked inside the daisy out of the sun.'

'And been half drowned for my pains?' she ground out. 'Of all the filthy tricks to play....'

'What d'you mean, drowned?' He paused and frowned down at her, and his glance sharpened. 'Your hair's wet,' he observed. 'Are you really as hot as all that?'

'I'm boiling over, like the engine,' she snapped back. 'You....'

'Lee, I'll be free in a few minutes to dance with you.' Vince waved the local brass band to start marching and lead the troop of dancers along the roads the floats had just taken, and approached her with a confident look on his face.

'Go away!' she wiped it off abruptly. She was being abominably rude, and she did not care. She had probably ruined Polrewin's growing strawberry trade with the hotel, and she did not care about that, either. She was wet, and hot, and furious, and determined to make Haydn pay for what he had done. She turned her back on Vince's startled, 'But I say....' and faced Haydn grimly.

'You did it deliberately,' she accused him, her voice tight with anger.

'Did what deliberately? I don't know what you're talking about.' His frown darkened. 'Go away,' he told Vince over his shoulder, and his jaw jutted ominously. Across the background of her mind Lee heard Vince's splutter of protest, heard Haydn repeat his command in a tone that brooked no opposition, and after a pause, Vince's footsteps receded across the tarmac. They sounded sharp, and hurried, and angry, but it did not matter. She was through trying to keep peace with people, she decided recklessly. Nothing mattered, except the choking misery which possessed her, through which she heard Haydn say with restrained control,

'Come and have a drink of lemonade or something, and cool down.' He reached out to grasp her arm, and as soon as the tips of his fingers touched her skin, something inside her seemed to snap. With a furious gesture she flung him off.

'Drink it yourself!' she stormed. 'And as for cooling down, it's a wonder I haven't got pneumonia. You must have got the hosepipe and nearly drowned the daisies with water, to make the backing drip like that. Look at the float,' she gestured towards it furiously, '—no doubt you think it's one huge joke. Well, I don't!'

Her voice broke, and with it her courage, and she took to her heels and ran before he had time to see the tears that streamed down her cheeks and made them wetter than the drips from the daisies. Her blurred vision made out the kaleidoscope of colour that was the gay dress of the crowd, who surged forward for a closer look at the floats now they were parked. They parted as she ran towards them, and Lee hurled herself through the gap like a rabbit bolting for the safety of its burrow. One or two of the people looked at her strangely, but no one tried to stop her, and the crowd swarmed round her, closing in behind her and shutting off Haydn, and Vince, and the floats. With a sob of relief she ran on, her one desire to put as much distance between herself and Haydn as possible. The sound of the music from the band mocked her, and the words to the familiar tune ran through her mind with painful poignancy.

Lonely I would have to be, in that quaint old Cornish town....

The dancers gyrated, following the intricate movements that had been danced down the steps of time, and fleetingly Lee wondered how many other girls had stood in previous summers, as she stood now, apart, on the edge of the crowd, watching other couples dancing, their arms entwined, eyes looking deep into one another's, while their steps moved in unison as they followed the music of the band, which drew more and more dancers to join them, like the Pied Piper, as they marched along the narrow, cobbled streets.

Lee drew apart, shrinking into a cottage doorway to get out of the crush, and feeling more alone than she had ever felt in her life before. Perhaps that was how the writer of the song had felt, she thought dully. Lonely, and miserable, and angry all at the same time. At last she could stand the noise and bustle no longer, and with feet that felt like leaden weights she forced herself to step out of the sheltering doorway. And straightaway collided with Haydn.

'So that's where you went to earth.' She tried to back away from him, but the press of people held her, and the door prevented her from turning the other way. He hung on to her arm, and this time she could not shake him off. His fingers closed like a vice round her wrist, and she tried to pull away, but his grip did not relax.

'You're hurting me!'

'Then stop struggling.'

He dragged her with him. She had no option but to go along, his strength was greater than her own, and his hold was unrelenting. So was the line of his jaw.

'Where are we going?' Lee gasped at last.

The crowds pressed about them, and her sandals slipped on the smooth cobbles, and she grew breathless and angry.

'Somewhere quiet, where we can talk.'

They reached the end of the harbour wall, passed the harbourmaster's office. The *Sea Mist* lay close by, keeling over on her side, waiting for the next tide to bring her upright. Haydn stopped. He loosed her wrist.

'You brute!' She rubbed it furiously. 'There'll be bruises in the morning.'

'Not half as many as I'd like to administer,' he growled back, and she had a fleeting vision of him spanking the boy on the beach. It was not reassuring. It caused her to bite back the words that trembled on the edge of her tongue. 'Now we can hear ourselves speak,' he maligned the efforts of the local band, 'you'll simmer down, and listen to me.'

'I won't!' She faced him defiantly. 'You can't have anything to say that will interest me.' She tried to step round him, but found she could not get far enough away because the edge of the harbour wall was too close, and the drop frighteningly long. She came within an ace of losing her balance, and Haydn reached out a long arm. She tried to sidestep his grip, and he grabbed her unceremoniously with both hands as she teetered on the very edge of the drop.

'Don't add diving over sea walls to your other silly tricks.' He pulled her back to safety with ungentle hands, and held her as she caught her breath in a hard gasp.

'My silly tricks!' She swallowed, fighting for composure. 'I suppose you think soaking the backing on the float was a sensible, adult thing to do?' she flung at him angrily. He still held her captive against the possibility of her trying to dart round him, but she was too angry to feel his hold, to care about his nearness.

'No, I don't,' he retorted harshly. 'If it was done to discomfort you, it was senseless and childish. And I didn't do it.'

'I don't believe you.'

'You're too stubborn to believe anything you're told.' He spoke through gritted teeth. 'Even if it's to the benefit of Polrewin, you refuse to listen. At least Jon's got the sense to listen to someone who knows what they're talking about,' he added bitingly.

'And you do, I suppose?' she jeered, and felt him stiffen.

'There's no point in even trying to talk to you,' he grated. 'Maybe you'll listen to this.'

His mouth had the same abrasive pressure as his fingers on her wrist. Hard anger fired his kiss. Lee felt it scorch through the muscular grip of his arms, holding her tightly to him. Through the forceful beat of his heart under the thin stuff of his shirt. Could he feel her heart beat, too? It fluttered in her breast like a wild bird beating its wings impotently against the immovable bars of a cage, and the pain of it agonised like the pain of fire.

'Now will you be quiet, and listen to what I've got to say?'

It was a pointless question. She could not speak anyway. Her lips hurt, not so much from the pressure of his, but because he had taken that pressure away. She gazed up at him, mute and white-faced.

'I don't know who drenched the backing on the float, but I certainly did not.' His voice was firm, compelling, and she had to steel herself not to believe him. 'I intend to discover who it was, though,' he went on grimly, 'and for your own sake I hope it wasn't you.'

'Me? Why should I do it?' She stared at him in astonishment. Why on earth should he think she would play such a stupid trick, and then blame him for it?

'I wonder....'

'Eh, Mr Haydn, but it's a bonny boat.'

From somewhere behind them Lee heard Nell's voice. Haydn checked himself abruptly, so she did not know what it was he wondered. The tautness went out of his body, as if a fire had been momentarily extinguished, and he dropped his arm from around her. And she felt curiously empty, and afraid.

'I brought Nell and Ben along to see the *Sea Mist*.' Jon appeared, with Ben behind him. 'Look, Nell, those windows on the side are the cabins.'

'Eh, but the curtains are right pretty.'

'You'll have to come back when she's afloat and have a look over her,' Haydn offered generously.

'I'd never dare,' Nell exclaimed. 'I've no use for going on the water meself. I like the ground firm under my feet,' she declared.

Lee sympathised with her. The ground under her own feet felt anything but steady. It seemed fraught with quicksands whichever way she trod. She forced her mind to concentrate on what Nell was saying.

'It's nice to be out of the crush in the town.' The housekeeper perched on a bollard. 'It was a lovely procession, though. I thought our float was the best.' She patted her hair into place complacently.

'The daisies kept lovely and fresh.' Ben joined in, and Lee tensed, but he went on innocently, 'It's a good job I put the hose over them again before you started off this morning. It stopped them from wilting in the heat, didn't it?' he asked proudly.

Lee dared not look at Haydn. The harbour, and the *Sea Mist*, and Ben's beaming, honest face seemed to revolve slowly round her. From what seemed a great distance away she heard her brother ask,

'What are you two going to do now? I'm taking Nell and Ben back to Polrewin, they've had enough of the crowds.'

'Lee and I are going to join the dancing.'

Haydn did not ask her if she wanted to. He caught her wrist again, and took her with him, and she had not the strength to resist. She had to trot to keep up with his stride, back across the harbour wall, and into the crush of the streets. The band was doing its second round of the town. Lee could hear it oompah-ing its way towards them, the music growing louder and more insistent with every second. A burst of cheering heralded its approach and it turned a street corner, and the cheering and the music made the din indescribable.

'I don't want to dance.'

'What did you say?' Haydn cupped his hand to his ear. 'I can't hear a thing in this noise.'

Lee could hear what he said, clearly enough. She suspected he could hear her, but there was no way of proving it, and pride made her refuse to raise her voice and shout again. He did not give her the opportunity to try. He reached out and swept her into his arms as the last of the dangers passed them, and spun her to join the other couples drawn to dance with those in costume.

'Lonely I would have to be, in that quaint old Cornish town....'

The words echoed like a drumbeat through Lee's mind. She danced, encircled in Haydn's arms, and she had never felt lonelier in her life. She felt as if she was on a little personal island by herself, isolated from the cheerful music, the bright sunshine, and the gay festival crowd. And worst of all, from Haydn himself.

Why didn't he say something? she wondered numbly. Even 'I told you so' would be better than nothing. How was she to know Ben had sprayed the float in a fit of misplaced zeal? She had automatically blamed Haydn. And he suspected she had done it herself. She stole a glance upwards at his face, but he was looking over her shoulder, guiding them both expertly through the intricacies of the dance, and all she could see was the square, uncompromising outline of his chin.

She followed his movements with ease. He was a superb dancer. His slim body took the beat of the music, became its instrument, and interpreted it into a lively step that brought a response from Lee's feet whether she wanted to dance or not. That was another thing she had inherited from her Spanish grandmother, besides her fiery nature. She was a natural dancer. Her lissom body swayed, her feet twinkled in response to the music, and with a gesture of surrender she gave herself up to the hypnotic, throbbing tune; to Haydn's arms, and the bright, hot sunshine that stirred all the inherited instincts in her blood, and brought her vividly alive.

Haydn must have sensed her response. His arms tightened round her, his steps quickened, and he sent her a quick, flashing, downwards glance. Her head tipped back with the sway of the dance, her lips parted showing the shine of her tiny, even teeth. His look kindled, and this time it was not with anger. He strained her to him, and automatically she adjusted her position so that their figures moulded, moving as one.

It was some time before she became aware that the music was growing fainter, the sound of the marching band farther away. It hardly registered at first, then their feet began to slow, the momentum of the music denied them, and Lee dropped her eyes from Haydn's face and turned her head. A white wall of daisies reared up beside them, and Haydn deftly guided her to a stop in between their own float and the one parked next to it. The crowds were gone, attracted away by the dancing in the streets, and temporarily the area occupied by the floats was deserted, except for themselves.

'I thought you wanted to dance?' Bewilderment and sudden disappointment took hold of Lee. They were at one, when they danced.

'So I do, but later. At the ball, tonight.'

So why bring her back to the float? Perhaps he wanted to go home?

'Not yet.' He sensed her question even before she asked it. 'You should have a flower for your hair.' He reached out lazily and plucked a daisy from the side of the float. He held it for a second or two, shook it to make sure it was quite dry, then carefully tucked it among the waves of her hair.

'You should always wear a daisy,' he told her solemnly. 'They become you.'

They would become anyone as naïve as she was....

'About the daisies,' she spoke haltingly. 'I'm sorry—I thought——' she stammered to a confused halt.

'Ben meant well.' His voice was amused, uncritical. 'Let's forgive him, shall we?'

'I feel I owe you....' She meant to say 'an apology', but she could not speak the words with Haydn's lips exploring her own.

'Owe me for the daisy?' He removed them for a moment. 'Now I come to think of it, you did say you'd pay for the daisies.' He looked down at her reflectively, and the glow in his eyes brought the warm, shy colour rushing to her cheeks.

'You took....' she whispered. He had taken a kiss beside the field of daisies, while they were still growing.

'So I did.' The glow deepened, and he bent his head above her, and his low laugh told her he remembered, too. 'But that was only on account,' he told her softly.

CHAPTER TEN

'I'LL put it in water.' Lee took the daisy out of her hair and stood in the middle of her bedroom floor, looking at it undecidedly. 'No, I won't, I'll press it.' Along with the piece of honeysuckle Haydn had plucked from the hedge for her, and one of the miniature red rosebuds she had brought from his nursery.

She felt in a curious state of suspension. Her mood on the way back from Tarmouth yoyoed wildly between bliss and misery. Haydn's kisses had held the same seeking demand as the ones on the day they had swum to the point; it seemed a lifetime ago now. They were not angry, like the one he took while they were on the island, or the one on the sea wall after the procession was over. Was his ardour the result of the festival spirit, in which kisses might be given and returned with no real meaning beyond a shared joy of the day, and no regrets afterwards on either side? She did not know, any more than she knew whether her own response had betrayed to Haydn the true state of her feelings. The uncertainty left her feeling confused and vulnerable, and she sought refuge in work as soon as they returned to Polrewin.

'There's no need for you to bother, Sis, now we've got Ben full time,' Jon refused her offer of help. 'By the way, Ben, about those stretchers. . . .' He hurried over to the older man, and Lee returned disconsolately to the house and sought out Nell.

'I can manage well enough on my own,' the housekeeper told her forthrightly. 'There's not enough to do in a place this size to keep one body occupied, let alone two.'

Lee wandered back to her own room, feeling in the way. She did not want to take the two dogs swimming again today. The calf of her leg ached at the mere thought of going in the water, and she shivered, and turned to her wardrobe. She had not decided yet what to wear for the ball tonight.

He thoughts wandered as she riffled through the dresses. It really did look as if Jon would not need her help now Ben was working full time. By pressing her brother into making a decision on the marketing arrangements, Haydn had virtually made her redundant. Strangely, she no longer resented his action. It did not seem to matter any more. The only thing that mattered was that she loved Haydn, and he did not love her.

She surveyed the possible dresses listlessly. The black one suited her mood, but it was too sophisticated to wear tonight. It had been bought for a formal occasion, and served her well several times since. But not for the festival dance. Perhaps, after all, Haydn did not care all that much for sophisticates? What did he care for? She did not know that, either, and the lack of knowledge only increased her confusion and uncertainty. She hesitated over a white dress, and her hand strayed on. That did not suit her mood, either. Her fingers paused on one she had not worn before. She bought it on impulse two years ago, because she loved the vivid, eye-catching colours, and so far she had not had an occasion to wear it. It would be just right for a festival ball.

She fingered the stiff, rustling silk, and her mood lightened a little. From a tight, sleeveless bodice, the skirt cascaded over her arm in a fan of pleats, jewel-bright with a forked lightning pattern slashed across them in a multicoloured rainbow display. She took it off its hanger and held it against her, then twirled round experimentally. The skirt billowed away from her slender waist. It breathed the snap of castanets, and the throb of guitars under warm, Southern nights. All the verve of the dance passed on to her from her Spanish ancestors tapped her feet in response, and she spread it lovingly across her bed. There was an ankle-length waist slip to go with it, somewhere.

Lee rummaged, with scant regard for the chaos inflicted on the orderly piles of everyday undies in her chest of drawers, until her fingers encountered stiff lace, and she drew it out triumphantly and laid it beside the dress. She did not question that either would fit, and when she showered and changed, and slipped into first the petticoat and then the dress, she found her confidence was fully justified.

Sheer stockings and slender strapped dancing slippers added a touch of luxury, and her mirror gave her morale all the support it needed when she surveyed the result. Her hair lay close against her head in deep waves, and her dark eyes glowed with a soft, inward light. She would need all the confidence she could muster at the ball tonight; to dance in Haydn's arms was like being torn apart. To smile and talk and respond to the bright, laughing banter that made the atmosphere of the yearly festival ball would require all her determination. The dress gave her courage. She clipped a pair of gold rings to her ears, completing the exotic flavour of her costume, and had the satisfaction of knowing she looked her best. She could not know how closely she resembled that earlier, Spanish beauty whose looks had been renowned. She only knew she had done her best for Haydn—and he probably would not notice, or care if he did.

A fit of shyness took her as she was about to go downstairs, and she turned back and reached for a silk coat to cover her dress. She would need some form of wrap when they returned; although the evening was still hot now, it would be early morning before the ball was finished, and cool by the water. The high mandarin collar and loose folds of the heavy silk cloak shimmered green and gold as she moved, and enveloped her from throat to ankles, giving her a feeling of cosy security that bolstered her confidence as she joined Haydn downstairs. She felt his eyes upon her, but he did not say anything, and he was unusually silent on the journey back to the Royal Anchor.

'I wonder what the chef's masterpiece will be for the buffet table?'

She spoke nervously, unable to bear the silence any longer. Haydn, clad in casual slacks and shirt, however impeccably cut, she could stand up to, and even quarrel with. But this silent, aloof man beside her in the Mini, devastatingly handsome in the magpie colouring of evening dress, was a stranger, and a daunting one at that. He must have brought his evening clothes back with him the day they visited the Channel Islands.

She pleated the green-gold silk of her cloak in tiny folds, with restless fingers. She thought it would have been easier than this. Put on a bright smile and a brave face, and talk lightly about nothing. But you could not talk to someone who would not answer, someone who just looked at you when you spoke, so that you knew he must have heard what you said, but then looked away again.... They joined the line of other drivers heading in the same direction, and Lee gave up her effort at conversation and left Haydn to concentrate on driving.

Her fingers stopped pleating her cloak, and she smoothed out the material with a sigh. Tiny, sharp creases showed along the edge, betraying her nervousness to observant eyes. She felt Haydn glance at them, once, briefly, encompassing the fact, but not, she hoped, the reason, then he looked away again and the silence tensed her nerves until they felt at screaming pitch by the time they parked once more beside the daisy-covered float and joined the jostling, cheerful crowd in the foyer. The ballroom at the Royal Anchor was capable of holding three hundred dancers, and it looked as if it would be full tonight.

'I love your dress, Lee.'

A girl of about Lee's own age called across the powder room as she handed in her cloak and shook out the folds of her dress, and another joined her with frank envy.

'That should pin Vince down, if nothing else does!'

Lee smiled, the smile she had vowed she would wear whatever happened during the evening, and it must have worked, because the two girls smiled back, cheerfully friendly. She did not want to pin Vince down, whatever that meant. She did not even want to meet Vince, and the same reluctance to rejoin Haydn kept her paying unnecessary attention to her hair until the two girls swept her out of the door along with them.

'There's Vince.'

'I'm not with Vince.' She had to quieten them, in case Vince heard, and came up. In case....

'She's with me.'

Haydn came across to claim her. He was easily the most

handsome man in the room. Lee felt, rather than saw, the two girls stare, heard the one breathe, 'I say!' in a way reminiscent of Betty, the greengrocer's daughter, as Haydn towered above her, his hand on her arm, guiding her towards the ballroom, and she should have felt glad and proud; but instead she felt miserable, and uncertain. But somehow she managed to keep the smile on her face, and respond to the greetings from her many acquaintances. She had not had time yet to make any real friends in Tarmouth.

Curious glances slanted in their direction as they passed through the crowd, but Haydn seemed impervious to them, although Lee's heightened sensitivity made her acutely aware. Just as she was aware of Haydn looking down at her, although she kept her eyes lowered, she felt the power of his. Felt his hand leave her arm and slip to her waist, the better to ease her passage through the dancers, and those standing on the edge of the ballroom just watching.

'Let's go and see how the flowers are faring.'

Instead of walking her round the edge of the room to where the flowers were, he drew her into his arms and danced her there. It was a quickstep, and he swung her so that her dress billowed and flowed about her feet like a moving rainbow, and she did not even notice when they passed the massed flowers they had worked on together only that morning. Haydn's dancing was exhibition standard, and her own not far behind, and she surrendered to the rare pleasure of performing with a partner who equalled and surpassed her own prowess.

She wanted to dance like this for ever, floating on a cloud of illusion that she knew would shatter when the music stopped. The tempo changed, and a tango took the place of the quickstep, and all except one other couple deserted the floor, but Haydn and Lee danced on, oblivious to their surroundings, conscious only of the dance, and of the joy of moving in perfect harmony, until the music drew to a crescendo and stopped, and a burst of spontaneous applause broke from the circle of people lining the walls of the room. She looked up at him, then, the heady excitement of the dance still in her eyes and her flushed cheeks, which deepened into a rosier hue at the expression on his face.

'The chef asked if you'd like to view the buffet table, sir, before it's opened to the guests.'

A waiter made his way towards them, and drew them to a door at the end of the ballroom.

'He wants us to see his masterpiece,' Haydn guessed with a smile, and Lee descended from her rosy cloud and managed to answer him.

'It must be something very special.'

It was. In all her demonstrating experience, Lee had never seen anything like it before. A large swan, fashioned from icing sugar, sailed majestically across a sheet of mirror glass, and in the hollow of its back, between arched wings, reposed a dish of the best strawberries delivered from Polrewin that morning. A flotilla of miniature paired wings surrounded the large swan, making individual strawberry-filled dishes for the delectation of the guests. Cunningly placed gladioli served as coloured rushes, reflecting in the mirror surface like a pool. The chef had created a fairyland, and Lee stood entranced.

'You miss it, don't you?' Haydn asked, his eyes on her face.

'Yes.' She did not try to deny it. 'But Polrewin comes first.'

'And after Polrewin,' Haydn asked softly, 'what then?'

'I can return to my old career, I suppose.' Her voice was flat. Her old job would be gone. It would be difficult to pick up the threads again. As if she was with them in the room, Lee could hear Moira Scott's voice speaking with wisdom learned from experience.

'Don't give everything to the nursery. Keep something of yourself alive, for afterwards.'

'I don't want to go back inland,' she admitted slowly, 'I should miss the sea.' The sea, rather than Polrewin, she thought with a flash of honesty. Her particular niche there was filled more ably by Ben and Nell. She had given twelve months to the nursery, and she could leave her investment in it to give Jon the backing he needed. Her practical help was no longer necessary. She expected it to hurt, but it gave her a strange sense of release.

'I, too, should miss the sea now.' The chef took up her remark, and Lee grasped at the diversion. She did not want to answer Haydn's question, not even to herself. Not tonight....

'Your art is wasted here.'

'I thought so too, once, but now—I wonder?' The chef looked thoughtful, and Haydn's glance keened interestedly.

'You've got something in mind,' he guessed shrewdly.

'Your strawberries put it there,' the man smiled at Lee. 'With supplies of top quality material, an independent caterer could supply not one hotel, but many. The big resorts along the coast would get to hear. They have conferences, and balls. Their own staff could do the standard meals, and I would provide the specialities. Like this,' he nodded towards the buffet table. 'It would be an all-the-year-round trade. Mr Merrick—I mean Mr Vince's father—is delighted with what I've done tonight, and he's brought some of the more important guests to see it, the same as yourselves. I've already had a number of enquiries.'

'If you set up in business on your own, you'll need help,' Lee realised with sudden hope.

'Occasional help, at first,' the chef agreed. 'I did hope you might be able to join me now and then, if you have any time to spare away from your nursery?'

'We'll think about it.' Haydn answered before Lee could speak, and the chef nodded, and hurried away.

'It doesn't need any thinking about.' Lee's temper erupted, and she spun to face Haydn. 'It's just the opportunity I've been looking for. And what do you mean, we'll think about it? Since when did you include this kind of thing in your repertoire?' She waved an angry hand towards the swans.

'It's a bit outside my scope,' Haydn admitted, and she interrupted him impatiently.

'Well, it's not outside mine,' she fumed, 'and I don't need you to answer for me. I've put up with your interference at Polrewin because that partly belongs to Jon, but this is my affair. It's got nothing to do with you.'

'I wouldn't dream of interfering,' Haydn assured her, and Lee bit her lip. If anything, he was more infuriating when he agreed with her than when he didn't. 'Vince might try to, though,' he added mildly.

'It's got even less to do with Vince than it has with you,' she retorted sharply.

'He'll lose his chef,' Haydn pointed out.

'It'll serve him right,' Lee snapped. 'He should treat his staff properly.' She broke off hurriedly as the buffet room doors were flung open and the guests began to stream in, preceded by Vince himself. He gave Lee and Haydn a surly look; evidently he had not forgiven them for telling him to go away that afternoon.

'I suppose the chef let you in here?'

His frown showed that he knew of the chef's plans, too.

'It's a superb arrangement. Congratulate your chef,' Haydn said wickedly, and drew Lee unresisting towards the door under cover of the admiring exclamations from the other guests who hurried forward to see the table.

'Would you like some refreshments?' Haydn paused, as if about to turn back.

'No. Thank you.' Belatedly, Lee remembered her manners. 'For goodness' sake let's get out of here, the crush is awful.' She wanted to get away from Vince, not the crush.

'Not even strawberries?' Haydn persisted.

'I hate strawberries,' she retorted vehemently.

'You'll have to make an effort and eat some,' he told her blandly as they gained the ballroom again. 'It looks as if the chef might have sent some out specially for us.' A discreetly beckoning waiter caught his eye, and he steered her in the direction of a small table by the bandstand, on which reposed a tray bearing a selection of dainties. Lee's heart sank; she felt she could not swallow anything more solid than lemonade.

'You two are honoured. How did you manage it?' The owner of the boatyard strolled across and greeted them cheerfully.

'By knowing people in high places,' Haydn grinned.

'Vince, I suppose?' The man slanted a glance at Lee.

'No, the chef.' Haydn put his priorities right, and the man laughed.

'If he lays on spreads like this, he'll get the Royal Anchor quite a name. But I'm glad he's sent your share out here,' he addressed Haydn. 'I wanted to see you, and there's too much of a crowd in the buffet room to talk comfortably.'

'Have you given our discussion some thought, then?' Haydn looked up, suddenly alert.

'Quite a lot,' the owner of the boatyard replied. 'So far as we're concerned you'll make an ideal neighbour. I told you I didn't want to sell the yard to another boatbuilder.'

'We'll call it a deal then, shall we?' Haydn held out his hand, and the boatyard owner took it and shook it heartily. 'We can settle all the details later.'

'Any time,' the other man told him accommodatingly. 'Now we know where we stand I can go ahead and settle the details of our own move to the new premises. In the meantime, feel free to use our private mooring at the present yard,' he offered, 'It's as good as yours now, except for the formalities.' He nodded in a friendly manner to Lee, and rose to his feet as the orchestra began to reassemble.

'Do you intend to take over the entire town, eventually?' Lee's voice was tight.

'Not the entire town.' Haydn steered her skilfully back on to the dance floor as the orchestra struck up the first bars of a waltz. 'I have got one more—er—item in mind,' he admitted, 'but the boatyard is ideal as a distributing centre for our mail order business.' He did not enlarge on what the other item was, and Lee determined not to ask.

'I thought you'd decided on Polrewin as your distributing centre,' she said drily, and he shook his head.

'You're really not very businesslike,' he reproached her. 'A mail order business requires a warehouse, where the goods can be packaged and transported from. With a private mooring, the boatyard is ideal for running the stuff across from the Islands straight to the packing sheds, with no second handling necessary. Polrewin will be a customer for salad crops and so on, a sort of middleman, nothing to do with the mail order business at all.'

'I don't see why you couldn't build your warehouse on Guernsey,' Lee said stubbornly. If he had done, she would not have met him, and would not feel so wretched now. She might even be dancing with Vince. She wrinkled her nose at the thought.

'Why pull such a face?' She had forgotten Haydn could see.

'My nose itches.' She could not explain the real reason.

'I'll rub it for you.' He leaned down and touched her nose lightly with his own. 'That's the way Eskimos kiss,' he informed her solemnly.

'Not in here.' She pulled her head back hurriedly. A passing couple gave them an amused look, and she went scarlet.

'Let's go outside, then,' he suggested.

'You haven't answered my question,' she digressed hurriedly, her colour rising still further.

'Why don't you expand on Guernsey?' He repeated it. 'We can't. There's no room,' he said simply. She had not thought of that. 'I told you, you're not very businesslike.'

'I don't want to be businesslike. I want....' She could not tell him what she wanted. She leaned her forehead against his stiff shirt front, hiding her face, and let the sentence go.

'I wonder what you do want.' He addressed the top of her head, and when she did not answer, added provocatively, 'It looks as if Vince wants to dance with you. He's hovering at the end of the room.' He did not need to add, the end in which direction they themselves were heading.

'I don't want to dance with him.' That brought her head up, her eyes imploring him. 'Steer us the other way, do.'

'You're sure? You won't change your mind?' Maddeningly he continued on his course. If she baulked, she would cause a collision with the other dancers, and some badly trodden on toes.

'They might turn this into an excuse-me dance....' If they did, Vince would grab his chance, and her, and she shrank from the thought of him touching her. 'I don't want to dance with him,' she insisted.

'I just wanted to make sure.' He changed course with an expert twirl, and she breathed freely again.

'You haven't got a flower in your hair tonight,' he observed. 'Did your daisy wilt?'

'No, I pressed it.' As soon as the words were spoken, she wished them unsaid.

'Pressed it?' His eyebrows rose.

Why, oh, why did she have to say that? Why couldn't she have said she'd left the daisy at home? Carelessly, as if she might have simply forgotten it. As if it was of no importance.

'Yes, as a souvenir.' Perhaps he would think she meant a souvenir of the festival. But it was after the procession was over that he had given her the daisy. Just before he kissed her, by the float.

'I wanted to keep just one. The others will fade.' It should have come out sounding bright and matter-of-fact, but instead it merely sounded forlorn.

'The daisies won't fade. Every time you close your eyes, they'll always be there, bright and fresh as ever.'

So would Haydn's face, and she would be afraid to close her eyes because of it. The strains of The Blue Danube sighed across the room, haunting, nostalgic, and he lowered the hand that held her own, guiding her fingers to his waist, then he put both his arms right round her and held her close to him, dancing as she liked to dance, as if they were one.... Lee let her hand rest where he had put it. She could feel his movements, lithe and effortless beneath fingers that felt warm from his touch, and she laid her cheek against him, suddenly too weary to fight any more. The lights dimmed round them, so she did not need to guard her expression, and her lids dropped, drugged by the soft notes drawn from the throbbing strings of the wandering violinist, now close to them, now a lifetime away.

She felt a light touch on her hair, and another, but she did not stir. Haydn had kissed her before, but it did not mean anything, at least not to him. How could you go on dancing, she wondered, when your heart felt as if it was breaking in two? Would she ever hear The Blue Danube played again, and not feel the agony of this moment in his arms?

The lights went up, a low murmur of laughter rippled round the room as more than one couple were caught in a closer embrace than was strictly necessary, and the tune changed to a quickstep. The M.C. announced an excuse-me-dance.

'Let's sit this one out,' Lee began, but she was too late. Vince pushed through the crowd and laid a hand on her arm.

'My dance, I think.' He glared at Haydn belligerently, and Lee's eyes widened with dismay.

'Don't. . . .' she began nervously, and glanced apprehensively at Haydn. He must not make a scene, not in here. But he merely smiled, and bowed, and let her go, and contrarily she felt abandoned. Vince took her triumphantly on to the floor.

'It's about time somebody else had a chance,' he muttered as he steered her away. He was heavy-footed, and his hands were hot. Lee put the one firmly back to her waist where it belonged, and held it there so that it should not stray again, and her lips tightened. 'I haven't set eyes on you all evening,' Vince went on petulantly, without bothering to lower his voice. 'You promised me a dance.'

'Which you've just had, so that releases the lady.' Haydn stepped towards them as they completed their first circuit of the room. Vince's hand tightened on Lee's arm, and he turned to the other man with an angry exclamation. Momentarily his move loosened his fingers a little, and Lee took the opportunity and twisted away from him before he tried to detain her, as she knew he would.

'Thank you, Vince,' she smiled at him nervously, and ducking under his arm she fled to Haydn's side. His arm came up and circled her confidently, and swept her away from Vince and his angry protests, and lost them among the other dancers, but not for long.

'Where are we going?'

Instead of circling the room in the approved manner he spun her away towards the exit. Dimly she became aware that over his other arm he held folds of cloth that shone green-gold in the lamplight.

'Put it on.' Haydn held her cloak towards her, and deftly turned her so that he could slip it across her shoulders. She stood still and watched his face while he bent over her, intent on the task of snapping the slender gold fastening across the high mandarin collar, his fingers slim and cool against her chin.

'Let's go.' He did not say where. He put his arm round her and turned her towards the door. For a mutinous second Lee thought of refusing. They had come to dance, and the ball would not be over for another two hours at least. But the words would not come. She shrugged, and walked beside him silently down the hotel steps. She heard him wish the hall porter goodnight; so he did not intend them to come back. Resentment stirred in her, that he had not asked her whether she wanted to leave, but she thrust it aside resignedly. She did not really want to dance any more anyway. The decorated floats, parked in front of the hotel, glowed pale in the summer moonlight. She paused beside their own.

'It seems a shame they ever have to fade.' She raised her hand from inside the folds of her cloak and touched the daisies wistfully. 'They've kept fresher than most of them, though.' The flowers on the float next to it showed obvious signs of wilting.

'Thanks to Ben.' Laughter threaded his voice, and his teeth flashed white in the dusk.

'Thanks to Ben.' She could laugh about it too, now. 'That was about the wettest ride I ever had!' She strolled on, propelled by his arm across her shoulders, not really conscious of where they were going. 'Don't you like dancing?' she asked him idly, not caring about his answer, but afraid to let the silence drop between them, and allow room for her thoughts to torment her.

'Yes, but I don't like crowds,' he answered, 'and I thought you'd probably had enough of the opposition.'

It was a second or two before his meaning dawned on her.

'There isn't any opposition,' she told him stiffly.

He gave a low chuckle. 'I'm glad to hear it.'

'I didn't mean....' she began confusedly, then stopped. What use to try and explain what she meant? Haydn was deliberately provoking her, and she refused to be drawn into another argument with him today. She invariably lost.

'We're at the harbourmaster's office,' she realised. 'Are

you going to the end of the hard and back?' The sea wall was a long one, and the thin leather of her dancing pumps was not made for treading rough stone.

'Only as far as the *Sea Mist*. I'm going to put her into the private mooring for the night—you heard the man from the boatyard offer me the facility.'

Lee stopped short at the top of the harbour steps. 'I'm not going in a rowboat and climbing up rope ladders in these clothes,' she told him indignantly.

'You won't have to go in a rowboat.'

'And I'm not going to be left alone here while you look after your precious boat!' She clung to him, suddenly nervous, not hearing what he said. In bright sunshine the harbour wall was an attractive place to be. Now, the moon cast only a faint illumination. The slapping of waves against the wall made an eerie accompaniment to the faint sigh of the wind which was never long absent from the water. 'I refuse to stay here on my own.' What if Vince followed them? She swallowed, and her voice trembled in spite of her efforts to keep it firm.

'I don't intend you to,' Haydn said calmly. 'You're coming with me.' With a swift movement that took her completely unawares, he picked her up in his arms. He held her with one arm while he tucked her cloak round her with his other hand, effectively preventing her from using her hands. The enveloping folds of material swaddled her like a child's shawl, and she gave a gasp of fright as she felt the ground give beneath Haydn's feet. What if he fell? She closed her eyes tightly, and opened them again when she realised he was merely running down the harbour steps, lightly, as if he had both hands free, and no burden to carry.

'I told you we shouldn't have to use the rowboat.' With a long stride he spanned the distance between the steps and the deck of the *Sea Mist*.

'Let me go!' She tried to push away from him, but her cloak made a very effective bond.

'You'll lose your shoes if you kick,' Haydn warned her, and there was an underlying laugh in his voice that made Lee redouble her efforts to get free. She drew in her breath on a hard, angry note, and kicked just the same, although her feet touched nothing but empty air. She felt the shoe on her right foot come loose, and curled her toes frantically to try and keep it on, but perversely her move made it slip further until it hung right on the end of her toes. At any moment it would drop into the water.

'I told you to keep still.' Haydn paused and propped her against his upraised knee, then removed her shoe from her foot.

'Put it back!'

'When you behave yourself.' Calmly he pushed her shoe into his jacket pocket.

'Put it back now. And put me down!' she shouted furiously.

'I will if you want me to,' he offered easily, and tipped her so that she could see the width of dark water over which he straddled between steps and deck.

'I d-didn't mean....' She gulped into silence. He was more than capable of dropping her, if she insisted. She closed her eyes and turned her head into his shirt front, and felt as much as heard a laugh shiver through him.

'You—you——!'

Fright stopped the words in her throat as she felt him step across the strip of water dividing the boat from the wall, then she relaxed slightly as he straightened up with both feet on the deck. He moved forward again, and she tensed. Where was he taking her? Below decks, to his cabin? But his feet kept on the even deck, and she felt him edge sideways as if into a narrow space. She opened one eye in an apprehensive peep, then the other as he tipped her the right way up and stood her on her feet beside him in the cockpit of the *Sea Mist*.

'I'm going back.' She spun away from him and ran to the rail, but Haydn made no move to detain her. With an unhurried hand he reached towards the controls, and the engine of the boat purred into life.

'Go ahead, if you want to swim for it,' he told her mildly. He spun the wheel, and Lee gripped the rail convulsively as the width of water doubled between themselves and the harbour steps.

'I hate you!' she gritted furiously.

'So you told me, once before.' He sounded completely unperturbed.

'Give me back my shoe. My foot's cold.' It was not. The layers of petticoat, long dress and cloak dropped right to the floor and insulated her with cosy, protective warmth.

'I'll keep it until you listen to what I've got to say.' The steps on the opposite side of the harbour loomed close, and he let the *Sea Mist* drift gently into the private mooring to the boatyard, and cut the engine into silence before he turned to her. 'You can have your shoe back afterwards, and walk away, if you still want to.'

'What makes you think I won't want to?' she ground out. The conceit of the man! 'I want my shoe now.' She could see it, sticking out of the top of his jacket pocket. If she could reach it, she could slip it on and jump on to the steps up to the boatyard. The *Sea Mist* had come to rest right against them. She held her breath and grabbed. Her fingers actually touched the coloured satin toe of her shoe, then his hand descended on her wrist. His other hand left the wheel of the cruiser and grasped her round the waist, and spun her to face him. She loosed her shoe with a furious exclamation.

'For two pins, I'd use it to give you the spanking you deserve,' he threatened roughly.

'Let me go!' She beat at him with her one free fist. 'Let me. . . .' His lips closed on her mouth and cut off the rest of the sentence. They sought, demanded, and found. They kissed her eyes, her cheeks, and returned to her lips again, and she was lost. An aeon passed, during which the only sounds were the lapping of the water against stone, and the soft sigh of the wind. An aeon in which Haydn's hand captured her free one and drew it to him, and instead of beating against him it remained where it was, of its own accord.

'Let me go!' It was only a whisper now, and it had no conviction behind it.

'I'll never let you go,' he told her roughly. 'Never, so long as I live. I love you, do you hear me?' He gave her a little shake to make sure she had heard.

Lee nodded, unable to speak.

'And you love me,' he told her; he did not ask. 'Only you've been too stubborn to admit it. Tell me you love me,' he demanded, and tipped her face up so that she had to look at him.

'I love you,' she whispered, and her heart was in the glow of her eyes, 'but I didn't know—I thought——'

'You thought—what?' he asked her softly, but his voice was gentle now, and he gathered her to him, but this time she did not resist, and his lips sought her cheeks, and the small, soft hollows of her throat. 'Tell me,' he demanded huskily.

'I thought you wanted Polrewin.'

'I wanted Polrewin to be a success.'

'You wanted that to help Jon.'

'At first, yes. And then I wanted it, so that you could be free,' he told her astonished ears. 'You said you wouldn't leave Polrewin until it was a viable concern, so I had to try and make it one. Fast.'

'And all the time I thought....' It didn't matter now what she had thought. She nestled back contentedly in his arms, and the wind crooned a gentle melody, and the long, slow minutes ticked by unheeded.

'Did you know my rose bush was a red one?' Lee asked, at last. She knew in her heart what his answer must be, but she wanted to hear him say it.

'Of course I knew.' Haydn looked surprised. 'I picked it specially for you.' He sat her upright on his knee and looked at her sternly. 'I've tried to tell you in a dozen different ways that I love you, practically since I first set eyes on you, but you've been so busy suspecting me of trying to wreck Polrewin, you wouldn't let yourself listen,' he accused her.

'I'm listening now.'

So he told her again, until he was quite sure she believed him. And the *Sea Mist* rocked gently, sharing their secrets.

'There isn't a glow round the masts tonight.' She let her eyes follow the pointers rising black against the soft light of the summer moon.

'There's no storm about tonight. At least, not up there.'

'What do you mean?' She eyed him suspiciously, and his teeth flashed in a quick grin.

'St Elmo's not the only one who's holding fire,' he laughed.

'I'll blow the flame out if you like,' she offered demurely.

'Don't ever do that. Promise me,' he begged her huskily. 'Without fire there'd be no light. At least, not for me.' His eyes went bleak at the prospect.

'I promise.' She could not bear the look in his eyes. She herself had felt the same way such a short while ago.

'You can help the chef if you want to,' he conceded, 'but not all the time. I shall want you myself.'

'And I'll help you build your mail order business.' A memory stirred. 'You said you wanted something else on the mainland, too.' She could not remember him saying what it was.

'When you marry me, I'll have it,' he told her softly. 'I could get a marriage licence tomorrow. We needn't wait.'

'We've got nowhere to live,' she objected.

'There's the *Sea Mist*. We could live on that until we've got a place of our own. We'd be on our own, on the boat.'

There did not seem anything to stand in their way.

'May I have my shoe back now?'

'Are you going to run away?' His hand hesitated over his pocket.

'Never,' Lee promised happily. And she let him put it on.

Also available this month
Four Titles in our Mills & Boon Classics Series

Specially chosen reissues of the best in Romantic Fiction

August's Titles are:

HUNTER OF THE EAST
by Anne Hampson

Kim's flighty young foster-sister was about to ruin her life by running off with a married man, and Kim had to do something drastic to stop her. She declared that the only thing to do was to kidnap the man in question. Unfortunately, Kim kidnapped the wrong man . . .

TIME OF CURTAINFALL
(Darling Rhadamanthus!)
by Margery Hilton

After her father died, Judy was somewhat daunted to find that he had consigned her to the guardianship of his old friend the forbidding Quentin Frayle. Then she found that there was a far more attractive side to him – and alas! it was all being turned on his glamorous cousin Crystal.

BAUHINIA JUNCTION
by Margaret Way

"You know, Gena," the cattle baron Cy Brandt told her, "there's the same easy magic in handling women as horses. Just show 'em who's master!" There was no doubt that Cy was good at handling horses, considered Gena, but as far as women were concerned, he had only just made her own acquaintance – and he would be in for a surprise.

DESERT DOCTOR
by Violet Winspear

It seemed as if the Lawrence-like Doctor Victor Tourelle must be a hundred per cent proof against young secretaries like Madeline. And yet he seemed interested in Donette, who was only one year older. But even if the Frenchman was out of her reach, Madeline could not stop herself hoping.

BUY THEM TODAY

Forthcoming Classic Romances

DARK ENEMY
by Anne Mather

Determined to revenge herself on Jason Wilde because of the way he had treated her sister, Nicola took a job with the oil company Jason worked for. To achieve her purpose, she determined to make him attracted to her. But things did not quite work out in the manner she expected.

MY HEART'S A DANCER
by Roberta Leigh

Melanie's marriage had ended before it had begun – but happily it was not long before she found herself in love once again. Yet even now happiness looked like eluding her, when her career as a ballet dancer began to come between her and the man she loved.

SECRET HEIRESS
by Eleanor Farnes

Young love is a pretty sight; but is it always strong and durable? Fiona's father had his doubts, and that was why he arranged for her to see a little of life outside her own small circle before becoming engaged to Guy. Would the experiment be successful, or might it lead her into real unhappiness?

THE PAGAN ISLAND
by Violet Winspear

In an effort to forget her grief over her beloved Dion's death, Hebe had gone to the lovely Greek island of Petra. There she met Nikos Stephanos, a man as different from Dion as he could possibly be. But a dark tragedy lay over Nikos's life. Would he bring tragedy to Hebe as well?

Mills & Boon Classic Romances

– all that's best in Romantic Reading

Available September 1979

Forthcoming Mills & Boon Romances

RETURN TO DEVIL'S VIEW *by Rosemary Carter*
Jana could only succeed in her search for some vital information by working as secretary to the enigmatic Clint Dubois – and it was clear that Clint suspected her motives . . .

THE MAN ON THE PEAK *by Katrina Britt*
The last thing Suzanne had wanted or expected when she went to Hong Kong for a holiday was to run into her ex-husband Raoul . . .

TOGETHER AGAIN *by Flora Kidd*
Ellen and Dermid Craig had separated, but now circumstances had brought Ellen back to confront Dermid again. Was this her chance to rebuild her marriage, or was it too late?

A ROSE FROM LUCIFER *by Anne Hampson*
Colette had always loved the imposing Greek Luke Marlis, but only now was he showing that he was interested in her. Interested – but not, it seemed, enough to want to marry her . . .

THE JUDAS TRAP *by Anne Mather*
When Sara Fortune fell in love with Michael Tregower, and he with her, all could have ended happily. Had it not been for the secret that Sara dared not tell him . . .

THE TEMPESTUOUS FLAME *by Carole Mortimer*
Caroline had no intention of marrying Greg Fortnum, whom she didn't even know apart from his dubious reputation – so she escaped to Cumbria where she met the mysterious André . . .

WITH THIS RING *by Mary Wibberley*
Siana had no memory of who she really was. But what were Matthew Craven's motives when he appeared and announced that he was going to help her find herself again?

SOLITAIRE *by Sara Craven*
The sooner Marty got away from Luc Dumarais the better, for Luc was right out of her league, and to let him become important to her would mean nothing but disaster . . .

SWEET COMPULSION *by Victoria Woolf*
Marcy Campion was convinced that she was right not to let Randal Saxton develop her plot of land – if only she could be equally convinced about her true feelings for Randal!

SHADOW OF THE PAST *by Robyn Donald*
Morag would have enjoyed going back to Wharuaroa, where she had been happy as a teenager, if it hadn't meant coming into constant contact with Thorpe Cunningham.

Available September 1979